BRENDA VICARS

POLARITY IN MOTION

DEDICATION

For Jane Swann Nethercut
(January 1, 1950 - March 15, 2013)

You taught us so much about making the playing field even for all kids.

CHAPTER 1

I WAS THE LAST STUDENT IN the freshman class to know. Well, almost the last—Ethan found out from me.

It all came out during sixth period, when the teacher left the classroom unsupervised. Danny, the big bad guy of Star Ninth Grade Center, leaned back in his chair and scratched his belly. "Yuck! Hill's got dog breath—ruff, ruff!—today."

Kids snickered, and immature silliness broke out all over the room. The computer lab desks were arranged in a big square, with everyone facing inward, and so even while studying my screen, I couldn't help witnessing some of the nonsense.

Across the room, Danny stood and stretched with a loud-groaning yawn. "Damn, Coach ran our butts hard this morning." He leaned forward and rubbed his hands on the front of his thighs.

Cynthia, the super-crimped blonde sitting next to him, pulled makeup out of her purse. "You know, you're just the water boy." She added another coat of mascara to her already loaded lashes.

Danny's grin drooped. His skin, usually the same straw color as his short spiky hair, gained a pink glow. "I'm in the relays. I'm running every day."

Drawing on fluorescent blue eyeliner, Cynthia crooned, "Ooooo, relays. Yippee."

"Yeah, Cyn, come watch me this afternoon. We can have a little sin after practice. Heh, heh, heh." He checked around the room, as if to see who got his joke.

I slumped lower to use my computer screen as a barrier. In the chair next to me, Ethan, the one black guy in the class, remained totally focused on his research. Not only did he act older than the other boys, but he looked older—more muscular and taller than my dad's six-foot-two. Ethan's strong jaw, straight nose, and deep, dark eyes conveyed an air of confidence.

I envied him because he automatically fit into a group—small in this school, but still a group. The group of black students. It was my fourth week at Star, and since there were only two weeks left until summer break, I had settled into the role of trailer-park outcast. I didn't see the point in trying to schmooze into a clique. I figured Mom would want to move again before school started, anyway.

Danny sat down, but unfortunately, his voice boomed over the drone of the rest of the class. "Hey, Aiden, Sean—did you hear that Hill has dog breath today? Ruff, ruff!"

Coincidentally, I had just Googled "how to tell if you have bad breath." I hated never knowing for sure whether I had it. I surfed for some way to give Mr. Hill a hint, so maybe he could find a remedy. I hoped before I reached the making-out phase of my life, someone would invent a bad breath detector, so I could know how my own breath smelled.

Arvey, one of the few girls in the school who seemed as unpopular as I was, tapped my shoulder. My breath thoughts halted. With her trademark glum expression, she angled her head toward Danny, where every other student except Ethan had clustered. They were whispering about something on Danny's screen.

This school district had pathetic filters compared to Houston and all the other schools I had attended—students could cruise any site they wanted. I figured whatever he pulled up kicked because even the good students crowded around his computer with their mouths dropped open. I glanced at Ethan, who was still absorbed in his work. No way would I get up and go over to the other side. Like Ethan, I didn't care to hang with Danny's group.

Arvey stood next to me with a small, thin-lipped smile, as if waiting for my reaction. She lived in a trailer near mine. Hers, a big rusting, double-wide, seemed to be falling apart, and so many children and visitors drifted in and out all the time, I couldn't tell who actually lived there.

"What is it?" I asked her.

She tilted her head downward so that her curtain of long dark hair covered her eyes. She shrugged and started walking toward Danny. She usually didn't hang with a clique, but whatever Danny displayed clearly grabbed her interest because she drifted right back to the enthralled crowd.

In spite of my effort to keep my eyes on my halitosis article, Cynthia's gasp caught my attention. She smirked at me while coating on a layer of hot pink gloss. "Ooooo." She smacked her lips. "Hardcore."

I figured Cynthia targeted me with her grooming display because my super-diligent, opinionated parents didn't allow me to wear makeup.

A girl standing behind Danny gaped over his shoulder. "I can't believe it."

Though everyone's eyes were drawn to Danny's screen, they kept sneaking peeks toward the side of the room where Ethan and I sat. Ethan, with his strong, detached demeanor, scanned his article and jotted notes.

Before class, Danny had griped out in the hall about this civil rights assignment—except dumb, disgusting, dirtbag Danny used the N-word in place of civil rights. He had also barked like a dog to all of his friends. So I assumed Danny had pulled up some site that joked about civil rights or dogs, and as soon as Hill came back in, everyone would chill.

Cynthia giggled and repeated, "Hardcore." A heartbeat later, she added, "Polarity!"

Sara, whose crimped blond hair and fluorescent blue eyeliner mirrored Cynthia's, edged closer to Danny's screen. "What'd you expect?" she asked in a not-soft-enough whisper. "She's just trailer trash. Doesn't even have a double-wide."

7

Since no other single-wide trailer person on the planet has my stupid name, Polarity—bestowed in a classic borderline moment by my ever-unraveling mother—I gave up hoping they weren't talking about me.

Danny, now pinker and happier than ever, imitated Cynthia's giggle and pointed at his screen. "Whoa. Poetic Polarity."

I scooted my chair back, but before I could get up to see what Danny ogled, a crash jolted the room.

Ethan, with clenched fists, had stood so fast his chair landed sideways.

His furious scowl deflated all the smirks. Instead of gawking at me or the computer, everyone tracked Ethan as he started toward them.

Danny, eyes popping, paled and melted back into his chair. No smirks or giggles now.

The classroom door opened, and Mr. Hill stepped in. Slight in build, probably about five feet four, he wore a white shirt and dark necktie. Ethan, halfway around the room, froze with his fists still clenched. Everyone else scrambled back to their places. For the briefest moment, Mr. Hill and Ethan made eye contact.

"What's going on? Arvey and the rest of you, get back to your seats," Mr. Hill said needlessly, since everyone except Ethan already scurried in rapid retreat. Mr. Hill headed toward Danny. "Danny, what have you got?"

"Sorry, sir. I don't know how it happened—just popped up from the history." Danny had plenty of time to switch his screen. He wanted Mr. Hill to see.

Mr. Hill saw the screen. His eyes widened, and he went pale. "Oh no! Polarity, oh no!"

It seemed like an eternity. Mr. Hill standing with his mouth dangling open. Everyone looking at me.

I glanced down at myself to make sure I didn't have something spilled or buttons undone on my pale turquoise shirt, even though the room's reaction must have resulted from something on the computer screen. Heat crawled up to my face. I couldn't stand the silence. "Yes, sir?"

His bulging eyes boomeranged from the screen to me and back again. "Go to the office. Now."

"Sir?"

"You heard me." His voice shook. "Pack up and go to the office." His eyes stayed on the screen, as if glued to something terrifying. "Wait for me there."

I started shutting down and picking up my stuff, relieved to be getting out of that room but a little queasy with fear about why he was sending me to the office. I assured myself that I'd never been in trouble before. All my visits to the office had been about routine things—schedules, paperwork, even a poetry award once. So whatever Danny displayed on his computer would get straightened out.

"Get up!" Mr. Hill ordered Danny. "All you kids in this row—go stand by the back wall." Mr. Hill moved everyone able to view the screen. He ripped a sheet of paper out of Danny's notebook and started writing something, probably the web address.

When I reached the door, he was still writing, and everyone else except Ethan was frozen and gawking at me. Ethan returned to his seat, picked up his chair, and set it down with a loud thump. For a second, his concerned, kind gaze locked with mine. I didn't want him to worry, so I shrugged and smiled at him before I left.

I shut the door on the classroom and leaned against it. *What just happened?* Fortunately, it was near the end of the period, so the halls were deserted. I took a few deep breaths before heading to the office. The waiting area was empty except for a secretary typing, and I slipped in, trying not to be noticed. A large aquarium covered the side wall, so I faced away from the secretary and pretended to study the fish. The aquarium had a clear divider in the middle, with a single red and blue betta on one side and a few dozen black mollies on the other.

The secretary sighed, lifted her dull eyes from her computer screen, and smoothed back the light brown hair that had strayed from her ponytail. She could have passed for a student herself. The nameplate in front of her computer was labeled Miss Regina Smart, Administrative Assistant. "Where's your hall pass?"

"I don't have one, Miss Smart."

She cast her eyes back to her screen. "You cannot be in here without a hall pass." She didn't look up again. "Go back and get one."

"But Mr. Hill told me—"

"Out."

I went back into the still-empty hall and stood by the door.

She noticed me through the glass and came stomping out. "You cannot be in the hall without a pass. Go back to your classroom and get one. Now. No more stalling, or I'll write you up."

It was pointless to argue with her, but I was desperate. "Miss Smart, may I please make a phone call?" I wanted to let Mom or Dad know I'd been banished to the office, and even in this little town, I was probably the only living ninth-grader with no phone of my own. Well, I did have a 911 phone, but my parents obsessively feared that I'd be harmed by social media. There would be no real phone or unsupervised Internet for me until at least tenth grade.

She sighed and pushed back her stray hair again. "No. Not without a pass." She folded her arms.

I started down the hall, but as soon as she went back into the office, I cut into a bathroom. I decided to wait a few minutes and peek into the office again. Maybe by then, Hill would be there.

Within three minutes, the school-wide intercom clicked on. "Attention, please. Attention. This is Mrs. Sanchez speaking. Polarity Weeks, report to the office. Polarity Weeks, report to the office immediately."

Never, in any of the many schools I attended, had the principal ever called me by name over the intercom during class. Never.

How did I get into this nightmare?

Danny must have pulled up some news blurb about my mom. She must have finally gone too far and done some unspeakable thing that made the news.

The trailer park where we rented a space was less than two blocks away. Plus, at five feet eight, I had long, skinny legs, and I was wearing jeans and sneakers, so I could get there fast. Whatever the bad news, I didn't want to hear about it in the school office.

I dashed out the door, down the empty hall, and out of the

building, heading home. I was about halfway through the parking lot before my P.E. teacher and the security guard cut me off. This all felt surreal. I couldn't believe I, Polarity Weeks, had been captured while attempting to escape from school.

The bald, chubby guard, Raymond, was red-faced from his sprint to catch up with me. He caught my arm, spun me around, and started walking me back toward the school while he yelled into his walkie-talkie, "Female youth apprehended headed southerly in the easterly parking lot. Repeat, female—"

"Polarity Weeks," interrupted my P.E. teacher, Mrs. Moorman, grabbing my other arm.

"Acknowledge. Acknowledge," the guard shouted even louder into his unresponsive speaker. He paused to pick up his blue cap that had slipped off his head during his run toward me.

"Officer, I think your battery is dead," I said. Most of the students called him Raymond, but he preferred to be called officer.

He adjusted his cap, rattled his walkie-talkie, and repeated his alert, including my ID, even louder. The bell rang for the passing period. *Oh, great. Now the whole school will witness me being hauled to the office.*

Mrs. Moorman rolled her eyes at him. "Raymond, yelling won't make a difference."

We marched back toward the entrance.

"All right, young lady," Mrs. Moorman continued to me. "Let's go into the office. You must have heard the principal call you on the intercom. Where did you think you were going?"

Dozens of students gawked at our show. Instead of the usual flow of bodies migrating to seventh-period classes, a group clumped at the open double entry doors, and heads peered out the windows all along the building. The principal, Mrs. Sanchez, was shooing the mass along, and she relieved Mrs. Moorman of my right arm at the entrance into the main hallway. Raymond still held my left arm as the three of us trudged through the rubbernecking students lining our route to the office.

Mrs. Moorman, following behind us in the hallway, blasted her whistle and roared, "Move it. Anyone not hustling on my count of three gets laps after school. One... two...."

Students started trying to move, but the crowd was thick as Jell-O. As bodies oozed by us, their stares—some curious, some sneering—made my face hot.

Finally, we reached the glassed-in waiting room, and Mrs. Sanchez left the guard and me while she and Mr. Hill went into her private office and shut the door. Mrs. Moorman had successfully emptied the hall, so at least no one gawked through the office windows at me. With his walkie-talkie back in his side holster, the guard stood directly in front of me, as though he thought I might flee. Miss Smart eyed me suspiciously while she pulled out a hairbrush and redid her ponytail. Then she got very busy straightening up the waiting area.

Sweet Tilly, the Down syndrome girl, and her teacher aide came in to deliver some papers to the office. Tilly beamed and patted the polka-dot hair ribbon I had helped her tie in her fine, reddish hair at lunch.

The corners of her lips fell. "Mean girls." She pronounced it *gulls* instead of *girls*.

Almost every time Tilly saw me, she remembered the torture of the day I first enrolled here—the jokes about my name, my skinniness, and my trailer. On that first day, at the end of last-period P.E., I had lingered in the gym, waiting for the grounds to clear, so I could walk home free from the herd of girls in my class. I was sitting on the bleachers, thinking I was alone, and I gave in to a brief bawling episode. I didn't know that Tilly, who took longer in the locker room than the rest of us, was still there. She came and sat beside me. I acted as though everything was okay and helped her put on her pink fanny pack—somehow the expandable waist band had gotten disconnected, and she couldn't get it back together by herself. I guess I didn't fool her because after I helped her, she patted my shoulder and said, "Mean gulls."

Now, sitting in the office, Tilly's sympathy broke my control over the tears, even though I never cry in public. I willed my eyes not to drip, but they filled anyway. I made my mouth keep smiling at Tilly, but she took a deep breath and held it as she peered closely at my eyes. Before I could distract her, she started gasping and crying herself.

She patted both my shoulders and rocked her head from side to side. "Mean gulls."

The teacher aide, who had been whispering with Miss Smart, and the guard jerked forward to get a close-up of Tilly.

Raymond narrowed his eyes at me. "What did you do to Tilly?" He gripped his walkie-talkie as if it were a gun.

His attitude stopped my tears. "Nothing. Tilly is talking about some other girls."

Raymond pulled out his little black pad and a pencil. "What other girls?" Before I could answer, he glanced at the aide as if to see whether she knew anything. She shrugged, and he zeroed in on me again. "Well?"

"I'm not sure. I'm new, and I didn't know their names."

He slid the pad back into his pocket. "What exactly did you see them do to Tilly?"

Tilly's gaze flitted between Raymond and me. Frantic worry lines twitched around her eyes. I laid my hand on her shoulder, to comfort her. The nosy aide was focused on me rather than on her job of distracting Tilly.

"Nothing to Tilly." I tried to figure out how to explain Tilly's sympathy for all the tricks of my first week, especially in P.E.. But I didn't want to leak embarrassing details about girls yelling stuff like, "Whoo-hoo, bean-pole Polarity... poet of the park—the trailer park!"

About this time a police officer—not a school officer—arrived, and Miss Smart instantly dropped her housekeeping chores and ushered him out of sight, into Mrs. Sanchez's office. My stomach dropped. Some catastrophe could have happened. Mobile homes burn faster than regular houses. Even though ours is new and Dad does regular safety checks on all the alarms, I envisioned our cozy trailer in flames.

Tilly, the aide, Miss Smart, Raymond, and I froze. Mrs. Sanchez opened her door and motioned for me to come in.

I hugged Tilly. "Don't worry about me anymore." I looked directly in her eyes, to be sure she listened. "Everything is just fine. No more crying. Okay?"

She gave her happy, squinty-eyed smile, and she hugged me back. "Kay, Pohlee."

I forced myself to turn away from Tilly and go into the private office. After Mrs. Sanchez closed the door behind me, she pointed to a chair next to her desk. "Please sit here." Mr. Hill and the officer, a stocky, gray-haired man, were seated on the other side of the room, and both were studying their shoes.

"What happened to my parents?"

The officer must have known, but he kept his head down.

"Are they okay?"

Mrs. Sanchez was the only one in the room who seemed to be listening to me.

"Did my mother do something?"

Mrs. Sanchez looked more like someone's cookie-baking grandmother than a principal. "The authorities haven't done anything yet." With her roundness, her curly black and gray hair, and her soft voice, it was weird to hear her talk about authorities. "That's why we need to talk to you first. Polarity, we understand that some very bad things have been going on in your life." She paused as if she wanted me to say something. "And I know it's hard to tell outsiders, but I need you to tell me the truth. And I promise no one will hurt you."

Could they know about last Christmas, when Mom disappeared for four days, or about her arguments with our neighbors in Houston? "Where are my mom and dad?"

Mrs. Sanchez patted my shoulder, just like Tilly had. "As far as we know, your parents are fine. They haven't been informed about this yet."

"Informed? About what?"

"The fact that we found a nude picture of you on the Internet."

I laughed with relief. My parents were fine. "No, ma'am. That's not true." That must've been what Danny had on his computer—some porno picture that resembled me. "There's no nude picture of me on the Internet."

"Would you like to see a printout?" She placed her hand on a blue folder on her desk.

"Okay."

She slid the folder across so that it rested directly in front of me. I glanced at Mr. Hill and the officer, who both quickly averted their eyes. Mrs. Sanchez slowly opened the folder, but she kept her eyes on me.

My first thought: *That naked, skinny, brown-haired girl has a pitiful flat chest just like mine.*

My second thought: *That has to be me. It's my narrow face, brown eyes, wavy hair that almost reaches my boobs, the V-neck tan lines from our fishing trip to the coast, but I never posed for that picture.*

She—I—was giving a big toothy grin. I hated my big teeth and always smiled with my lips slightly parted. And she—I—was dancing and waving both hands at the camera. I never posed like that, even dressed. And if I were naked, I'd try to cover my private parts, not flash them forward.

Am I totally crazy? Was I drugged? Have I entered an alternate universe? Do I have a twin I don't know about?

Someone had used Photoshop to draw a party hat on her—me—and write all kind of graffiti stuff. A layer of pink and yellow zigzag lines completely covered the background, and on top of those lines were school mottos, written in orange and green: "Go Shooting Stars," "Blaze to Win," "Burn the Mustangs." Intermixed were some phrases about me: "Bean-Pole Polaritey," "Polaritey of the Park." And right across the feet, the only covered part of the body, a textbox said:

Hi, I really need my own special hotie.
Come and get me. Poetic Polaritey.

I couldn't stop staring at the picture. Every time my brain tried to rationalize that this couldn't be me, another detail screeched, "Oh yes, it is you."

On my first day at this school, the English teacher, Mrs. Mitchell, asked me to introduce myself to the class. I made the fatal error of mentioning that I liked Emily Dickinson's poetry, and some clown dubbed me Poetic Polarity on the spot. Even if there were another girl identical to me, she couldn't also be named Polarity *and* be dubbed "Poetic." It had to be me.

I hated that people would think I wrote such a pathetic two-line poem, with no iambs or mature rhyme scheme. And how weird that my name was spelled wrong. But the worst thing of all was that Ethan may have seen it. He seemed to be the one person who wasn't in on the picture. He'd tried to help when Danny mouthed off about me in class. What if Ethan saw it? He'd lose all respect for me.

I could barely trust my voice. "I want to call my dad."

Mrs. Sanchez rolled her chair closer to me. "Polarity, did your father take this picture?"

"No, of course not. He would never, *never* do anything like that." My dad, a hero in every way, was the most conscientious, protective father I'd ever heard of. I felt sick to my stomach. *This can't be happening.*

"How about your mom? Why did you ask if your mom had done something? Did she take the picture?"

"No." I wanted to destroy the picture, but I made my trembling hands close the folder.

Mrs. Sanchez sighed and looked down at the closed folder. I expected that now she would grill me about why I ran out of the school.

She raised sad eyes back to me. "Then tell me, who took the picture?"

I guess fleeing school isn't even worth fretting over, in light of a naked picture.

I told her the truth. "I don't know. None of this makes sense." I met her gaze, hoping that somehow she'd see I wasn't lying. "I never posed for that picture."

The police officer sent Mr. Hill out and asked me hundreds of questions, mostly about my parents. Why did we move so much? Why did we live in a trailer if we have a house in Houston? Why were we in Garcia, since my dad didn't have a construction site here? A second officer, wearing a static-popping speakerphone on his shoulder, came, and repeated most of the same questions. His speakerphone, tuned into a dispatch operator, allowed the officer to listen to my answers and the ongoing police reports at the same time.

After the last bell of the day, Miss Smart stuck her head in the door. "Would you like for me to stay late, Mrs. Sanchez? I don't mind if there's anything I can help with." She eyed me with curiosity. "Anything at all."

Mrs. Sanchez ushered her out with clear instructions to leave. While the office door was open, the two officers left, saying they'd be in the conference room. They crossed the secretary's area and went into a room a few steps past Miss Smart's desk. They shut the door, and I could no longer hear what they were saying, but the electronic racket of the shoulder-mounted speaker still bleeped through the quiet office.

"May I go home now?" I asked Mrs. Sanchez when we were alone. "My mother will be worried. She's probably on her way here now or maybe outside already."

"I'm sorry, but no. You can't go home. The police still need to ask questions. They're probably talking to your parents now. Tell me what you'd like for supper?"

Supper. She thought I was staying for supper. I stared at her in silence.

She put her hand on mine. "You must eat, dear. How about something from Wendy's?"

I could barely speak, much less eat. But I forced out an answer. "Plain baked potato."

"Okay, we'll—"

A girl called from the reception area, "Mrs. Sanchez, come quick! It's the Boy Scouts in the gym. Someone's hurt."

"Oh, my goodness. What now?" She went into the front area for a few seconds then stuck her head back in. "I'll be just over in front of the gym. I'll be within sight of the reception room door, so don't leave. I'll be watching the whole time. Is that okay? Will you be okay a few minutes?"

17

I nodded and laid my head on her desk. Almost as quickly as she shut the door, it opened again. I raised my head, expecting that she'd forgotten something, but Ethan stepped into the room.

I stood. "What are you doing here?"

"What's going on?" He approached me and raised his hands as if to put them on my shoulders, but he stopped and lowered them to his sides. "What did Danny have on his computer?" His eyes showed concern, and something like anger tensed a muscle in his jaw. "Why are you still here? Why the cops?"

I didn't know where to begin.

He moved even closer to me. "Are you okay?"

I looked down.

He took my chin and raised my head so we were face to face. He had never touched me before. The feeling sent a buzz through my body. "Polarity, you can tell me. It's Danny, isn't it? Maybe I can help, but we have to hurry. Mrs. Sanchez will be back in about two minutes."

I reached to the folder on the desk and opened the bottom edge just enough to slide the picture down, so that the lower half of my legs could be seen. He took his hand away from my chin, and I had to resist the urge to pull him back. My voice came out in a hoarse whisper. "I don't know how this picture was taken, but it's me with no... no clothes on." I ripped the printout and held up the bottom half, with my legs and the textbox across the feet.

Ethan put a warm, strong hand over my trembling one and took the sheet from me. "I'll figure it out. Don't worry."

Through the partially opened door came the voice of the loud-talking girl, still exclaiming about the scouts, alerting us that she and Mrs. Sanchez were coming back toward the office.

Ethan squeezed my hand and whispered, so close that I could feel his breath on my face, "Don't worry." He shoved the picture of my legs into his pocket, slipped out the door, left it ajar, and jerked open the cabinet below the aquarium in the waiting area.

"Ethan, you're still here," Mrs. Sanchez said as she entered the office.

"Yes, ma'am. Just checking the water filter." I watched his strong back through the cracked door. "Fish food clogged it this morning—want to make sure it's good for the night."

"Thank you, Ethan. I appreciate your dependability. I can always count on you."

I agreed with her. Even in my few weeks at Star, I had figured out that Ethan always defended the underdog. And no one—not even Danny—messed with him. I guessed that I was probably the most desperate underdog on the planet. A new mission for Ethan.

Mrs. Sanchez asked, "Do you have a ride home?"

"Yes, ma'am. Shanique's mom is giving me a ride." Shanique must have been the loud-talking girl.

While they said their good-byes, I opened the blue folder. Under the picture I had just ripped lay a duplicate, so I took the torn one out, folded it, and shoved it into my back pocket as Ethan had done with his half. I hoped Mrs. Sanchez wouldn't miss the top picture. Maybe she'd assume a police officer took it.

Through the window behind the principal's desk, I watched Ethan and Shanique walk quickly toward the street. I had seen Shanique on campus before even though we didn't have any classes together. She was as tall as me, but she was all curves and toned muscle. The Star orange-and-green gym shorts and shirt she wore meant she was in track, but she moved more like a dancer than an athlete.

Mrs. Sanchez's soft-soled shoes shuffled back into her office, but I couldn't pull my eyes off Ethan and Shanique. He kept his face forward as they walked, and Shanique swerved closer to him, talking with her hands flying. Her skin, rich and dark as his, glowed with amber highlights compared to his chocolate tones. She briefly put her hand on his arm and faced him with a bright smile, giving me a perfect silhouette of her long, elegant neck and artfully angled haircut. *They must be a couple.* How could two people be so gorgeous? So perfect? So lucky?

Mrs. Sanchez sat behind her desk. "Sorry for that interruption—the Boy Scouts are fine. How are you holding up, dear?"

"Okay."

Ethan and Shanique rounded a corner, and I could no longer see them.

When I turned towards Mrs. Sanchez, she started to say something else, but a third police officer, this one in plain clothes, came in, and we went through all the questions again. Finally, after he finished, yet another officer brought me a baked potato from Wendy's. He and Mrs. Sanchez left me alone to eat while they went into the outer office.

I picked at the potato, hoping that at any moment, Mom and Dad would show up and shut this craziness down. My parents suffocated me with their protectiveness, but Dad was strong and competent. He could run major construction sites across the state, so these small-town officials would be no challenge to him. And Mom, even with her issues, would fiercely defend me. When they arrived, I'd be finished answering these questions.

The officer who brought the food left the door open a little when he went into the outer office, where Mrs. Sanchez talked on the phone. Aside from her soft voice, the office area was deadly quiet—no students, no more police radios, nothing. It was night. Everything looked strange, with darkness at the windows instead of the usual sunlight and dozens of ninth-graders.

Mrs. Sanchez dropped the office phone into its receiver with a soft click. "I can't believe they're picking her up tonight."

You don't know my parents, if you can't believe that. I was amazed they weren't here already. At any moment, they'd burst in and get everything cleared up, and we'd go home and laugh about this circus.

But the officer said, "Think about it. They're living in a travel trailer. They could be in Mexico in a couple of hours. The department can't risk it."

Who were they talking about? Who was going to pick me up?

"But," Mrs. Sanchez said, "I believe it's a prank. That's all."

"Maybe," the officer answered. "But why do they move so much? It doesn't add up. The father claims he owns a construction company, but he moves every few weeks or months and lives in a little trailer."

"But the services are usually slow. Picking her up tonight... I'm just surprised, I guess."

"They've got the picture—that's concrete evidence that someone did something. How could they let her go home and—"

I pushed the door all the way open. "Who's picking me up?"

Mrs. Sanchez, her pained gaze burrowing into my own, started to say something but stopped as if she couldn't find the words.

The officer looked down at the floor.

I stepped forward. "Who's picking me up?"

No one spoke. Mrs. Sanchez moved closer to me, but the officer slinked farther back. Their silence was scarier than anything they could have said.

I took a deep breath and kept my voice steady and firm. "I want to know who, and I want to know where my parents are."

Mrs. Sanchez put her arm around my shoulder. "I'm so sorry to have to tell you this. I know this is so hard for you. Please remember, Polarity, that in the end this will all get—"

The officer tilted his head toward the outer door. "I think she's here now."

Relief flooded me. *Yes. Mom.* But a young, dark-haired woman came in. She wasn't in uniform or anything—just ordinary jeans and plaid shirt.

"Where's Mom?" I asked.

Everyone shuffled around, talking at once. No one answered my question.

Mrs. Sanchez introduced me to the woman, Lacy Wright. I lost track of most of what they said, but phrases punched through my confusion and sent chills up my spine before my brain could process them. "... Child Protective Services... young people like you when they have to be taken from their families for a while."

I stopped breathing. *This can't be happening—stuff like this happens only in movies.*

"... safe house in another town... until the police have figured out what is going on."

Mrs. Sanchez and Miss Wright studied me, as if waiting for a reaction.

My stomach clenched. The food I'd just eaten pressed like a rock, ready to be thrust out. I tried to keep my voice firm, but it quivered, just as it had with Ethan. "But what if it's just students playing with Photoshop—someone playing a trick?"

Miss Wright shook her head. "The police are considering that, and they'll trace the IP address and send the picture to a lab for analysis." She spoke softly, as if there were a sleeping baby in the room. "But for now, especially since you aren't giving us any explanation, we can't risk sending you home." She stepped closer to me. "You'll be in protective custody for your own safety."

Long moments passed before I could make myself speak. "Okay." The hours of questions, the principal, the social worker, the police, and the picture itself had clustered, as if into a massive boulder that shut me down. I couldn't get my voice to say more. I followed Lacy Wright toward the exit.

"Wait," the police officer said.

I froze in the doorway that led into the reception area while he whispered something to Mrs. Sanchez.

She listened to the officer, and her pained eyes shifted towards me. "Polarity, dear, I need to search your backpack before you leave."

I handed it to her, turned my back on all of them, and listened to my belongings clatter onto her desk. Keeping my gaze on the aquarium while she shuffled through the stuff, I felt as trapped and alone as that red-and-blue betta. *This is unreal. My bag is being searched, I'm leaving the school at night with a stranger to go someplace I've never been, and no one believes me. Except Ethan.*

CHAPTER 2

"POLARITY, WAKE UP."

As soon as I looked around the car, my living nightmare came rushing back. I must have been asleep for at least an hour because my hair stuck to my cheek from perspiring on the vinyl covered seat.

Miss Wright jiggled my arm. "We're here—at the safe house where you'll stay."

She opened her door. We were in a regular neighborhood. Near the car was a bright blue tricycle some small child had probably forgotten to take home.

I followed Miss Wright out of the car and up the sidewalk, which was bordered with marigolds. The cracked old walkway led up to a weathered white wood house with a gated area, like a courtyard, in front of the door. Miss Wright pushed a button on the speaker box.

Someone answered, "May I help you?"

"Hi, Hannah. Lacy Wright here with Polarity."

A sharp click broke the silence as the gate unlocked, and after we got inside the courtyard, the gate shut behind us, and the front door of the house snapped open. A lady about my grandmother's age, with long gray braids and wearing a T-shirt and sweats, stood in the doorway.

"Come in, Polarity. I'm glad you're finally here." She beamed as if I were a Christmas present. "You must be so tired. I know this has been a long, awful day for you." Her lotion-scented arms, tattooed with several different flowers, wrapped around me before I could say anything. "My name is Hannah, and I'm going to help you while you're here."

Somehow her sympathy made me want to cry, so I gave a short answer, to keep my voice normal. "Thanks." *I shouldn't be here. This is all a mistake.*

Stacks of board games, all kinds of drums, and beanbag chairs filled the musty-smelling front room. I waited while Hannah did some paperwork with Miss Wright. The rest of the house was dark except for little nightlights plugged into the wall sockets, along a hall that stretched all the way to the back end of the house.

After Miss Wright left, Hannah whispered while she led me down the hall. "These old walls are thin—not very sound-proof—and the other girls are sleeping in these two rooms we're passing. We have five girls right now, other than you. They wanted to stay up to meet you, but it got too late. We're going to go all the way to the end of this hallway. The room where you'll sleep tonight is a small one next to mine. But tomorrow we'll settle you in a regular room with the other girls."

We passed through her room with a mussed bed, and she pointed out the bathroom and my room. "Here we are. Your digs for tonight. It's small, no furniture except the bed and no windows, but you'll get a better room in the morning." She held up a pair of pajamas. "I think these will fit you. Now, are you hungry or thirsty?"

I mumbled, "No thanks."

"Do you have any questions?"

"How long?"

"What do you mean, Polarity?"

I sat on the bed and gripped the fluffy comforter with one hand to steady myself. "How long will I be here?"

"Not more than thirty days. This is just an emergency placement facility—until foster care is finalized or you're allowed to return to your parents."

Thirty days. Foster care. Crashing fear, the same as I'd felt earlier in the day when I thought Mom and Dad might have been in a fire, left me shaking. Hannah dropped to the edge of the bed next to me. "Is there anything else you're wondering about?"

No one would allow me to call Mom or Dad. "May I call my grandmother?" My voice cracked.

"I'm sorry, but until your case is assigned, you won't be allowed to contact anyone."

"Assigned?"

"Yes, you'll be assigned a caseworker who'll figure out who you can have contact with." She stood again. "What else can I help you with?"

Questions swirled in my mind, but I didn't want to cry, so I shook my head.

She put her hand on my shoulder. "You'll be safe here, and I'll be sleeping right in there. If you need anything, just call out 'Hannah,' and I'll be here, lickety-split. And things will look better tomorrow. They always do." She clicked on the little plug-in nightlight. "Are you ready for the top light to be turned off?"

"Yes, ma'am."

The door squeaked as she closed it with a soft thud. I set the pajamas on the foot of the bed. With all my clothes and shoes still on, I lay on the bed with my backpack hugged to my chest. I listened to Hannah move around, settle into her bed, and—a little while later—start to snore softly.

The nightlight gave a little pop—the bulb had burned out. It left the room so dark that it looked the same whether I had my eyes open or shut. I used to be afraid if I couldn't see, but that day's living nightmare made the darkness less than nothing.

The door of my room squeaked open, and the dark outline of a person appeared. It couldn't be Hannah—she was still snoring. *Oh, no. What else is going to happen?*

I gasped to holler when the intruder whispered, "Don't be scared. I'm Zada—I stay at this house, too." She quietly shut the door and found her way to the bed.

When the edge of the bed shifted with her weight, I sat up, too, still holding my backpack to my chest.

"Do you want your nightlight on?" she asked.

"I think the bulb burned out."

"Well, that's okay. Sometimes it's nice not to see. I'm fifteen. I live with my grandmother, but she had a stroke." She talked fast—she had told this story many times. "Until she gets on her feet, I had to come back into foster care. I've been to this facility before, and it's a good place. Hannah's okay—means well. You can trust her."

She stopped talking and waited as if she wanted me to tell my story. I couldn't make out her features, but from her shadowy outline, she seemed shorter than me. I didn't know where to start. I didn't think I could say out loud everything that had happened.

After a silence, Zada asked, "How old are you?"

"Fifteen."

"Oh, we're the same. Are you scared?"

Her simple, basic question comforted me. With the hundreds of questions today, no one had asked if I was scared. It was a breath of air. "Yeah."

"Brothers and sisters?"

"No. Just my mom and dad."

Her we're-in-this-together tone made me want to tell her everything. "Your real dad or your mom's boyfriend?"

"My real dad."

"What happened to you?"

I took a deep breath. I wanted her to know, but the words didn't come.

Finally, she asked, "This is your first time, isn't it?" Her warm voice made me feel connected.

"Yeah." The room was so dark that I gave up trying to see her face, and in a way, it was easier to talk without seeing anything.

"It will help if you tell what happened." She paused, and from the shifting on the bed, I sensed that she scooted closer to me. "Telling takes the sharpness out of it. And each time you tell, it gets easier."

I eased my backpack off my lap onto the bed, and in a whisper in the pitch-black room, I told her about the day, starting with sixth-period history. She had been right—it did help to tell it. Especially to tell someone who really heard me. Other than Ethan, she was the first person to ask for my side of the story.

"Maybe somebody cut your head off a photo and stuck it on a naked body."

I remembered that crazy moment when I saw the picture. "I don't know. It looked like my body."

"Well, if they blame your parents for taking the picture, you'll be placed in foster care. But if they blame a student, you'll both be kicked out and have to go to alternative school."

"But I didn't pose for that picture. That's the truth." I wrapped my arms around my stomach, hugging myself.

"I know this sucks, but they won't believe you."

"But they can't prove anything. I can't be blamed if I don't even know about it."

"All the proof they need is the picture."

I couldn't speak or move. I bit my lip and sat, frozen in my own embrace.

"You have to stand strong even if no one believes you." Zada's voice went inside me. "When I was five and first went into foster care, I thought I'd die. But I'm still here—still myself. Don't worry about what they think—just tell what you know to be the truth. Just think about the next step you will—"

A cry came from another part of the house.

"That's Natasha—probably having nightmares again. I'll go check." The mattress shifted as Zada moved off the bed. "We'll talk some more tomorrow."

When she opened the door, the outline of her back slipped out. I drifted in and out of sleep through the crying, Hannah's snores, and the creaks of the old house.

Something startled me awake. For an instant, I tried to convince myself the voices coming from the front of the house fit with our trailer and my little fold-out bed in the front room. But the 3-D nightmare of my naked picture flashed in my mind, and I wished it was a dream and I'd wake to see Mom in the kitchen mixing a smoothie for me.

Every awful thing from the day before hit me at once. I started crying. Loud, out-of-control sobs rocked my body. I clutched the sheet up to my salty tear-covered face. With all my experiences in changing schools and dealing with Mom's issues, I excelled at putting on a stoic front. But at that moment, my front wasn't big enough to hold back the tsunami: my naked picture on the Internet, my parents blamed, not knowing what town I was in or when I'd see Mom and Dad again.

Hannah came in and sat on the bed beside me. She tried to hand me a washcloth and a glass of water, but I didn't take them. "Polarity—there, there. Here, drink some water." She sat beside me for a long time and said nice things that made me cry harder. Finally, she sighed. "It's okay if you need to cry." She hummed softly for a few minutes. "When you're ready, let's go have some breakfast, meet the other girls. Maybe we'll get some news today about your case."

As soon as she mentioned the other girls, I thought about Zada—my thin lifeline, who'd come in the night. Knowing I could talk with her made me feel like getting out of bed to face the next threat.

I drank the water and wiped my face with the cool, damp cloth. "Do I have time for a shower?"

"You betcha." She handed me a blue T-shirt and underwear. "Here's a clean shirt and undies for you. You'll probably want to wear your own jeans—I don't think we have any in your size."

I nodded and took the clothes, unsurprised that she didn't have jeans long and skinny enough for me.

"And when you're done, just follow your nose to the kitchen, just up the hallway. We'll all be in there."

After my shower, the smell of bacon and the sounds of clattering and voices led me to the kitchen, where Hannah and five black-haired teenaged girls in pajamas were working on breakfast. One of them asked, "Why do you think she's named Polarity—like an electrical charge, positive and neg—"

I stepped into the room, and they all turned toward me. One of them was pregnant. She was the shortest of the group—probably close to Mom's five feet two—and she had long braids coiled around her head.

"Hi," I said. *Which one is Zada?*

All five girls froze and stared, mouths gaping open. I looked down at myself and checked my clothes, just as I had the day before in history. Chills sickened me. Had they seen my naked picture?

Hannah broke the silence. "Everyone, meet Polarity Weeks. Polarity, this is—"

The gate buzzer interrupted.

"One moment." Hannah went to the intercom speaker on the wall. "Yes, may I help you?"

"Hannah, good morning. Deputy Gonzales. Need to speak with you, please."

"Be right there. Girls, introduce yourselves, and go ahead and eat," Hannah said as she started up the hall toward the entry room.

The five girls had stayed frozen the entire time, their eyes stuck on me. I wished I could disappear. *They must have seen me on the Internet. Maybe it's gone viral this morning.* The tallest girl—as tall as Dad's six feet two—said, "Zada, why didn't you tell us she's white?"

It took a moment to register that they were staring at me because of the color of my skin, not because they saw the naked picture. Two of these girls, the pregnant one and the tall one, were black, and the other three looked Hispanic.

"I didn't know. It was too dark to see," answered the pregnant one. *Zada.*

Zada was pregnant. When her silhouette passed through the open doorway last night, I hadn't noticed the baby bump. We'd talked about only my problems. We hadn't even touched on being fifteen and pregnant.

The tall girl shrugged, and her brows lifted. "I didn't know they let white kids in here."

They continued talking as if I weren't there.

Zada cut them off. "Hey, Polarity. You can sit here. Have some pancakes and bacon." She added to the tall girl, "Well, where do you expect white kids to go?"

29

"Hi, Polarity," said the tall one. "I don't mean to be rude, but I never saw a white kid in the system before."

Another girl, wearing Betty Boop pajamas—I think the same one who had been talking about my name when I came in—said, "I've seen them before, but they don't stay in long. Hi, I'm—"

"Polarity," Hannah called from the front of the house. "Could you come here, please?"

The girls continued their preparations as if that kind of request was routine.

I went to the entry room, where Hannah stood with a wide-faced young man in a police uniform and a middle-aged woman wearing black slacks and a blouse with embroidered roses circling the neckline.

"This is Deputy Gonzales and his assistant, Tammy." The assistant, smiling and nodding, stood behind the deputy. "They're going to take you to the sheriff's office to review your case."

The deputy smiled, but I guess I looked scared because Hannah put her arm around my shoulder and squeezed. "This is a good sign, Polarity. It shows that things are moving forward quickly. Someone is investigating. Sometimes you have to wait weeks before the authorities even get started. You go get your things, and I'll pack you some fruit to take."

I left the room, hearing the deputy say, "Yeah. There's a big push on this one—been getting calls since last night."

After I gathered my stuff and made sure I hadn't left a mess in the bedroom or bathroom, I went back to the kitchen, where Hannah waited with a bag of oranges and bananas. All five girls stopped in mid-sentence or mid-bite. Hannah offered a paper plate of pancakes and bacon, but I told her no thanks.

"Bye," I said, glancing around at them.

They mumbled good-byes, and Hannah led me back toward the entry.

As we walked away, one of the girls in the kitchen said, "You were right. Whites get out quick."

Before we reached the front door, I stopped and returned to the kitchen. "Zada, thank you for talking to me—you really helped."

Her face lit up in a big, beautiful smile, and she came and gave me a hug. She whispered, "You're going to do fine. You'll kick butt." She squeezed harder. "But remember—things will get worse before they get better." When she pulled away, her expression had saddened, and she looked at me with old eyes.

What had she experienced to make her look so much older than me? Am I going to learn those things, too?

CHAPTER 3

I N THE FRONT RECEPTION AREA of the Baker County Sheriff's office, an older lady heaved herself up from a stuffed chair and grabbed a large, battered briefcase. "Good. You're here. I'm Nelda Sims, state-level case administrator for Child Protective Services"— she thrust a business card into my hand—"assigned to determine your temporary placement. Let's go to the conference room."

Deputy Gonzales, Nelda Sims, and I went into a room labeled in bold black letters, Holding A2. A large part of one wall was glass, letting me see Tammy sit at a desk right outside the door. Like interrogation rooms in the movies, the only furniture was a square metal table and the three chairs where we sat. The scrape of our moving chairs echoed off the bare walls and tile floor. There was no spare chair, and the table was small, so I kept my backpack on my lap. I didn't see a two-way mirror or camera, and fortunately, there was no computer or folder that could be holding my naked picture.

The deputy removed his cap and rubbed his hand over his black, buzzed hair while he set an old-fashioned tape recorder on the table and pushed record. "Would you like to begin, Mrs. Sims?"

I figured we'd spend the next hour hashing through what happened.

Mrs. Sims rubbed her eyes from underneath her glasses. "Polarity, tell me about your food intolerances. Explain what foods you can't eat."

Why is she asking that? "I can't have anything with gluten or soy. Where are my mom and dad?"

"I don't know. They're not in custody right now." She plunked her briefcase in front of her on the tabletop.

"Can I go home?" I looked from her to the officer, hoping one of them would say yes or nod or give a glimmer of hope, but his expression showed pity, and hers seemed curious and annoyed.

"No, I'm afraid you won't be able to go home until the police have completed their investigation of your parents." She rested her hands on top of her case.

What does she have in there? "But they didn't do anything."

"I've been working cases like this for over thirty years, and in order to get this resolved as quickly as possible, we need to do two things this morning." She snapped her case open and pulled out a folder.

Please, not the picture.

"One, we need to decide where you're going to stay during the investigation, and that's why I want to talk about your food intolerances." She opened the folder and skimmed over a form. "And two, we need to get to the truth about who took the picture of you. Which one shall we cover first?"

The picture topic would be a dead end, so I picked the first one. "Well, if I eat gluten or soy, I get sick. Depending on how much I eat, it might be as simple as a stomachache or as bad as total dehydration, dizziness, hives—"

"Dizziness?" she cut in.

"Yeah, dizziness." I pulled my backpack up from my lap and hugged it.

"So do you ever forget things?" She and Deputy Gonzales glanced at each other with raised eyebrows.

"No." *Duh. Kind of a stupid question. How would someone remember that they forgot stuff?* And I was sure that I didn't forget because I didn't have time gaps in my memory.

"Are you sure?"

Why is she asking me this again? How is this going to help clear up this mess? "Yes, I'm sure. It's just dizziness."

She checked more boxes. "Okay, so what's the everyday name for gluten?"

"Gluten is protein that's in wheat, rye, or barley. I guess most people just call it flour, though not all flour has gluten in it."

She nodded for me to go on.

"Gluten is in almost every processed and fast food there is—ketchup, mustard, mayonnaise, salad dressings, processed meats. Any processed food that doesn't have gluten probably has soy."

She cleared her throat, lurched forward, and peered into my eyes as if she'd find my next answer written there. "Did you tell anyone about this—Hannah or the Garcia officers when they questioned you at your school?"

"No, no one asked me about it."

She frowned. "What have you eaten since you've been in custody?"

"Yesterday I had a baked potato, and this morning I ate an orange from Hannah and some nuts that I had in my backpack."

"That's all. You're sure?" Nelda Sims didn't act like the social workers I had read about. People in protective services were supposed to side with the victim. This woman was gruff and repetitive.

"Yes, that's all."

She and Deputy Gonzales looked at each other and smiled—as if relieved of a big problem. She shifted her attention back to me. "Thank you, Polarity, for being responsible and careful. We would not want you to get sick from eating something that's bad for you."

Why would she thank me for doing what anyone would normally do? I didn't know what to say, so I waited for her to go on.

"I guess it's pretty hard not eating the things that other kids do."

"Not really." My voice wavered. "My mom always makes healthy stuff that tastes good. Sometimes other kids want to have what I get."

"Who took the picture?" she asked.

Zada's secret-in-the-dark talk with me the night before made it easier to retell. And it was no shock when they didn't believe me.

After I explained that I knew nothing, she said, "If you're protecting someone, sooner or later we'll find out who that is. If you tell us more now, we might not have to investigate your parents anymore."

"I wish…" I had to stop and regain my voice. "I wish I could tell you. I want to go home. If I could tell you, I would. I don't want to be away from my parents. And I don't want them to be investigated. But I don't know anything about that picture." I clutched my backpack tighter and made myself meet her glare. "I know it sounds crazy, but that's the truth."

Her next question shot into me like a bullet. "Did you do the background—all the graffiti?"

Somehow, her single-minded aggressiveness made me calmer. I looked away from her and spoke to the tape recorder. "I never saw the picture until Mrs. Sanchez showed me."

"Did you write the poem or did someone else?"

"If I had written it, I would have spelled my name right." My voice stayed steady. "I don't know who wrote it."

"You're a creative girl—a poet, right? Maybe you misspelled your name to throw us off. At least tell me where you were in the picture. That will help the police figure out who did it."

I didn't answer. She wasn't hearing or believing anything I said anyway.

For a long time, the only sounds were the air conditioner, our breathing, and muffled voices and laughing from the front office.

Finally, she shuffled through more forms. "Okay. Let's talk about something else. Why is it that you and your parents move around so much, even though your dad owns a home and construction business in Houston?"

"I knew you'd ask this." *Where to begin?* "Do you know what BPD—borderline personality disorder—is?" They both nodded, but I learned a long time ago that most people really don't understand it. "Mom has a borderline personality disorder. We moved to Garcia because her support group told her about a *curandero* who helps borderlines."

Mrs. Sims held up one hand. "Back up. What's a *curandero*?"

Deputy Gonzales said, "That's a Mexican healer—uses herbal remedies and meditations and prayers—who treats all kinds of sickness. They've got a couple of well-known ones in Garcia."

She jotted something onto a form. "Okay, Polarity. You relocated to Garcia for the healer. What about the other moves?"

"We went to Arizona because her doctor said that her disorder might be aggravated by allergies to pollens. Before that, we lived in

Austin for a while because there's an acupuncture group that treats borderlines. She's done all the traditional therapies, and we go to counseling a lot." Talking about this made me miss the times when we first moved to a new place. We would be happy, upbeat, and hopeful. But every new place eventually ended in disappointment. "But Mom doesn't want to take medication, so we keep searching for treatments that will help her. And we like living in our trailer—it's cozy...."

I had to stop. I loved Mom and Dad so much. I regretted that, only a few days ago, I had griped to Dad about wanting to go home to Houston, where I had my own room and old friends.

The deputy and Mrs. Sims waited, but I didn't go on. I didn't tell them about the time that Mom freaked because she thought the neighbors were evil spies, or about last December when she disappeared for four days while Dad and I were at a support group for families dealing with BPD. We didn't get home as soon as she expected, and she imagined we had left her for good, so she ran away rather than face being abandoned. Mom is smart, so very smart with a degree in anthropology, but she couldn't see her own paranoia.

"I love your name, Polarity. Is there a story behind that?" Deputy Gonzales asked, changing the subject. Maybe he could tell it was hard talking about Mom.

"Mom knows that BPD can cause her to see people as perfect or evil. She named me Polarity, spanning positive and negative, to remind her that I'm not one or the other."

The deputy and Mrs. Sims froze, surprised and listening.

"She wanted to be sure that she never judged me the way that borderlines tend to do." I hardly ever tell people that, but I guess the hundreds of questions yesterday and today were wearing me down.

For once, Mrs. Sims didn't write on a form. She and Deputy Gonzales sat in silence, as if waiting for more. There was nothing more to say.

He cleared his throat. "That's beautiful. It sounds like your mom loves you very much."

"So does my dad." I wished I could take back all the times I griped about my name.

Mrs. Sims asked, "Who were you dancing for and waving at in the picture?"

Her question jerked me out of my moment of sadness. "Do you want me to say it all again? I can't tell you any more than I already have."

She dropped her forms into her briefcase, clicked it shut, stood up, and opened the door. Tammy laughed loudly at someone she was talking to on the phone.

"Let's go make some calls," Mrs. Sims said to the deputy. She turned to me. "We're going to leave you for a while."

"Want a soda or snack?" Deputy Gonzales asked as he picked up his cap and the tape recorder.

I shook my head.

"You just let Tammy know if you need anything."

Relieved to be alone, I wondered what they would have thought if I had told them about our family counseling session a couple of months ago, when the psychologist asked Mom to explain why she named me Polarity. After Mom answered, he straightened tall in his chair and frowned at her. "Mrs. Weeks, don't you see that by giving your child a name that services your own personality disorder, you have indulged in a classic borderline act—you gave your child a name to serve your own needs. You completely negated her right to have a name for herself."

His words had surprised me. I've often griped about my weird name, but I'd never thought of it as self-serving on Mom's part. Of course, Mom then dropped into her dark zone and spewed out her most disturbing fears between gasping sobs. "Everyone must hate me... I'm such an evil person... What have I done to my daughter?"

We spent part of the session trying to get her spirits back up. I hated it when she called herself evil. Guilt engulfed me each time I couldn't fix her, couldn't make her stop thinking that.

Toward the end of the session, Mom asked, "Doctor, is mankind a borderline collective?"

He peered at her with a frown. "What do you mean?"

"Spaniards used their word for black to label a race of dark-skinned people. Is Negro used to label the race, or is it used to appease those who selected the name?"

"Your rationalization is not analogous—it is quite normal for culturists to assign descriptive categorical names. Completely misaligned with naming your child."

"But," Mom persisted—borderlines never, never lose an argument, and surprisingly, the psychologist let her suck him into this—"the people are brown, not black, so it isn't a purely descriptive name. And if races are named with a descriptive framework, then why is the light-skinned race, Caucasian, named after a mountain?"

Maybe the psychologist was also BPD because the debate continued until our time ran out. People with the disorder have a hard time with gray areas—they get trapped into needing to have extremes: good or evil, black or white, right or wrong. Mom and the psychologist both demanded to be right only minutes after they had discussed that my name was a reminder to be open to middle ground.

Afterwards, Mom, Dad, and I went to eat Indian food. I think we were kind of numb from the session because we were pretty subdued for a while.

Dad grinned at Mom. "Hon, I think you're smarter than the psychologist."

Mom's outraged gaze zeroed in on Dad. Every muscle in my body tensed. She twisted in her chair, frowned, and said, in a voice that totally sounded like the psychologist, "Could you rationalize that with an analogous example?"

We all cracked up laughing. Even though that session could have been labeled a failure, I loved to see Mom and Dad laugh together. And after that grueling hour with an outsider, we three had felt closer and happier.

After twenty minutes or so, Mrs. Sims came back in, this time alone. She patted my hand as she sat beside me. "Polarity, I'm just so impressed with how smart you are about food intolerances and bipolar disorder."

I wished she would just level with me. I'd rather have her rude questions than this kissing up. "Mom's not bipolar; she's borderline. Bipolar is a brain disorder. Borderline is emotional."

"Oh, yeah, that's right." She nodded and spieled off how it's okay for freshmen to pull pranks that go too far, how all students make mistakes, and how telling the truth makes everything better. Finally, she leaned in too close, and her voice got so low I could barely hear. "Polarity, dear, is this the first time someone made you do something like this, or has it happened before?"

I repeated my same story. Her lip curled, and she puffed up in aggravation. There was nothing I could say or do to convince her, and that sickened me. I could simply follow Zada's advice: tell the truth.

"You are clearly waving and smiling at the camera in that picture." She folded her arms. "Clearly. You must have some idea when and where it was taken. Even if you had not seen the camera, you must know who you were looking at when you danced naked and waved. The longer you wait to tell the truth, the worse it'll be for everyone."

I had never danced naked. "I'm sorry. I've told you all I know."

She unfolded her arms and put both hands on the table in front of her. "I don't believe you."

"I know."

She shoved herself up. "This is your last chance. If you're not going to give me any information about the picture, I'm leaving, and I won't be back."

I wanted to say *good*. "Good-bye."

As soon as she left, Deputy Gonzales came and stood in the doorway. "Look what I found for you over at the drug store." He held up an energy bar with a gluten-free label. "Thought you might like a snack."

I hated to disappoint him because he was trying. "Thank you, I appreciate it. But I think it has soy in it. Every bar, ice cream, gum, cookie—everything labeled with 'natural flavoring' can contain soy."

"What the...." He put on his glasses and squinted at the ingredients. "Yep. There it is. What do you eat?"

"All fruits, vegetables, meats, and dairy—as long as they have no additives—are fine."

"Well, I guess you never thought it would be a good thing to have your complicated food issues, right?"

Mystified, I stared at him.

"Your parents have convinced the state that you need to be with family immediately because of your extreme diet needs, so your grandmother is coming from Dallas to take you home with her." The word *grandmother* released a rush of joy even before my brain caught up with his words. "You'll still be restricted from contact with your parents until the investigation is finished."

"Thank you." I felt as if I were breathing again after being underwater for too long.

"In a little while, Tammy and I will drive you to the San Antonio airport to meet her. First, we've got to figure out what you can eat."

"Either Wendy's baked potato and salad, no dressing, or convenience store fruit and unseasoned nuts," I blurted, not wanting to waste time on food decisions. I had learned long ago how to sustain myself in all kinds of places. "Or we can skip it. I'm not hungry."

"Well, I am. We'll stop at Wendy's." He turned to Tammy, who was still at her desk. "Tammy, you ready?"

At the San Antonio airport, we waited for Grandma near a security office. She arrived sooner than I expected, in one of those little cars that they run through airports for handicapped people. The driver and Grandma were both having a big belly laugh. Grandma in her colorful, flowing clothes, made me think of what Dad always said about her: "Abby is a painted bunting among sparrows." Dad, an expert on birds and their calls, always labeled the small painted bunting as the most colorful in our region.

When the cart stopped, I stepped up and hugged her. "Thank you for coming for me."

"Oh, my little Polarity. You don't have to thank me." She called me little, but both she and mom were five foot two and barely weighed a hundred pounds. I had been taller than them for years. "I'm sorry for the trouble that brought us here. But I am so happy that you're coming to stay with me." She hugged me closer and whispered, "We can talk about everything later if you want to, but let's try to relax first."

She reached for her walker, and I lowered it to the ground and unfolded it for her. Grandma's legs were badly injured when Mom was four years old and their house burned down because of an electrical short. Two of Mom's sisters and her dad died in the fire. Grandma could manage without a walker, but she needed one for long periods of walking. Her legs were not only scarred but also shriveled with lots of muscle loss. Even with therapy, she never was able to fully replace the lost tissue.

She maneuvered herself into the walker with her strong arms. "Polarity, dig in my purse and hand me my cell phone. Before another second passes, I've got to send a text message to your parents, letting them know you're with me now."

When I handed her the phone, she located her text—already drafted—and pushed Send. "Okay. Let's get this show on the road."

Deputy Gonzales and Tammy introduced themselves while I put Grandma's phone back in her purse. We went into the office, and it took about thirty minutes for them to go over all the documents for Grandma to sign. I sat next to her the whole time, relieved that they didn't talk about the picture.

After they finished the paperwork, Deputy Gonzales, with his wide friendly face, stood. "Polarity, come here."

He had me stand next to Grandma's chair, and he put his hands on my shoulders. *Don't talk about the picture again.*

With a kind smile, he said, "Your grandma just signed an agreement that says the two of you will have no contact with your parents—no text, e-mail, phone calls, no messages through friends—nothing." He pointed at Grandma. "That text she sent your parents letting them know she is with you is the last communication she is allowed during the investigation. If you break that agreement, your case will be worse for everyone."

Grandma took my hand and squeezed it. When I glanced at her, she nodded, as if to say, *We can do this.*

"If there's an emergency need to communicate with your parents,

41

your grandma has the contact info for the Dallas caseworker. Any communication will have to go through that channel. Do you understand?"

"Yes, sir."

He made me say it all back to him. After he was satisfied that I understood, he said, "If you want to give us new information or help clarify who took the picture, let your caseworker know. That would help move things along."

"There won't be anything new," I said. "But would it be possible for me to get a mailing or e-mail address for Zada?"

He tilted his head, his expression puzzled.

"She's a girl I met at Hannah's."

"She won't have e-mail while she's there. I don't remember Hannah's mailing address offhand, but here's my card. If you e-mail or mail letters to me, I'll take them by Hannah's."

He and Tammy wished us luck and left.

Grandma asked, "Who's Zada?"

"She's a girl I met last night in the safe house. She listened to me and told me what to expect. I want to thank her and see how she's doing."

The next few hours were like a holiday adventure rather than the continuation of a nightmare. We had four hours before our flight to Dallas, so we got a wheelchair, explored the little shops in the airport, bought some magazines, and had a feast of Mexican food. The whole time, Grandma talked about all the fun we'd have in Dallas.

To my relief, she never once asked me about the picture. For now, we just enjoyed our time together.

Once we were sitting in the boarding area, I asked, "Grandma, how did you get here so fast?"

"Fast. I didn't get here fast. Fast would have been yesterday. Your mama and daddy tried their darnedest to get you and me hooked up last night. According to them and all the agencies across the state they've been hounding, today is pitifully late."

"How are Mom and Dad?" I asked.

"They're okay. You know when your mama gets a project, she is so focused that her other troubles fall away. Each time I've talked with her, she's been researching Internet tracing. I expect she'll be an expert by the time this is finished." She pointed to a model in the *Teen Vogue* we had picked up in the bookstore. "Oh, now look at this outfit. Do you like that? I could sew that up in no time. See how simple the top is—almost like a sheath. I've got a Simplicity pattern from the eighties that is the exact cut. What do you think? You know this would be a good outfit for you to learn to sew on."

"Sure, that would be great."

Grandma was trying to distract me from worrying. "And wait until you see all the new fabric I have."

I loved to go to Grandma's. Trunks of fabric, big jars of buttons, and baskets of trims and laces filled the sewing corner in her living room. When Mom was little, Grandma sewed for a living. She didn't have to support herself any longer because Mom and Dad helped her out, but she still sewed for fun. Her own clothes were always made of wildly colored, soft fabric that didn't hurt her tender skin, with long skirts that covered her legs.

"Oh, and when we're not working on your high school wardrobe, we can zone out on movies. You still don't have streaming movies yet? Right?"

"Of course not."

Mom and Dad allowed only limited amounts of monitored media. We spent most evenings reading or playing games, and much to my ongoing angst, we didn't even have cable. However, they had given Grandma Netflix and an Internet-connected television for Christmas.

"I didn't think you did—I know how strict they are about your brain development. Woo-hoo, girlfriend, you're on vacation now! We'll have double or triple feature every night—the world to choose from. Won't it be fun?"

It did sound fun.

The airport started boarding the handicapped and parents with babies. I helped Grandma stand and carried her purse and my backpack.

43

The friendly lady scanning our tickets, asked Grandma, "Is this your granddaughter?"

"Yes, ma'am. Isn't she a doll?"

"Yes, she is." She handed me our boarding passes. "And how nice she is to help you travel." She reached for the ticket from the person behind us.

But Grandma is the one helping me.

We got on board and ended up in a two-seater row together, so I offered to rub her legs. She always said I gave the best massages. She handed me her special lavender-scented lotion from her purse, and I spent the short flight massaging her scarred legs. The slick, rippled scars didn't feel like skin, and her muscles underneath were hard and stringy. I always forgot what a difference the normal layers of tissue made until I touched her limbs—they were just muscle and bone.

"Oh my gosh." She sighed. "You've always had a wonderful touch. You're going to spoil your grandma." She dozed because she jerked when the pilot gave an update on our progress over the intercom.

After we landed forty-five minutes later, she pulled out her phone and waited for the okay to use it. "I'm going to call my friend, Scooter. He'll pick us up. You'll be the first in the family to meet him." She grinned and shrugged the same way my best friend in Houston used to when he told yummy secrets. "Polarity, I have a boyfriend!"

I could hardly believe my ears. As far as I knew, she'd never had a date after my grandfather died. "You *do*?"

"Yes, and he's just the nicest man. I was planning to introduce him to everyone in June when you were all supposed to visit. I didn't want to tell your mama ahead of time because she'd worry about me spending time with a man she doesn't know. So, now you'll be the first to meet him."

"Wow." I thought I'd had all the surprises possible for a while. "Where did you meet him?"

"Yoga class. He has quite a bod. And he's really smart—used to be a Dallas County prosecuting attorney."

They gave the okay to use electronics, so Grandma made her call. A twenty-minute de-boarding process and two shuttle rides later, we arrived at the exit labeled Passenger Pickup. Grandma was tired by now, so we picked up a wheelchair for the last trek of the journey.

"That way." As we rolled outside, she pointed to a red Buick LaCrosse.

The man standing next to it smiled and waved. He reminded me of Dad because they were both tall and fit and suntanned as if they spent time outside. But Scooter was older, with loose, white hair that hung down to the collar of his denim shirt.

I rolled her chair toward him.

"Welcome home, Abby." He hugged her as she stood from her chair. "And this must be your beautiful granddaughter, Polarity. So happy to meet you." He clasped my hand with a firm, warm grip.

"Hi."

"You can call me Scooter." He opened the door and helped Grandma into the front seat. "I know it's a funny name for an old man, but it's what everyone calls me."

"Okay." He acted nice, but honestly I didn't relish getting acquainted with one more person or making small talk. And I didn't want to talk with him about the naked picture.

New-car smell and white leather greeted me when he opened the back door. He arranged for an attendant to take back the wheelchair, and we were off. We chatted during the ride home, which was lengthened by heavy traffic. Luckily, Grandma and Scooter had enough to catch up on without asking me too many questions.

The comfortable back seat of Scooter's car, the calm rhythm of Grandma's and Scooter's voices, and later the familiar tree-lined streets near Grandma's condo neighborhood made me more relaxed than I'd expected to be that day, when I awoke that morning at Hannah's. Grandma's home had always been a special place, filled with memories of good visits, sometimes with my parents and sometimes by myself.

The sun was setting when he pulled up in front of her condo, and he came inside with us while they continued to talk about their day. *Does he live with Grandma now?*

He reached for my hand. "Polarity, while you're here, I hope that you'll come swimming at my house." His smile was kind as we shook hands. "Your grandmother and I do laps several times a week, and I'd love for you to join us."

"Sure. Thanks."

He turned toward Grandma, gave her a hug, and left. He was easy to talk with, but I exhaled in relief when the door closed behind him. Maybe I was selfish, but I wanted time alone with Grandma, whether we just hung out or talked about the picture or watched movies.

Grandma liked to go to bed early, so after we had a quick snack, she gave me a layered pink gown to sleep in—silk underneath, with chiffon trimmed in lace on top. Luckily it was loose and long, so it would work for me in spite of the six-inch difference in our heights. "You'll sleep dressed like an old lady tonight. But we'll go on a shopping spree tomorrow."

I hugged her. "Good night, Grandma. I love you."

"I love you, too—more than I can say. And I'm so happy you are here—even if you had to come for a bad reason. I love having you with me."

Her bedroom was directly above the guest bedroom, so while I changed into the nightgown, I heard her shuffle around the room a few minutes and settle into the squeaky bed. I waited until I thought she was asleep to get my jeans that I'd left on the desk chair and pull the folded, torn picture out of the pocket.

I opened it slowly, and a sinking, sick feeling sucked at me. *How can this picture exist?* It had been carefully cut across the top—someone, the police or Mrs. Sanchez, hadn't wanted me to see the web address.

I hadn't been alone with a mirror since the picture showed up. I locked the door and checked the windows as I always do to be sure that the blinds and curtains were shut and no one could see in. I stood in front of the full-length mirror hunting for the girl in the naked picture.

First, I smiled like the picture—it was hard to get my lips up that high off my teeth. I raised my arms and waved my hands. *No. I never did this. Never. I never did this pose ever.* Even if someone pasted a naked body under my head, the mouth didn't match. I lifted my gown enough to show my skinny legs. How close was the body to mine? I thought of stripping and posing, but I couldn't make myself.

What do I do with the printout? I could have folded it and put it under the mattress or somewhere in my backpack. But sooner or later, someone on the planet would find it. Yes, it was on the Internet, but I didn't want to leave one more copy to be seen by anyone. I ripped it down the middle, tearing apart the two sides of my body. I ripped again and again until there were only tiny, unrecognizable confetti-sized pieces. I flushed them in the guest bathroom adjoining my room and snapped off the light.

Fear immediately nagged that I should have kept the picture—some clue might have lurked in the graffiti or the background or my body.

I lay in the dark on the cool sheets for a long time, but I couldn't go to sleep, so I clicked on the light again and found some paper and sat at the small desk in the corner to write a letter to Zada. Hannah had mentioned that no one stayed there more than thirty days. I wanted to send the message to Deputy Gonzales tomorrow in hopes that it would catch up with her before she moved on.

Dear Zada,

Two days ago, I would not have believed that I could be taken away from my parents and placed in a strange house. I knew that things like that happened, but I never dreamed they would happen to me. All day, I've thought about how nice you were to come and talk to a stranger and to give me advice.

I want you to know that when the deputy and the social worker questioned me, it helped that you and I had talked the night before. You were right when you said it gets easier each time you tell it.

I'm going to live with my grandma in Dallas until the investigation is finished. I hope your grandma is better soon, and you get to go home with her.

I'm sorry we didn't have more time to talk. I would like to know all about your life, and I hope we get to meet again.

Your friend,
Polarity Weeks

I left the letter on the desk, shut off the light, and got back into bed. In the darkness, I thought about what I didn't say in the letter—that Zada had been wrong when she said, "Things will get worse before they get better." For her, first entering foster care at five, things had gotten worse. But things were already getting better for me. Even with the worry about Mom and Dad being investigated and the picture online, tonight was heaven compared to the hell of yesterday.

Wrapped in Grandma's silky pink gown, cuddled in her pretty guest room filled with purple, red, and lavender-blue pillows and curtains, warm hope blanketed me. In the dim glow of the streetlight coming through above the blinds and curtains, happy pictures of Mom—graduation, proms, Halloween costumes, her wedding with Dad—covered the walls.

Surely, within a few days, Ethan would get the truth about how Danny made this happen. And I'd ask Grandma to let me use her computer and find the URL myself. *Maybe there's some new porn-creating monster online that allows people to undress and distort someone in a photo.* Somehow, I would find a clue.

I thought my hell was over.

CHAPTER 4

THE NEXT MORNING, AS I dressed in one of Grandma's shirts and the same jeans I'd worn since I left Star, I realized that I was totally crashing into her life. I had been so focused on myself yesterday that I hadn't considered how she must have had plans of her own, especially with Scooter in the picture. But now she was stuck with me.

I found her at the kitchen table, and she popped up and hugged me. "Oh, Polarity, we're going to have fun today." Almost hopping, she squeezed me in rhythm with her words. "You're going to love the new mall." She released me and peered up into my face. "Any thoughts about what you'd like to buy?"

"Not really." I couldn't help smiling at her enthusiasm. "What were you planning to do today before I came? I don't want to interrupt. And I may not need much—maybe I'll go home today or tomorrow."

"Interrupt! You? Never." She gripped my arms. "There is nothing I'd rather do than have a day with you. Having you here is like a surprise Christmas-plus-birthday-plus-Fourth-of-July for me. Now"—she ushered me to the table, where she had rice cereal and fruit sitting out—"I think to start you need at least one more pair of jeans, some shorts, and a few shirts." She set a bowl and a carton of milk in front of me as I sat down. "Then you can sew some more shirts. How does that sound?" She didn't wait for me to answer. "And, of course, a swimsuit and undies and PJs and whatever else we find.

Oh, and a journal—I know how you love to write." She sat down with me at the table. "What do you think?"

Before I could answer, her phone rang, and concern flashed across her face. She squeezed my hand, squared her shoulders, and picked up her phone. A heartbeat later, she mouthed, "Scooter."

I felt relieved that it wasn't bad news but sad that it wasn't Mom or Dad saying the picture mystery was solved.

Grandma nailed it about the new mall in her neighborhood. I loved it. In addition to finding everything she had planned, I found the best jeans of my life, and I filled out a size larger than the two-long I'd been stuck in since seventh grade. I was getting slightly less skinny.

After we came home from shopping, Grandma let me go through her trunks of fabric to see if she already had something I liked.

I found some beautiful multicolored cloth in shades of cream, so different from the colorful fabrics she wore. "Why did you buy this?"

"Oh, a good friend of mine wanted a dress that color. I planned to surprise her with it, but she bought one ready-made before I started it. You like it? It's kind of drab."

"I think it's beautiful. Can I make a layered shirt like that one in *Teen Vogue*?"

"Let me find my pattern. Go get the magazine, and let's make sure they match."

Minutes later, she showed me how her old Simplicity pattern had the exact same lines as the new style. She pulled the thin paper pieces of pattern out of the envelope and told me to set up the ironing board and press the fabric. She sat in her special chair that vibrated her legs and instructed how to lay the pattern pieces on the fabric, so the grain ran in the right direction and no fabric would be wasted. With the soft humming of her chair in the background, I pinned the worn, old pieces onto the smooth fabric. How many shirts had this flimsy, frail paper touched?

Once we agreed on the layout of the pattern, she let me cut it with her electric scissors. I figured she'd take over the actual sewing, but no. She gave directions, step by step. Every time the needle had to be rethreaded or my stitch got out of line, she explained what to do. Grandma had always let me do little sewing projects, but this was the first time I'd done a shirt from start to finish. I loved it.

Her cheerfulness and the sewing were good distractions, but the undercurrent of disorganized worries, which had been rippling around since yesterday, surfaced and grabbed my full attention: *Has Ethan seen a whole photo of me by now? Why did he get furious when Danny called out "Poetic Polarity"? Why did he sneak in to see me in Mrs. Sanchez's office? Did he set up the whole Boy Scout thing with Shanique? Will I ever again get to experience a wonderful moment like the one in which he put his warm, strong hand on mine? Is Shanique his girlfriend?*

I didn't know Ethan well—I didn't know anyone at Star well—but he had an evenness that lifted him above the dumb stuff that went on in school. Once in the cafeteria, two loud, goofy boys were clowning around and backed right into Ethan, almost knocking his tray out of his hand. I gasped, half expecting Ethan to be angry, but he just grinned, shrugged, and steadied one of the boys who had lost his balance in the collision.

I met Ethan on my first day while Mom and I were waiting in the office to get checked in. He had come in to feed the fish. At first glance, I'd thought he was a staff member. His face was angled away from us, and his height and muscular build made him seem older. But when he slid his Star orange-and-green backpack to the floor, I realized he must be a student.

Mom, who always tried to help me make friends in new schools, chatted him up. "Oh, hi there. Are you in charge of the aquarium?"

He rotated his handsome, full face toward her and flashed an easy, slow smile. "Yes, ma'am." His low, smooth voice made my breath catch. His eyes, chocolate brown like his skin, met mine. "New student?"

"Yeah." I saw flecks of gray in his eyes. I had to resist the urge to move closer to him, to see him better.

"I'm Ethan. Welcome to Star." He stood still, comfortable with himself, and waited for me to answer.

"I'm Polarity." I clutched my backpack on my lap. "Thanks."

Mom said, "Hi, Ethan. How did you get the job of taking care of the fish?"

"He won it based on our point system," the secretary piped in from behind the counter.

I expected Ethan to roll his eyes or be embarrassed, but he continued his work at the aquarium as if unaffected by her.

"It's one of the honors the principal gives to students for good citizenship." She pointed to a citizenship-chart poster behind her desk. "We know we can depend on Ethan."

He opened a cabinet door below the aquarium, pulled out a test tube and dropper, and started dropping aquarium water into the tube. His hands were steady as he let the water drip, drip, drip until the level satisfied him.

While he dipped strips of yellow and pink paper into the tube, Mom asked, "Do you have that divider in there to keep the betta from eating the mollies?"

Ethan tilted his head thoughtfully. "I guess that could happen, but what would happen for sure is that the mollies would gang up on the betta and start nipping at his fins."

"Well, the little brats," Mom said. "Just like their own little mob, picking on the outsider."

The secretary said, "Okay, Mrs. Weeks and Polarity, you can come sit back here now, and we'll get your paperwork started."

As Mom stood and started toward the secretary's desk, she asked, "Miss Smart, why do you have only ninth-graders on this campus? We drove out to University High School first, thinking that's where Polarity would enroll, but they don't have freshmen."

I trailed behind Mom. Our path would take us even closer to Ethan. He was placing the equipment back into the cabinet.

"Oh." Miss Smart stood and waved her pencil as if giving a lecture. "The research shows that ninth-graders have the highest dropout risk, so the school board established our Star Ninth Grade Center with lots of special supports. You know, *star*, like *rising stars*?"

I had attended many different schools in the past two years in our search for Mom's cure but none with such a cheesy name.

Mom passed Ethan and pushed through a little swinging half-door that separated the waiting area from the secretary's corner. "Interesting."

Miss Smart, nodding and ratcheting up her pencil motion, continued to talk about the advantages of having ninth grade only, but her babble escaped me.

When I was beside Ethan, he peered into my eyes and gave a slow grin, sort of lopsided, that touched something deep inside me. "I like your name, Polarity."

Warmth hummed through me, and I wanted to say something back, like *thank you* or *I like Ethan, too*—anything. I guess I froze because the swinging door popped the fronts of my legs, and I jumped backwards. I think I said, "Oh."

Ethan reached out with his strong, thick arm. I thought he was going to touch me, but he grabbed the little door and held it open for me. I stopped breathing as I passed through. The next thing I'd known, I was sitting by the secretary's desk, watching Ethan walk out the door.

Has he seen the whole picture on the Internet by now? Please don't let him see it.

By midafternoon, I finished the bottom layer of the shirt and was ready to start the top, vest-like layer.

"Try it on," Grandma said. "Let's see how you like the fit before you go any further."

Its perfection dazzled me. I couldn't think of the right words to describe it, but I loved the way the smooth fabric draped on me. And the creamy colors made my skin look tanner.

"Oh," said Grandma when I showed her. "It is classic and understated, yet totally in style—perfect for jeans or a black skirt. And you have plenty of growing room—which is a good thing to remember while we're working on your wardrobe. I think you've got your height. Now you're going to fill out. You might be like your mama. She went from being a little girl to a B cup. Seemed like overnight." Grandma could say things like that—or anything—and it didn't embarrass me.

I started back toward the bedroom to take off the shirt, but the doorbell interrupted. I paused to open it, but Grandma hurried past me. She must've wanted to answer the door herself. I waited in the hallway.

A very young woman with two long black braids stood in the doorway. She held up an ID card and explained that she was a caseworker from the state protective services. "Mrs. Johnson, please give me a tour of the house." She had a Spanish accent. "I know this may feel strange to you, but I need to verify that the environment is safe and appropriate for Polarity." As she came into the hallway, she took my hand. "You must be Polarity."

I nodded. "Is there any news? About my parents? Have they figured out who did the picture?"

"No, I'm sorry." She sounded soft, kind. "If there are any new developments, I don't have them yet."

We showed her around. She wanted to see where I slept and where I kept my clothes. The weirdness of a stranger in our private space made me feel uncomfortable. She even snooped in the refrigerator. I hoped she'd inspect us and leave. I prayed that she wouldn't show the picture or talk about it in front of Grandma. Even though Grandma knew the basics, I wanted to shield her from the ugly details, and I wanted to shield the world from the picture itself.

But after we went through the whole house, the caseworker asked if we could sit at the table and have a taped conversation. We had to go through every detail and all the questions as if I had never told it to the principal, all the officers, and the administrator of the social workers, Nelda Sims.

And Grandma had to hear every word. I hated bringing something so ugly into her world. And I felt ashamed. Even though I hadn't done anything, I felt ashamed that it had been done to me. I was a part of it.

Grandma sat beside me quietly the whole time. For minutes, tears streaked down her cheeks. No sound came from her, but the tears were there.

When the caseworker finished, she said she would visit weekly from now on. I was so stunned by everything that she'd said, I didn't think to ask which day or what time. Suddenly she was getting into her car and driving away.

After I closed the door, Grandma wrapped her arms around me. "I'm so sorry you have to go through this. If I could do anything to make it all go away, I would."

"I wish you didn't have to know about it," I said.

We talked for a long time about the picture and about Zada's idea that it was a photo trick. Grandma thought Zada made sense. I did okay talking about everything that happened until I tried to ask, "Why doesn't anyone—" I had to stop to keep my voice.

Grandma said, "Why doesn't anyone what, Polarity?"

"I told the principal and police officers and everyone the same thing I told you and Zada, but only you and Zada believe me." I wasn't sure why I didn't mention Ethan.

She pulled me closer to her and laid her head on my shoulder. "It doesn't have anything to do with you. Let's think about this for a minute." She held onto me. "What if... Just imagine, what if your parents were awful people who really did take bad pictures of kids? I know it's crazy to even think about it. But what if they were? And what if you were afraid to tell the truth? What if your parents had threatened you that something awful would happen if you told the truth? And what if the all the officials let you go home because you said your parents didn't do it?"

"I see what you mean," I said. But even though there were logical reasons for Mom and Dad being investigated, I had to do something. I couldn't just stand by while authorities suspected my parents of a crime. I had to find a way to get to the truth.

"And think about this—nobody in Garcia knows you or your parents. And it probably looks fishy that you've been moving around so much for the past two years. You wait and see. Everything will work out. I just know it."

I loved her confidence, but I needed to do something. "Grandma, may I use your laptop?" A whisper of guilt nipped when I asked because Mom and Dad would never, never, never let me have free rein on the Internet. They monitored my computer use and had every imaginable protective filter. "I want to research photography and try to figure out how someone could make that picture and get it online."

Without a heartbeat of hesitation, she said, "Of course. As much as you like. Go get it off my desk. You know your dad set me up with wireless, so you can use it anywhere in the house."

I didn't feel guilty enough to remind her about my parents' overly protective views. "Thanks, Grandma."

First I Googled *Polaritey*, but the search engine showed results for *polarity* instead and led me to thousands of articles. For the next hour, I searched for ways to alter photos and post them on the Internet. I figured out that anyone with an e-mail address can post pictures on a number of sites. And there are lots of sites that will let you crop pictures, insert textboxes, and do graffiti. I didn't find the monster I imagined that let you undress people or distort their faces.

I also Googled Ethan Rawls in Garcia, Texas. Nothing. Even a search of the online phone directory didn't list any Rawls in Garcia. I had no way to ask him if he had learned anything.

After dinner that night, Grandma wanted us to watch a movie together. But I guess neither one of us really felt in the mood because we couldn't decide which one to see. It was as if another person invaded the room—someone we really didn't want to visit with but who wouldn't go away and let us be our normal selves. I stopped scrolling Netflix.

"Grandma, how can you be so happy?" How could she always stay so upbeat in spite of her burned legs? Before her tears that afternoon, I didn't remember ever seeing her cry.

"It is a wonder, isn't it?" She gazed at me a long time, as if thinking over something. "Are you ready for a long story—a true story—instead of a movie?"

Instantly curious, I said, "Yes."

"Let's go in your room. I'll show you some old pictures while we talk."

I figured she meant the pictures of Mom on the walls. When we got there, she plumped the pillows up on my bed, sat down, and settled back. "Before you sit with me, can you reach that top shelf in the closet?"

I opened the door. Luggage filled the top shelf, and my new

clothes hung on the hangers. A vertical row of shoe shelves remained empty. I touched the top shelf. "This one?"

"Get that old wooden red case, about the size of a wide shoe box, pushed way back in the corner."

There was a small step stool in the closet that I used to reach the little case. I brought the mysterious container to the bed and sat beside her.

She raised the lid, releasing a musty scent into the room. Old yellowed papers, documents, and photographs were stacked inside. "I used to have hundreds of pictures, but they were lost in the fire. So now there's only a few. This family picture is one that my mother had at her house." It was a picture of Grandma, Grandpa, and three little girls wearing identical ruffled yellow dresses with full skirts. The photo had been made in a studio. The three girls were sitting on a tall, cloth-covered bench between the parents, who were standing on each end of the bench. With a forest in the background, the photo looked like a storybook picture.

"You are all so young and happy," I said.

She kept quiet for a long time. "I never forget for one second how much we lost in the fire—three lives and your mama's peace of mind. But seeing this picture makes the loss sharp again."

I huddled closer to her and pointed to the middle sister. "This is Mom, right?" Any of the three blond girls could have been Mom, but she once mentioned being a middle child. They were all smiling, holding hands, and posed as if they might bounce off the bench any second.

"Yes, that's your mama. So sweet with her sisters. Loved to hold the baby. They were six, four, and one in this picture."

"You made their dresses?"

"Yes." She picked up an old, brown, musty-smelling envelope. "When you look at all the pictures on the wall, you see your mama's smile." The paper envelope crinkled in her hands as if it hadn't been touched in years. "The pictures in here are different, taken in the years after the fire. I will never have the heart to destroy them, but it's painful to see them."

She showed me the first one. "This is her school picture from first grade. She was in foster care. I was still in a burn center."

Foster care. Burn center. "I didn't know about that."

The information shocked like a bucket of ice water poured over my head. Grandma's grieving eyes stayed on the first-grade picture, as if she were reliving the memory.

"Mom never talks about any of that stuff," I said.

I'd known Grandma must have been in the hospital after her burns, but I had never thought about the length of time it took or what happened to my mother during that time.

In the first-grade picture, Mom had the same blue eyes and button nose she had in the family picture before the fire, but she was thinner. Instead of sitting up with bouncy energy, her shoulders were hunched, her sad and teary eyes hooked into me, and there was no smile—not even a faked one that a child might force in a school picture. I wanted to put my arms around the sad little girl.

The rest of the school pictures up until middle school told the same, sad story. The happy pictures from later years were on the wall. *When did her borderline personality disorder start?* Before I could ask, Grandma started talking again.

"After the fire, your mama lived with my sister's family for almost a year. As soon as I was released and had my own apartment, I brought her home. But after a few weeks, I got an infection and had to go back into the hospital. By this time, my sister's family had moved to California. I didn't have a way to get your mama out there." Grandma took a deep breath, and her voice shook. "So she was in foster care several months."

For as long as I could remember, I'd been troubled by certain questions. *What caused Mom to have BPD? Was it the fire? Was she born that way?* I whispered, "Do you think these years made Mom have her... problems?"

Grandma continued to look sadly at the picture. "Maybe. I don't remember her being any different from other children before the fire. In the years afterwards, there were so many problems that we were just surviving most of the time. I had never even heard of borderline personality disorder until a school psychologist mentioned it to me." Tears welled up in her eyes. "I think she was in middle school before I realized how much she needed constant reassurance. And that the way she could be so irrational at times wasn't... normal."

"But she looked so happy in high school." I glanced up at the wall at Mom beaming in her red formal.

Grandma released a sigh toward the prom picture. "She was just better at faking it by then."

We went through all the pictures, and Grandma told stories about each one until we closed the red case.

She sat still for a moment, with her hands resting on the closed wooden container. She lifted her sad gaze to meet my own. Resignation settled over her face.

A chill passed over me—something in her demeanor told me that she was about to say something hard. Something raw.

"We were asleep." Her voice was a husky whisper. "The house was small—only two bedrooms. My and Sam's room was on one side of the living room, and the girls' room was on the opposite side. Sometime during the night, your mama had come into our room because of a bad dream. We had a little sofa next to our bed where the girls could lay if they were sick or not sleeping well."

With her soft, warm hands, Grandma squeezed my hands together into a prayer-like position—her hands outside of mine. "I think you're old enough to hear this."

Chills skittered up my spine. I nodded. Nothing could stop me from hearing, even though it would be too awful to imagine. I'd always wanted to know more about the fire, but Mom got weird when I asked. She would either ignore my questions or go on a rampage about me being disrespectful. When I probed Dad about it, he said it was better not to delve into bad memories. So I had stopped asking.

"They say the fire started from an electrical short in the wall between the girls' room and the living room."

Now it was my time to listen with tears in my eyes, as Grandma had done when she heard my story.

"Sam woke us up, shouting about a fire—he pushed your mama

and me through the living room toward the front door, and he went to the girls' room. I took your mama into the front yard and left her standing by a tree next to the road, and I ran back in to help Sam get Margaret and Stephanie. Your mama screamed, 'Mommy, don't leave me! Please, Mommy, don't leave me!' I left her there screaming—I had to help get the others out."

I held my breath. The image of my mother alone by that tree, watching the fire squeezed my heart. The flames and the smoke must have been more terrifying than any nightmare a four-year-old could handle.

"By the time I got back into the house, the wall between the living room and the girls' room blazed in solid flames, and Sam came walking out, carrying both girls. He was burned so bad that he didn't look human, and the girls weren't moving. I reached for his arm. He was too hot to touch."

The sound of gasping ripped through the room. I didn't realize at first that it was me. Grandma and I were hugging—our arms around each other, our heads touching.

"That's the last time I saw Sam and Margaret and Stephanie. I don't remember anything else until I woke up days later in the hospital. The firemen said that the ceiling and attic caved in and must have trapped the lower part of my body." Her voice dropped to a trembling whisper. "Neighbors witnessed Sam bring Margaret and Stephanie into the yard and go back into the house and carry me out."

We were still hugging, and for a while, we just breathed together.

My voice scraped out, rough and raw. "Grandma, how could Grandpa have carried you after he was already burned so bad?"

"No one knows how he did it. I've read that people with deep burns stop feeling pain. He was a strong, brave man—a dear, loving man."

"What a terrible thing for Mama to see. She must have been so scared."

"We don't know what she saw. During the confusion, she disappeared. I guess neighbors assumed she was still in the house, so no one thought to look for her outside. They say the hot fire residue prevented a thorough search for her remains that night. The next morning a neighbor boy—" Grandma cut herself off and wiped her eyes. "He found her sitting in his bike shed behind his house."

I was gasping again.

Grandma handed me tissues and squeezed me tighter. "I know, I know," she said. "It hurts my heart, too. The idea of a four-year-old spending the night out alone is its own kind of pain—different from the three deaths. That neighbor boy was your dad."

I pulled back a little so I could see Grandma's face better.

"He was thirteen. Going out to throw a morning paper route."

I must have looked surprised because she nodded. "Your dad was the one who found her."

"Wow. That's like magic. But that's not when they started getting to know each other, is it?" Mom had told me they met when Dad did remodeling work in a store she went to.

"Oh, no. I don't think she even remembers the morning he found her—and, of course, we moved away from the neighborhood after the fire. They didn't get to know each other until years later, when your mama was in college. Your dad was working on a construction project in the store where I did alterations. He recognized me because of my legs. Your mom would come into the store after her classes, and one thing led to another."

I pointed at all the pictures on the wall. "Mom looked so happy in high school and later. Like none of this"—I picked up the envelope of sad pictures—"ever happened."

"She tried. We both did. But she struggled and had her dark days. My fears for her never settled until she met your dad again. I'm so thankful for him. Your dad is a big, unexpected bonus in my life. I knew I would love a grandchild, but I never would have guessed how much I would love a son-in-law. He changed the world for your mama and for me. A big-hearted, patient man. I am so happy they found each other—not just because of you, but because of how they are as a couple."

"I love you, Grandma." I hugged her.

"Well, Miss Polarity, this has been a long answer to your

question—how can I be so happy? I guess the bottom line is I can't change the past. But I control whether I bring the misery of the past into this moment. Why would I want to make my time with you sad? It wouldn't undo the loss and death. If you ruin your good times thinking about the bad times, you'll never really have good times."

"You remind me of an Emily Dickinson poem. I wish I had my book with me. She talks about how you can't understand something painful while you're in the middle of it. You might begin to grasp it after the hurt is over and you've stopped questioning. But you may never fully know during your lifetime."

"I love you," she said. "And if I were a poet like you and Emily, I'd write a poem about how much I love you."

After Grandma went to bed, I wished I had asked her to let me bring her laptop into my room, so I could keep searching while she slept. It was back in her room now. I would ask her the next day—I could get a lot done at night while she slept. I got out the journal she bought me on our shopping spree that morning. I'd always kept journals, and I wrote often, either poems or just reflections about things. I opened to the first blank page and imagined writing about the whole picture nightmare.

Instead, I wrote a poem about Grandma.

> *With happy photos on her wall*
> *And sad ones saved for honored times,*
> *She fills each day with love and light.*
> *Her grief and loss and pain remain*
> *Encased on the shelf of her heart.*

CHAPTER 5

EVERY SPARE MINUTE OF THE next morning, I searched the
Internet, including TeensterBlast—the favorite forum for most
of the kids I knew—to find Ethan. His common name sparked several
flutters of hope that I'd found him, but it was always someone else.

I did find other students from Star. Cynthia's clique driveled
on with commentary and photos on TeensterBlast. They'd been my
leading tormentors from day one, so they could be responsible for the
picture—or at least they would know who was. I scanned the pages of
her friends, hoping to find something, some clue, some connection.

Grandma came to the doorway of my room and reminded me
it was time to go to Scooter's house to swim. I had just cut back to
Cynthia's page and was zipping down her posts when my gut squeezed
and my heart sped up.

The very day that my naked picture showed up in sixth period,
someone named Tracey posted, *Sup with cops at school?* At least a
hundred responses followed.

"Did you put on sunscreen?" Grandma asked as she came into my
room.

Somehow, my voice said, "Yes, ma'am."

Responses to the cop question jumped out. Each phrase stabbed
me.

Check your texts
WTF!!!!!!!

Slammin

Sup—someone text it to me

OMG—she's crazy

A boy dubbed Jack O' Lantern posted a picture of himself with my same crazy smile and waving hands—except, of course, he had clothes on.

Some poet.

Is she in jail?

What a retard

So skinny.

Grandma said, "Well—"

I shut down the computer as she came closer.

"I think we're ready. Shall we head out?" As I stood, she put her hand on my forehead. "You're pale. Are you okay?"

Feeling as if someone else were talking, I said, "Feel great. Let's go get some sun."

The picture being so casually joked about by so many students deepened my shame. A hard knot formed in my stomach and crawled up my throat. *Ethan must have seen it by now.* My breath started coming out in short spurts. I bit my lip to keep myself from crying.

I battled to keep up a conversation with Grandma on the drive to Scooter's. She asked several times if I was sure that I was okay about going to his house. Fortunately, when we got there, Grandma and Scooter stayed busy swimming laps for a while. They later relaxed and talked in the shady end. And like the night he drove us home from the airport, they had so much to talk about with each other that I didn't have to contribute much to the conversation. I alternated between swimming and sunning myself while I replayed the TeensterBlast horror in my head.

"Polarity, I'm afraid you've been lying in the sun too long," Grandma said, breaking into my thoughts.

"I want to have a tan when I go back to school." *Whenever or wherever that might be. A dark, dark tan that will make me look like a different girl and eradicate my fishing trip V-neckline in the picture.*

"Well, let's space it out, not get you burned. You can sun again tomorrow morning."

Scooter suggested, "How about you ladies let me take you on a quick tour of my garden? Then we can go inside for a snack."

I mustered up a cheerful response. "Sure."

While he led us through his basil, parsley, zucchini, tomatoes, and hybrid roses, Grandma asked, "Isn't it interesting how Scooter has veggies and flowers all mixed up together?"

I nodded and forced a smile. "Yeah. Beautiful. What are those baby plants?" I made myself sound interested.

After he named all the seedlings, we went into his big kitchen, where he pulled a platter of veggies and carton of hummus from the fridge.

"I love your garden-fresh veggies," Grandma said as we settled around the table.

I felt too agitated to eat, but I put a few carrot sticks on my plate to nibble so Grandma wouldn't worry. I sat facing a wall of funny family pictures, not the posed studio kinds.

Scooter noticed me looking at the photos. "That's my family—four kids and nine grandchildren, so far. My wife died in a car wreck."

The wreck must have been when their children were still in elementary school. There were several pictures of the early years with her big smile and short curly hair. She usually wore jeans. You could tell by the size of the children that there were years with no pictures. When the kids reached middle and high school age, the family photos were missing the curly-haired mom.

"Beautiful family, isn't it, Polarity?" Grandma asked.

Scooter pointed to an early photo. "That's my favorite. Grand Canyon. Great car trip that year. Kids loved it."

I nodded. Did their smiles, as they stood along a rail overlooking the canyon, come from their hearts? Were those children really happy, and were those parents free of crazy moods? Or were people in those pictures like Mom, beaming big, fake smiles? Or, worse, were they like my face in the crazy Internet picture, caught in a nightmare? Misery and dread washed over me, and I had to force myself to swallow the carrot stick I had just chewed.

"Are you okay?" Grandma asked me for the millionth time that morning.

"Sure. Maybe just a little homesick today." I should have told her what I found on TeensterBlast, but then she might restrict me from her computer. And I didn't think I could make myself talk about it.

After we ate, Grandma said, "Let's show Polarity the rest of the house, especially your office. I want her to see the work you do."

It was a relief to get up and move around and not be stuck face-to-face at the table with both Grandma and Scooter. In his office behind the desk, law school diplomas and other certificates hung, but displayed on a separate wall were some unusual photos. A young African-American man's mug shot caught my eye. His ID number, the date and time, and the stark brick wall behind him formed a cold backdrop for the fear and disbelief in his stare. Next to his photo, a framed newspaper article's headline read, "Ross Jones Freed After Nineteen Years Wrongful Imprisonment."

"An innocent man went to prison?" I asked.

Scooter nodded at the picture. "Yes, Jones was the first case that I helped with in the Dove Dove Project, after I retired."

There was a small plaque on the wall engraved with two doves. I asked, "Why two doves?"

"We wanted to remember that these people are innocent of the original crime, but beyond that, they're innocent pawns of the system." Deep sadness tinged his voice.

I scanned the newspaper article. "How can that happen? How can someone be found guilty when they're innocent?" I guess I'd heard these things happened, but it never seemed as real to me as it did now, when I was being blamed for something I didn't do.

Scooter shook his head sadly. "We have one of the best justice systems in the world, but we're people, and people make mistakes." A picture of Scooter standing next to an older, smiling Ross Jones hung below the newspaper article.

Other mug shots and articles dotted the wall. "Did you help get all of these people out of prison?"

"Some. Most of these people are still in prison." Sadness crept into his eyes as he scanned the pictures. "We're working on their cases."

"Scooter," I said. "You know what happened to me?" With all those people he'd helped who no one else had believed, maybe Scooter would believe me. Maybe he'd have advice for me.

He gave me his full attention with alert, questioning eyes.

"Right?" I prodded.

Grandma put her hand on my arm.

"Your grandmother told me that a nude picture of you was found on the Internet, that you have no idea how it got there, and that the police are investigating your parents." An edge—an intellectual, sniffing-out-curiosity—slipped into his friendly kindness. "Sounds like a frustrating situation for you."

Grandma stepped closer to me. "We don't have to talk about this if you don't want to, Polarity."

I patted her hand, still on my arm. "I do want to talk about it. I want his opinion."

Before the words were completely out of my mouth, Scooter grabbed a yellow pad and pencil from his desk and motioned for us to sit on the small sofa that faced his wall of mug shots. He rolled his desk chair forward and sat facing us.

Grandma and I barely made it to the sofa before he said, "Start at the beginning."

His blue eyes took on a keenness. As I recited the story, beginning with sixth-period history, he listened intently with his pencil moving steadily, stopping me only to ask an occasional clarifying question. Grandma sat up straighter, this time, as if she'd picked up on Scooter's analytic mood.

"May I ask you some questions?" Scooter asked.

I nodded.

He glanced at Grandma for her approval then looked back at me. "Legally, your grandmother is your temporary parent. Otherwise, we would not be able to discuss this. You understand?"

I nodded.

"Do you think your parents had anything to do with the creation of the picture?"

"No. It's not possible." I said. When everyone else had asked me this question, my defenses soldiered up, but somehow when Scooter asked with his let's-figure-this-out approach, it came across as a valid question, even though my answer stayed the same.

He switched his gaze to Grandma. "Abby. What do you think?"

"I agree with Polarity."

"Does Jennifer or Seth have any criminal background?"

"No," I said.

But Grandma drew in her breath. "There's one thing. But it happened when Seth was just out of high school, before he even got to know Jennifer."

My dad, a criminal background? "What?" *Did I mishear her?* I froze, dreading her explanation. I didn't want my image of Dad to be tarnished.

Scooter nodded without as much as a raised eyebrow. "Let me have the details." He was already jotting on his pad.

Grandma looked at me with regret in her eyes. "He told me about it before he even proposed to your mama. He wanted there to be no secrets or surprises. It was just typical wild oats stuff. Probably isn't even in a record anywhere."

Disbelief gripped me. *Wild oats? My dependable, steady, responsible dad?* "What, Grandma?"

"Well, he used to drink a lot, like a lot of young guys do. But he doesn't drink anymore. Hasn't drank at all since he got with Jennifer. He even goes to AA from time to time, I think." Her eyes darted from Scooter to me, as if seeking a way out.

"We need all the facts, so we can get to the truth," Scooter said.

Grandma nodded. "He told me he wrecked his truck, and his blood alcohol level was high. He got a DUI and had to take courses and do community services."

"Okay," Scooter said, unaffected. "The police will have that info. Now, how about Jennifer?"

DUI seized my brain, but I made myself talk because I knew recent details that Grandma didn't. But first I had to give him an overview. "Mom has a borderline personality disorder, and she gets emotional and sometimes does erratic things. She gets a lot of therapy and sometimes takes meds to relax her, even though there's no med that will cure her disorder. She gets mad at people—neighbors, people in stores—" I forced an inhale and squeezed out the rest. "Dad... me. But she's never done anything illegal."

"Are there police records on any of her incidents?" Scooter asked.

Grandma said, "No."

This time I had the surprise to tell. "Well..."

As I expected, Grandma gaped at me, wide-eyed.

"Last Christmas, Dad called the police because Mom was missing. They searched for her right away because Dad told them about her mental health issues." I asked Grandma, "You remember Dad calling to talk about New Year's plans?"

"Yes," she said, realization dawning on her face.

"He didn't want to worry you unless we had to. But he was really just trying to figure out if Mom had contacted you. She came home after four days—she'd gone to a spa in Florida."

Grandma's eyebrows shot up, and she opened her mouth as if to deny the spa escapade, but she slumped a little and sighed.

Scooter zipped right along. "Erratic emotional history will be a red flag to the police. My guess is your parents are their prime suspects. And now that you're out of danger, authorities will take their time, thoroughly checking into your parents' activities and background."

"But it was students at Star. It had to be. That's why they all know about it. That's why they're texting the link to each other and talking about it on TeensterBlast. That's why Danny showed the picture." Even as I made these excuses, the truth nipped in the back of my mind, so I added what Scooter must have been thinking. "But just because the picture is viral with the students now doesn't prove they made the picture or posted it first."

"Right," Scooter said. "But what you can do is continue to watch social media." He reached for his desk, pulled his keyboard onto his lap, and flipped the monitor around so that we could see it. "Start a chart of all the postings you find." He logged into TeensterBlast. "What's the student's name who has all the posts?"

I told him.

"You'd be amazed at the number of people, especially kids, who incriminate themselves through social media." He found her page and, without my help, scrolled to the entry about me. His intense curiosity as he scanned the posts was contagious. "Here. Oh and here." He pointed out various comments. "Good information—might eventually roll into circumstantial evidence."

He opened a second desktop and started a Word document. "Your job, Polarity, is to track social media daily, and maintain a detailed log with posts pasted in. And go back to the first day you attended the school. See if anyone mentioned the photo in the weeks before the incident." In the document, he typed *Polarity Weeks*, *#*, *the date*, and *Social Media Evidence*. "Here's a sort of template you can use. Insert your case number." As he continued to talk, he typed a summary of what we were finding on TeensterBlast, quickly pasting in the posts. "Also, in a separate document, you should write an incident report, a minute-by-minute account of everything that happened that day—especially during the class. Not only including what people said and did, but also think about the people who didn't say or do anything. Sometimes the guilty keep silent and get overlooked."

As Scooter charted out the things I could do, a weight slid off my shoulders. I had a direction, clear action to take.

"And let me see it when you get finished." He glanced at Grandma, "Do you have business cards of the CPS caseworker and the lead officer on the case?"

"The caseworker, but the lead officer must be the sheriff of Garcia County. I don't have his contact information."

"I think that's still Stanley Chapa. I'll get his contact info for you. After we finish this report on the TeensterBlast info, let's fax it to both departments. And every time you find new information, we'll fax again."

"Couldn't we could just call them?" Grandma asked.

Scooter nodded while he continued composing his TeensterBlast report. "Call them as often as you like. Develop a relationship with them. That will keep you on their minds. But we'll also fax because the return receipt will be our proof that we sent them information. It's not as easy for authorities to forget or postpone a case when facts are reported in writing and there's verification of receipt. They know this." He glanced up at me as if we were partners on a project. "Polarity, I'll e-mail this draft to your grandmother. You can reword or add info as you like before we fax."

"Thank you, Scooter." No wonder Grandma thought so highly of this man.

He stilled his hands, and something shifted in his clear blue eyes. His energetic curiosity still glinted, but gentleness coated over it. "My guess is you'll be kept from your parents for a long time. Photo analysis and Internet tracking can be slow, expensive, and challenging."

Grandma said, "But in that movie last week, it took a guru just minutes to unravel the whole Internet thing."

Scooter chuckled. "Yeah. That was a good movie. But this case just won't take precedence or get the level of resources devoted to it that the competing violent crimes are getting. And real-life Internet gurus aren't as fast as they are in the movies. Polarity, what you need to focus on is ferreting out everything the kids know, so when the police get through exhausting their leads against your parents, you've got a new direction ready for their attention. And, who knows? If you find something concrete, we may get the police on the right track quicker. What do you think? Sound like a plan?"

"Yes," I said. "I like having clear-cut steps to take." *I'll finish the Word doc he e-mailed. I'll continue to search for the picture. If it's still on the Internet, I'll find it. And I'll keep searching for a way to get in touch with Ethan.*

"How soon until school is out for the year?" he asked.

"About two weeks," I said.

"That may slow things down even more. Even if the police get swayed from their focus on your parents, they may wait until school starts again to interview kids."

71

Grandma said, "You're kidding. That's awful."

"Yeah, but unfortunately, it's just more practical to talk to kids at school than it is to find them in the summertime."

I was chomping to get home to Grandma's computer, but she had a hair appointment, so I borrowed a yellow legal pad from Scooter and took it with me. I wanted to start writing my incident report while Grandma got her highlights.

At the beauty shop, I settled into a chair as the beautician started brushing through Grandma's pretty white hair that hung in loose, chin-length layers, with blondish highlights mostly around her face. She never went for the helmet or updos that some older ladies wear.

"Oh, Abby, what a beautiful granddaughter you have!" her beautician said.

"Oh, I know it. She's got her mama's pretty face and father's height and gorgeous brown eyes."

People always go on and on about you when you're with grandparents, and the praise is not as embarrassing as it might be around your peers.

The beautician stepped closer to me. "And look at this heavenly hair." She started picking up my hair, which hung below my shoulders. On good days, I let it hang; on bad days I rubber-banded it into a ponytail. I hated the color. Mom had bright blond hair, and Dad's was shiny, almost black. I wished I had inherited either of their colors. But oh no—I had the blah brown in-between color.

The beautician said, "This hair is the most wonderful color—it's like caramel—look how it gleams in the light."

While she trimmed and foiled Grandma, I made a list of every student I could remember in sixth period. There were several whose names I didn't know, so I described those students. I kept remembering what Scooter said about the guilty person staying quiet and going unnoticed.

And as I scanned the list of names, Arvey snaked into my thoughts. *Why did she tap me on the shoulder? Why did she point toward Danny with her eyes?* I couldn't be certain, but I didn't think I remembered seeing her on TeensterBlast or some other social media site.

Arvey lived in the same trailer park we did, and on my first day of school, she and I almost took the short walk home together after school. I was surprised that she was still around because I had stayed late in the gym, hoping everyone would be gone. She sat on the curb about a block from the school. When she spotted me, she smiled, stood, and fell into step beside me.

I had been about to ask her name when Danny rode by on a bicycle and said, "Well, it's Polarity and Arvey, the trailer queens." He exaggerated the Es at the ends of our names and in *queens*.

I usually ignore dumbasses who tease me but not when they are also bullying someone else, and I'd had enough for one day. "Danny." His was one of the few names I knew on the first day—he was such a total jerk, he got reprimanded constantly by the teachers. I stopped and glared at him.

His head swiveled back toward me, and his mouth dropped open in surprise as he wheeled farther away.

"Why don't you come back and tell me what you mean?" I turned back toward where Arvey had been. "He is so rude and...."

But she was running ahead toward home. I didn't blame her a bit. She had probably put up with the trailer jokes her whole life.

I checked Danny again. He slowed a little and continued to look back at me with a dumb, stunned expression. His mouth still hung open.

"Stop, Danny! I said stop!" I took a couple of steps in his direction, but he stood and pedaled away at full speed. "Coward."

I turned back toward the trailer park just as Arvey ran through the entry. By the time I caught up, she was out of sight. Her rusting double-wide sprawled just inside the main gate, and I had to walk past it to get to ours, which was parked all the way in the back end. In her yard, three preschool-age children sat in a plastic swimming pool full of sand. A few men, drinking cans of beer, lolled on the wooden steps of the trailer. But I didn't see Arvey. Most of the windows of the trailer were covered with aluminum foil. Was Arvey peeking out at me?

The next day after school, it was raining, so Mom met me in the parent pickup area with her car. On the short drive home, I spotted

Arvey starting her two-block walk. "Mom, that's the girl who lives in the old double-wide." Mom slowed down and pulled over.

I waved at Arvey through the back window. She started rushing toward the car. I opened the back door so she'd be able to dive in, and I pulled Gypsy, our honey-colored poodle-terrier mix, into the front seat with me. Sometimes Gypsy got overly excited about meeting a new person, and I didn't want her to overwhelm Arvey with licks.

Arvey, smiling and pushing her soaked hair off her face, put one foot into the car.

I said, "Arvey, you're soaked."

She froze with one foot still out on the pavement, and she glanced from me to Mom.

"Hop in, Arvey. We'll take you home." Mom said.

Arvey, with her smile morphing into a sullen expression, stayed motionless like a child in the swing-the-statue game.

Gypsy's low growl vibrated against my arm, shocking me. In the four years we'd had sweet, friendly Gypsy, she'd never made such a scary sound. I pulled her closer to me and shushed her.

"It's okay." Was I talking to Gypsy or Arvey or both?

Slam. Arvey crashed the car door shut. Gypsy barked crazily. Arvey stood in the rain and glared at us.

I started to get out of the car, but Mom stopped me. "She's upset about something—better to leave her alone." As we drove away, Arvey stood in the rain with her long dark hair and clothes glued to her body. Gypsy whimpered.

The next day at school, Arvey wouldn't look at me or talk to me, so in history class, I left a note on her desk. "I'm sorry about the ride home not working out yesterday. If we did anything to hurt your feelings, I'm sorry. Polarity." But she never spoke to me again until that last day in history class. Strange. *Could Arvey have something to do with the picture? Was she getting back at me for whatever we did to make her mad?*

I continued to puzzle over Arvey while the beautician started combing out Grandma's hair. "You know, Abby, the same highlights and cut would look lovely on Polarity. Longer, of course, but layered and with just a few lights around her face. The blond would make her caramel color even richer by contrast."

Yes! Another thing that will make me look different from the picture.

"Well, what do you say?" Grandma did her little girl shrugging-shoulder grin. "Wanna be a Grandma look-alike?"

I laughed out loud. "Sure."

"Well, let's just add it to our schedule."

Nothing. For over three months, nothing developed on my case.

I did constant Internet research, but after a few days of TeensterBlast gibberish about the police coming to school, the topic fizzled. In spite of our calls and faxes, neither the police nor protective services had new information all summer.

We continued to be banned from contacting Mom and Dad. Normally, months away from them with Grandma might have been a carefree, once-in-a-lifetime treat, especially now with my growth spurt demanding lots of new clothes. But the constant worry that Mom and Dad might be arrested because of the picture kept me on the edge of panic much of the time.

The young Dallas caseworker never came back to Grandma's house, even though she had promised weekly visits. Scooter said protective services were so busy with children in life-threatening situations that my case would not be a priority. Grandma called and faxed their office every week, just to keep them updated that I was still with her and doing fine.

It was a relief not to be inspected again.

Zada never answered my letter, and by now she would no longer be at Hannah's. And not finding a way to connect with Ethan wracked me. *Does he still even remember me? Has he seen a full picture? Does he think I'm disgusting?* Somehow I had to figure out a way to get into touch with both of them.

It was August, and I was preparing to enroll in a Dallas school. But one night at eleven thirty while I searched the Internet for the picture, everything changed. I found it on a photo-sharing site.

My stomach churned, and my heart thudded in my throat. Even though I'd seen the paper copy, the sight of the photo on the screen sent chills through my body. It wasn't just the nakedness. I hated the facial expression and the insane waving.

Wait. The textbox on this one is different. Someone had removed the original textbox and replaced it with a smaller one that said, "Sorry Polaritey." Along two edges of the new quote, between the textbox border and the graffiti, the background of the room was visible: the distinct checkerboard pattern of orange and green wall tiles of Star Ninth Grade Center.

Tears of relief blinded me for a moment. I wiped my eyes so I could see again and make sure I hadn't dreamed it. *Orange and green. This picture could only have been made at the school. That clears Mom and Dad.*

With trembling hands, I did a Print Screen and saved the picture onto Grandma's hard drive, in case someone removed the picture before I could report it. I also saved it to a thumb drive in case Grandma's computer crashed. Satisfied, I stood up and did a silent, twirling, jiggling dance as my best friend in Houston and I did when we were little.

I sat back down and composed my report to be faxed in the morning as soon as Grandma woke up. I kept it short and factual, the way Scooter had taught me. I stated the date, time, website, and significance of the picture. And in bold I wrote, "Evidence that the picture was made at Star Ninth Grade Center suggests that Seth and Jennifer Weeks were in no way involved with the production of the photograph." At the end, I added my own request, different from anything Scooter had instructed. "I request that investigation of my parents stop immediately and their parental rights be restored."

It was hard to wait until morning to share this news with Grandma and Scooter. The excitement and questions about this new textbox kept me awake most of the night. Why "Sorry Polaritey"? *If the creator were really sorry, wouldn't he or she cover up the nakedness?* It would be so easy to draw over the private parts. *Is this a new, sarcastic jab? Will this apology help with my case?*

Two days later, while I sat at the sewing machine facing a window with a view of the street, the unmistakable rumble of a diesel engine approached the condo. *Dad's truck.*

Through the window, I saw his large, white hood nose into the narrow driveway.

And there they were. Mom and Dad and our dog, Gypsy.

"Grandma, Mom and Dad are here!" I ran out to meet them. *Now my hell is over.*

"Well, who is this grown-up young lady?" Dad picked me up and twirled me around. His handsome face looked older. His dark hair gleamed the same, but new lines around his eyes triggered a choking I-could-cry feeling.

Mom grabbed me as soon as Dad set me down. "Oh, Polarity, my Polarity. I've missed you so much." She flounced around in a peach-colored sundress and, as always, looked ready to step into a *Vogue* model set for a photo shoot. "Give me a kiss."

While she held me close, she snapped in an angry whisper, "A padded bra? You are wearing a padded bra?"

I started to explain my growth spurt, but she pushed me away and put back on her fake-pleasant face. Now was not the time.

Grandma clapped. "Seth and Jennifer—come give me a hug, you two."

Gypsy was vibrating her curly coat and wetting herself and trying to leap into my arms all at the same time. I knelt down to pet her, and she bombarded me with big wet licks all over my face.

When we calmed down a little, I said, "It's over, right? You wouldn't be here if it weren't over?"

Dad gazed at the ground.

Mom's smile froze. "It's partially over. They're no longer investigating Dad and me. The judge gave us a court order this morning, ending your custody status. You can come home."

"Partially over?" The relief was a tease. A mean tease. "So, what's next?"

Mom gave me a not-now glare. "Let's go inside. I hardly recognize you. How much weight have you gained? You remind me of myself when I was a sophomore. Your hair."

I couldn't tell whether she loved it or hated it.

Three months ago, I would have reasoned with her—tried to get her to tell me what she knew, tried to get her to understand that I needed to know what happened—but I was far more patient with her since I'd been away. I kept reminding myself that the woman who had just given me the look was the same sad little girl in the first-grade picture. While Grandma's scarred legs were a visible reminder of the trauma of that horrible night, Mom's damage was just as deep, even though it couldn't be seen.

I didn't corner Dad and try to get information from him because he hated being pulled between Mom and me. I would wait for a while until Mom was ready to tell me.

The next hours were filled with me modeling my new clothes and Grandma bragging about how much I helped her around the house. Then Grandma dropped her man bomb.

Mom simultaneously dumped my latest sewing project and her public smile. She wrinkled her normally smooth brow and swooped onto Grandma. "You know, Mother, he may pretend to be very nice, but there are lots of untrustworthy people out there. You have to be careful. Does he have a job?"

"No, he's retired, like me."

I piped up. "Scooter's really nice, Mom. And if it weren't for his help, we might not even be together now."

I could see from Mom's worried expression that my opinion didn't make her feel better.

Dad, more laid-back about Grandma dating, grinned. "Well, when do we get to meet Scooter?"

Grandma beamed at Dad. "Tomorrow. He wants us all to come to his house for brunch."

From the moment Scooter and Dad met, they got along like old friends. They reminded me of each other—fit, smart, and soft-spoken. Mom relished in Scooter's credentials, house, garden and pool. And his Dove Dove wall fascinated her. She gave long talks to everyone about the anthropological implications of errors in institutionalized justice.

I was glad for Grandma's sake that everyone was happy, but the whole day, each time Mom and I had a moment alone, she showed me her angry edge. Once when I was talking to Scooter about writing incident reports, she watched me with narrowed eyes. But as soon as Scooter glanced at her, she flared her dazzling white teeth. Each time she and I made eye contact, she looked away from me. Waiting for her explosion reminded me that my time apart from Mom had softened my memory of her anger.

Just before we left Scooter's, I stepped outside to get away from Mom for a few minutes. I wandered over to the little vine-covered archway that led into the garden. Dad and Scooter were talking, and through the vines, I could see them leaning against the fence, looking out over the plants. They didn't notice me.

Scooter said, "You're lucky Polarity found that picture and they figured out you and Jennifer weren't involved before they charged and tried you."

"Yeah." I could see Dad's face—sad and worried as if observing a disaster scene that he was powerless to fix. "The whole thing has been the shock of our lives."

"You know, there may be tens of thousands of innocent people in prison, and I've seen wrongful convictions take thirteen years to overturn."

"Jesus Christ." Dad looked down at his feet.

He'd never said "Jesus Christ" in that helpless tone before. I hated seeing my strong, capable dad shaken. *Is this how he felt when he was younger and drank too much?*

They were silent until Dad cleared his throat and rolled his shoulders as if dislodging a bad dream. "Thank you, Scooter, for all you've done to help Polarity." He sounded more like his normal self. "We appreciate you."

Saying good-bye to Grandma the next morning was sad. When I hugged her, I whispered, "Thank you for everything. It was the best summer of my life. I love you so much."

She whispered, "We'll do it again and again. I love you a bushel and a peck and a hug around the neck."

We kept it quiet because it rattled Mom to hear things like this. BPD can make people feel left out and jealous even when there's no reason.

Dad held the truck door open for me while Mom and Grandma said their good-byes. When I started to squeeze into the backseat, he put his hand on my shoulder. "Get in the front."

So I hopped in and scooted over to the passenger side.

The lines around his eyes deepened. "No, in the middle."

This was off—Mom always sat in the middle, with me on the side or in the back.

As soon as we pulled out of Grandma's driveway, I asked, "Are we going back to Houston now?" I wasn't sure if I wanted to go to Houston and never see Ethan again, but I figured my parents were so fed up with Garcia that we'd never go back there.

Mom slowly targeted me with one raised eyebrow. "No, ma'am." Her voice turned icy. "We are not going to Houston now."

Her bad news tone quaked my stomach. "Then where?"

"Right back to Garcia." Her hate-filled eyes cut into me. "So you can clean up this mess you made."

Pow. This was the explosion I'd been sensing since yesterday. "What? I didn't do anything in Garcia, and you said they cleared you and Dad."

Mom started to answer me, but Dad interrupted her, keeping his eyes on the road. "Okay, let's back up and start at the beginning." He fell into his normal role of keeping Mom rational. "Hon, let's explain to Polarity what we've learned. She might be able to sort it out."

"Seth, the facts are crystal clear. Polarity posed for that picture and is covering for her friend who took it."

Her words squeezed my heart. *She can't believe this. She can't be my mother and believe this, no matter how BPD she is.*

Mom forged ahead. "She caused our computer and phones to be confiscated. She put me through more than three months of hell while she had a great vacation with Mother, got new hair—new body—new clothes, none of which I approved. I had to buy a new computer, spend countless hours Internet tracking, battle state agencies, be humiliated by endless questions." She glared at me until I met her eyes. "Polarity, everything you did was evil."

My voice scraped out in a whisper. "Mom, please, you're forgetting your limits." I glanced at Dad.

He gave a slight nod. This was the phrase we were trained to use when she got sucked down a BPD track and started looking at situations in black-and-white extremes. The use of the word "evil" was a big tip-off that she was having trouble.

Say something, Dad. Tell her she's wrong about me. Tell her I could never pose for that picture.

Mom didn't give him a chance. "I spied that secret look between the two of you. Go ahead, form your secret little club, but don't you use that psycho-lingo about limits with me. Using my condition to distract from your own evil is despicable."

"Jennifer." Dad rarely spoke in this take-charge tone. "Stop." Usually he gently coached her until she calmed down, but this time he raised his voice.

She folded both arms and glared ahead at the road.

He patiently started what I expected would be the first of many, many explanations—reminders of the trap ensnaring her. Each time this happened, he had to explain over and over to her—sometimes for days, sometimes even going in for a counseling session with her, until she got it.

"Jennifer, remember, this is not about you. Remember that we love you—you are a wonderful mother and my precious wife." He took a deep breath. "This is about Polarity and another kid. No one did it to target you. It hurts you because you love Polarity, but the reason it was done is not about you or me."

The world rocked. He thought I deliberately posed. They both thought I had done this and wasn't telling. My chest heaved, and I did my best to muffle the noise my weeping made. But my tears wouldn't stop.

Dad handed me a tissue from the dispenser on the visor. "They weren't thinking about us when they did it. Can you remember that, Hon?" He looked at Mom.

She blew out a loud huff of air and continued to stare ahead with her arms folded.

"Now, I'm going to tell Polarity everything that happened. Then she will tell us what she knows." He glanced at me. "When you didn't come home from school that day, Mom went to find you. Police officers were there, and they took her in to question her. At first, they thought Mom or I took the picture because they found it on a child porn site that is used mainly by adults."

I covered my face with my hands.

Dad put his arm around me and drove one-handed. "After they got nowhere with Mom, they let her call me to come to the station. They questioned me alone for hours before they let us be together. They let us go home but said that you'd be in protective services until they finished investigating. But now that they have the picture with a section of wall from the girls' locker room, they've cleared us." He paused and squeezed my shoulder with his arm, pulling me closer to him. He said gently, "But we still need to figure out who's responsible."

"So," Mom said. "You may as well tell us who you were posing for. I talked with the principal myself yesterday and she is going to interview all twenty-two girls in your gym class. I inspected the locker room myself, and there's no question that's the place where you staged that picture. You need to save everyone a lot of time and trouble. Spill it now."

I took a deep breath. "You have to believe me. You have to. I never posed for that picture. It's got to be a trick—different pictures stuck together, features enhanced."

"Don't be even more evil by continuing to lie!" Mom hammered out her words. "Don't you think that is the first, very first, possibility

I considered? I've analyzed the picture. The resolution aligns with a video still. Apparently, you didn't just pose for a snapshot. You put on quite a little show. I guess that's the next thing that will show up on the Internet—the whole video of your outrageous dance."

She narrowed her eyes. "Were there boys in the locker room? Is that why you won't tell? You were putting on a show for some boys?"

I gasped. I couldn't respond, couldn't believe she would suspect me of that. All hope drained out of me. There were no more tears, just numbness.

"Jennifer, stop now," Dad said. "You're for sure breaking the limits now." Dad was the only person who could talk to Mom like that and get her to listen.

Now she spoke with a new calmness that didn't fit this conversation. "Seth, I always take your guidance. But this time you're wrong. She's lying to us. And new hair, new clothes, and cozying up to you doesn't change the fact. She's lying, and if you won't see that, you're as evil as she is."

Dad said, "We don't know yet what happened, so don't draw conclusions until we've have the whole story. Polarity, now you can explain. Tell us everything you know about the picture. Help us understand."

I clenched my fists together and brought them to my lips.

I was supposed to have a structured "I feel" conversation with Mom. I was supposed to say something like, "When you say you think I danced naked for anyone—anyone, especially boys—it makes me feel sick, hurt, deserted. It makes me feel like my mother doesn't know me." I was supposed to say how I felt even if she didn't get it at the moment. It was important for me to express my feelings—for me not to be passive—so that we didn't get into a codependent relationship.

And more than anything, I wanted to make them know that I didn't do the obscene pose. I wanted to make the shame of it go away. *Somehow I will get to the truth. But not today.*

Gypsy whined from the back seat while Dad's question waited for an answer.

I moved my hands away from my face and unbuckled my seat belt. "I don't know anything. Nothing."

I crawled over into the back seat. No one talked all the way back to Garcia.

CHAPTER 6

"UP. NOW." MOM'S SHARP VOICE pierced my sleep at six the next morning. "We have an eight a.m. hearing with your principal. She's going to tell you what your consequences will be."

I opened my eyes to the peach glow of dawn coming through the windows along one side of our trailer. "Okay, I'm awake."

In the mornings, we raised the blinds along that wall because it faced a vacant field of tall weeds and mesquite trees. The windows stayed covered on the side that looked out on the other trailers because, to be honest, this park was a dump—rusting trailers, bare dirt for landscaping, falling down fences. I had been surprised when Mom consented to park here, but she was pumped to hang with the local *curandera*, and no other park in the area had a vacancy. She had laughed and said, "We're true anthropologists, living among the natives."

I stood, folded my sheets, dropped my pillow into its special bin, flipped the bed cushions over to cover the table benches, and clicked a switch that made the bed-base fold and rise into the table we used for eating. The aroma of coffee filled the crisp morning air, and Dad, already dressed in a white shirt and jeans, stood just outside the open door, holding his cup and Gypsy's leash. Usually Mom's cooking woke me because my bed was only a few feet from the stove, but this morning I'd slept through it. Food and plates on the counter waited for my bed to become the table. In spite of her rage at me, she had cooked my favorites: scrambled eggs with mushrooms and quinoa blueberry muffins. I headed toward the bathroom in the center of the trailer, and the loud grind of the blender punctured our silence. Mom was making her special smoothie, invented when I was a toddler to ensure that I'd start the day with enough nutrients.

We three ate together in the table nook with the morning sun streaming in as if it were any other summer morning. Only we didn't talk, and we didn't look at each other. I gazed out at the field. Someone had mowed the tall, wild sunflowers. For the first time, I could see a pile of junk in one corner—a rusted lawn tractor with a tattered purple umbrella, thousands of tangled Christmas lights, a peeling wooden "RV Resort" sign, several broken lawn chairs. Things that spoke of better days. Our rustic field view was really a dump. I just hadn't seen it before.

All I could think about was how disappointed Mom and Dad were in me and that we were going back to Star Ninth Grade Center. Maybe we'd see the picture again. The sweet smell of the muffins that I usually loved made me queasy.

When I got into the backseat of the truck for the two-block drive to the school, no one told me to get in the front. Dad started the engine but immediately cut it off. At first, I thought he'd decided that we'd walk. In the rearview mirror, his gaze locked with mine. The unspoken sorrow and worry etched in the shadowed reflection of my father's eyes found a direct link to my heart.

He broke our connection and slowly shifted his broad shoulders around in his seat until he faced me. "We don't understand any of this, but whatever happens from here on out, I want you to know that Mom and I love you." His voice grew huskier. "And we're going to help you through this."

"I love you, too." My voice caught. "I'm sorry you have to do this."

Mom kept facing the front, silent. She shook her head as if she were disgusted with both of us. She had smoothed her blond hair back into a twist, and she wore her black business pantsuit with high-heeled pumps. She carried her stiff black purse that was the size and shape of a briefcase. But with all her severity, she reminded me of a dressed-up child next to Dad.

For just a heartbeat, when I looked down at my own clothes, I smiled to myself. Grandma had bought me these jeans two days before I left Dallas because the other pair would barely zip. She had done her shrugging-shoulder grin. "Guess my good cooking is putting some meat on your bones." The thought of her made me touch a strand of my hair resting on my shoulder and remember the fun of getting highlights together.

The semester wouldn't be in session for a few more days, so no students were around. Miss Smart, with her ponytail super tight today, jumped up as soon as we entered the reception area and waved her ever-present yellow pencil. "Mr. and Mrs. Weeks, Polarity, allow me to conduct you to the conference room." She pointed her pencil to the right. Her little escort speech was silly, with the door into the conference room only a few steps from her desk. As we passed through the front office, the red-and-blue betta was missing from the aquarium. I did a double take—the divider that had isolated the betta was also gone. Oddly, the mollies acted as if the barrier were still there. They stayed on their side of the aquarium, just as they had in the past.

Mrs. Sanchez stepped out of her office, and she must have noticed my attention on the fish. "We're wondering when the mollies will figure out that they're no longer limited to one half."

Any other time I would have talked with her about the missing wall, but my nervousness squelched any small talk.

Mrs. Sanchez said, "Thank you, Miss Smart. I'll take them in."

Mr. Hill, in his routine white shirt and tie, sat tensely at the long wood table, which could have seated a dozen. He gave one solemn, quick nod in our direction and returned his focus to a notepad in front of him. A laptop, a tape recorder, bottled water, and a box of tissues rested in the center of the table. Mom, Dad, and I sat on the opposite side of the table from Mr. Hill, with me in the middle holding my folder of reports and a yellow legal pad from Scooter. Covering the walls, poster-sized photos depicted students doing all kinds of school activities—cheerleaders in a pyramid, a girl dreamily reading in the library, a boy with a blue ribbon and a white hog, the boys' basketball team posed around a trophy. I wished I could be one of those students who didn't have to think about a picture on the Internet. Their happy faces didn't fit the mood in the room.

A soft thud ended my wishing. Mr. Hill had stood and closed the door.

Mrs. Sanchez turned on the recorder and identified herself, gave the date and time, and said, "We are convened for the disciplinary hearing of Polarity Weeks. Before we begin, I'll ask each person present to say your name for the record and your relationship to the student."

After everyone did it, she turned toward Mom and Dad with her warm, grandmotherly approach. "Mr. and Mrs. Weeks, I appreciate your effort to get this hearing done before school starts." Her brown eyes burrowed into mine, just as they had that day in her office. Her voice softened. "I know this is not easy for you."

She started talking faster. "I'll review the procedure we'll use, take any questions, and we'll begin. We'll divide the hearing into four parts: first, I'll ask the campus representative, Mr. Hill, to explain why he brought the matter to the office."

I lifted the yellow pad from my lap and numbered one through four—ready to take notes on the four parts. No one else moved while she gave her overview.

"Second, I'll ask the family to respond to the actions described, giving any objections that you may have. In other words, give your side of the story. Third, Mr. Hill will have the opportunity to add or clarify any information that he feels is needed. And last the family will have the final opportunity to fill in any additional factors or clarification."

After we all agreed to the procedures, Mr. Hill, with his eyes on his notes, described how he spotted the picture on a student's computer.

Mrs. Sanchez interrupted him. "Polarity, I know that you're aware of who this student is, but during this hearing we won't name any other students. There are laws that prohibit us from identifying other students unless we have written parental permission."

I put my folder on the table beside my tablet. "I have incident reports with lots of names. Does that mean I can't talk about what I've written?"

"Oh no, dear. You and your parents are not bound by the same restrictions as Mr. Hill and I are. You can name anyone you please, but we won't be able to give you any information about those students. Okay?"

I nodded. Maybe this interruption made Mr. Hill forgetful because he zipped through his spiel without mentioning he was out of the room before he spotted the picture and that most of the students in class were ganged around leering at it. He talked about how he protected the picture from everyone's view, sent me to the office, and recorded the website location. Hearing that memory in his cold factual way brought a huge lump to my throat.

Each time I had talked about the picture, the experience grew more terrible. But now, with the sadness in Dad's eyes and the fury in Mom's everything—now was worse than all the other times. I didn't think I'd be able to talk.

He closed his notes and drew himself back in his chair as if pulling away from something that smelled bad. He shifted his gaze to Mrs. Sanchez seated next to him. "To make matters worse, she disobeyed my order to report to the office and was caught in the parking lot trying to leave school."

He never looked at me through his whole speech, as if he blamed me for everything and I was too despicable to observe.

"Thank you, Mr. Hill." Mrs. Sanchez's kind eyes moved to me in the same way they had that day in her office when she patted my shoulder. "Now we'll hear from the family. Tell us if Mr. Hill related anything that you have questions about and if you can clear up what led to these events. Our goal today is to understand the truth."

Her gentleness made the lump in my throat tighten—I knew the instant I said a word, I'd be crying.

"I like to hear from the student whenever possible, but it is the family's option who speaks, and, of course, you may all speak." I hoped Dad would say something, and he shifted forward as if he were going to.

Before Dad could say anything, Mom's voice bit the air. "Thank you, Mrs. Sanchez and Mr. Hill, I will speak for our family."

Dad and I both turned toward her. *Just bury me now.*

"First, Mr. Hill, although your procedures after your discovery were well-intentioned, they were minimal, and your procedures leading up to your students' blatant misuse of the computer were woefully inadequate." With her hands in her lap, her back stiff, Mom's eyes and words were lasers slicing into Mr. Hill. "Why is it you were not even in the classroom when this unspeakable thing happened?" Mom had gleaned that detail from my incident report. "And what kind of instructional climate allows students to assume that they can display a nude picture? What consequences did you apply to the student who did it?"

Everyone in the room remained frozen as she blasted her questions without a break.

"We wouldn't be here today if you had provided adequate supervision."

Mom could never, never lose an argument, and for once her stubbornness and skill at defending her own perspective were on my side. Somehow the circumstances in the room had made her switch positions. Hill's face began to match his red necktie.

"Second, no one in this school did anything to ascertain what sites the picture was on or how it got to the Internet. There are more than a million examples of child pornography on the Internet, with hundreds of new ones added each day. It's completely unacceptable for school staff to sit back and wait for some distant"—she moved her hands from her lap for the first time and did air quotes—"*institutionalized legal technology lab* to trace. If you"—her whole head jerked, as if to make sure that Mrs. Sanchez knew she was the *you*—"are going to give your students access to the Internet, then you must be responsible for monitoring it. It's easy for people to post and e-mail information anonymously. Proxy servers, floating IP addresses, wireless air cards— methods are endless."

When Mom latched onto a project, she was tireless. It sounded as if she had done the research.

"And court orders followed by records' searches take too long. If my family had not done months of research, the police would still have Polarity in protective custody, and my husband and I would still be under investigation. If, Mrs. Sanchez, you were serious about finding the truth, as you proclaimed in your opening remarks, you would have confiscated all of the students' phones and cameras."

Unlike the squirming Mr. Hill, Mrs. Sanchez faced Mom, remained perfectly still, and listened intently as Mom forged ahead.

"Third, who in this school is taking responsibility for the ineffective Internet filters? Mrs. Sanchez, who if not you is accountable for appropriate follow-up?" Again she didn't stop to let Mrs. Sanchez answer. "Fourth, who is supervising the locker room? How can something like this come out of the locker room with no adult at the school having knowledge of it? I could go on and on, listing the inadequate processes in this school."

For the first time, Mom shifted her rigid posture and leaned forward. She raised her right hand from her lap and her French-manicured index fingernail clicked the table with each word of "But. Here. Is. The. Bottom. Line."

She slowly looked between Mr. Hill and Mrs. Sanchez. I waited for her to tell them her final complaint, but she shifted her focus off of them and settled it on me.

My chest constricted, waiting for her ax to crash down. *Were the four complaints her twisted way to lead up to the theory that I danced for boys?*

"Polarity is completely innocent." She flipped back into her high-speed delivery mode. "She has a flawless behavior record in each and every school she has attended. Until we came to this poorly managed school, everything was fine. She has no knowledge of the event when the picture was taken."

Waves of relief rolled through my body. *She believes me now.*

"She was in a gluten-induced haze caused by the soap from the dispensers in your showers."

I think my mouth dropped open.

"When I inspected your dismal facility two days ago, I noted the brand of your product." Mom pulled a computer printout from her purse and slid it across the table to Mrs. Sanchez. "It is a cheap, phosphate, and gluten-filled formula. When I enrolled Polarity, not only did I list her intolerances on the health form, but I talked with you personally about how important it is that she not be exposed to gluten or soy."

Uh oh. Mom lied. I could use things like soap, lotions, and shampoos, and she knew it. Unlike people who have celiac disease, I'm not allergic, just intolerant. I have to limit only what I eat or put in my mouth—like food, gum, lip balm, or toothpaste. I glanced at Dad. He avoided my eyes. I couldn't read his expression.

Mom sped forward. "This entire incident is a farce of one error after another on the part of Star Ninth Grade Center. Your mismanagement and poor judgment have caused undue hardship on a child with a handicapping condition and her family."

I'd never thought of myself as having a handicap, but at least her freaking insane notion had blasted the lump in my throat. My urge to cry disintegrated.

Mom relaxed her back against her chair and folded her arms across her chest. "You both need to apologize, get your campus in order, and be grateful that we're not the kind of people who like to pursue lawsuits."

Mrs. Sanchez, instead of answering the accusations, gave Mom her usual kind expression. "Thank you, Mrs. Weeks. Polarity and Mr. Weeks, would you like to add anything to this segment?"

I almost stayed silent, but I wanted to say the truth to everyone at the same time. "I never posed for that picture or anything like it. I would never do that. I know that none of this makes sense, but that's the truth."

More silence.

Mrs. Sanchez said, "Thank you, Polarity. Mr. Hill, this is your opportunity to reiterate anything that you feel is important and clarify, if you can, any questions Mrs. Weeks raised."

Slumped and red-faced, Mr. Hill was a different person from the well-prepared man he had been in his opening. He stammered through everything he'd already reported and with a squeaky sputter added stuff about how hard it is to keep his eyes on twenty computer screens all at the same time. Two lines of sweat slid down his left temple.

When her turn came, Mom said, curtly and smugly, "No, thank you. Nothing I covered earlier needs to be repeated or clarified. It is now up to you to do the right thing for my daughter."

Mrs. Sanchez cast her eyes down at her hands and waited a moment. "I'm glad to see a family so committed to their daughter. Whatever happens, Polarity has the support she needs, and my hope is that she will come through this experience stronger and wiser."

She focused on me. "Polarity, I know this is the worst thing that has ever happened to you. I want you to remember that almost every successful adult on this planet, including the four in this room, can look back on their lives and point to at least one awful experience."

Everyone in the room held their breath. Mom's and Dad's gazes were locked on her. *Is Dad remembering his DUI? Mom her rampage yesterday?*

"But I also want you to know that as unbearable as the bad times may be, sometimes they help us in the future. The things you've experienced the last few months will pay off for you at some point. Your job is to make the most of what you've learned. Let it make you stronger and smarter."

I nodded. For some reason, her advice lightened my fears. What I'd learned from Grandma, Zada, and Scooter this summer had already made me stronger and smarter.

She asked, "Would you answer some questions?"

Surprised she would ask my permission, I said, "Sure."

By asking me, she was saying I was in control of something—which was weird, in view of the situation. I wanted to answer her questions. And I was glad I would be talking instead of Mom.

"Can you think of any way that the picture could have been taken without your knowledge? Could you have been playing around with a friend, and you didn't know the friend had a camera?"

I had thought about this a million times. "No. It couldn't have been."

She leaned forward with her hands folded in front of her on the table. "Tell me how you can be so sure."

I gazed down at my yellow pad with its one through four still blank. "Well, I don't even smile like that—so big and toothy. And if I were naked, I'd be covering myself. If someone walked in on me, I'd cover up, and I sure wouldn't wave—even if there were no camera. And I would never write such a stupid poem."

"What if someone slipped a camera in that you didn't see? I've thought about this a lot. Could you have been dancing in the shower stall with the curtain closed?"

She had just handed me the way out. From the corner of my eye, I saw Mom nod slightly. I could say, yes, it must have happened that way. It would be an easy, quick way to escape the nightmare, for it to be over. But I'd never find out the truth. "No, ma'am."

Silence, waiting to be filled by me, weighed down on the room.

I deflated like a balloon—drained as much by Mrs. Sanchez's kindness as by Mom's energetic arguments and Mr. Hill's dislike and Dad's silence—but I spoke. "I know it doesn't make sense to any of you. I don't understand it, either. The truth is I have no idea how the picture came to be. I would never have posed naked like that, and I never danced around like that even when I was alone."

My voice dropped so low that everyone edged forward a little. "In the locker room, all I did was hurry to get showered and dressed and out of there, so I could go home. If I had a way to explain this, I would. And I understand that none of you believe me."

Mom and Dad both put their hands on my arms. Gentle pressure on each of my arms—simultaneous, unplanned, warm. Something had shifted for them. I closed my eyes because I wasn't ready to see the emotion that would be in my parents' faces.

Mrs. Sanchez said, "Mr. and Mrs. Weeks, Raymond—he's our security guard—told me that Polarity was crying while talking with another student that day in the waiting area. Something about 'mean girls.'"

I looked up at her.

"Polarity, can you tell me what that was about? Could it be connected to the picture?"

Tilly talked about mean girls all the time. "No, it couldn't be connected. I wasn't even crying about the mean girls. Tilly always says that. I was crying because I thought something had happened to Mom and Dad. Like a fire or wreck or something."

Mom and Dad, still holding onto me, both squeezed my arms.

"Will you tell me about the mean girls?" Mrs. Sanchez asked.

"On my first day here, girls teased me a lot. They hid my shoes during gym class. They kept calling me 'bean pole' and 'poetic Polarity,' and they shook the curtain while I was dressing in the stall. Tilly noticed and called them 'mean girls.' Ever since that day, she's mentioned 'mean girls' almost every time she sees me."

Mrs. Sanchez sat up straighter. Her eyes widened. "Could the picture have been taken then—when they shook the curtain?"

"No. It was just an instant, and I didn't smile and wave at them."

Mom rapidly clicked her fingernail on the table. "Of course, that was when it happened. Of course, Polarity doesn't remember the details because she was in a gluten-induced haze. It's obvious."

Mrs. Sanchez raised her eyebrows at me. "Do you think you were in a gluten-induced haze because of the soap?"

I had been dreading this question. Mom wanted me to buy into the soap excuse. Her eyes were hard on me, but I said, "No, I don't think so."

Mom slapped the table with both hands and glared at Mrs. Sanchez. "Do you have any idea how utterly stupid it is to ask a child to remember something she has forgotten?"

I flinched at her voice, so much louder than Mrs. Sanchez's.

Mom continued even louder. "Think about what you are saying. How dare you question a child handicapped by your gluten-laced soap?"

Mrs. Sanchez, unfazed, listened calmly and turned to me. "Polarity, can you give me anything, anything at all, so that I can understand how this happened?"

I handed her my folder of reports. "Would you read these? There are some details that Mr. Hill didn't know about." She nodded. "Also, the person who did the textbox spelled my name wrong. Could you get students to write *polarity* and see if anyone spells it with an *e* added?"

She took the folder. "I had the same idea, and the day after you left, I went into that class and instructed all the students to write a one-to-two-page report about what happened. Every student in the class included your name in their report."

I scooted to the edge of my chair, hoping that at least one student's spelling stood out.

"And they all spelled it correctly."

Bummer.

"But I will read all this, searching for any clues about who else might be responsible."

Her *who else* stung, even though she said it in her gentle way. *She thinks I'm lying, covering for the others involved.*

She looked away from me and started talking to everyone. "Based on the evidence presented, I am removing Polarity from the regular campus to the alternative campus for thirty days based on reasonable belief of lewd behavior. This placement can be reduced to as few as twenty days with good behavior and academic responsibility."

Mom gave a sharp gasp. I stopped breathing and waited as much for her to explode as for the rest of Mrs. Sanchez's bad news. I—the quiet, poetry-loving nerd—was so not the type of person to go to alternative school. I had no clue what it was like. A girl in my class last year went to alternative school for fighting. On her first day back, she'd bounced into homeroom, beaming. "Slamming. Lots of hot, bad boys." A boy who went for having alcohol at school said he liked it better than regular school. Another boy said it was horrible—lots of scary gangsters.

Dad put his arm around my shoulder and pulled me close.

Mom's gasp didn't affect Mrs. Sanchez's composure. "While we're together, I will address the concerns raised by Mrs. Weeks, and I will outline options you have if you do not agree with my decision.

"First, for the concerns: Mr. Hill and the gym teacher both followed district protocol for supervision. They cannot see every student every moment."

Mom snatched my yellow pad and started writing hard and fast. Her pencil scrapes punctuated Mrs. Sanchez's words.

"And while we do require gym teachers to conduct walk-throughs of the locker and shower rooms, it would not be possible for them to stay in the shower room the entire time." Mrs. Sanchez paused and watched Mom for a moment, as if allowing her time to catch up. "We have done follow-up regarding the Internet filter. The district is in agreement with your concern about the flawed filter, and we are working with the vendor for a correction."

Mom rolled her eyes.

"You are mistaken in assuming that we have done no follow-up with other students and with our information systems to determine the origin of the picture. We have done both and will continue the investigation in attempt to find out who took the picture and who posted it. And as you've mentioned, we will continue to await the police reports to give us more direction."

She paused and perused the laptop screen. "Regarding the gluten intolerance to the soap, I do not find notes on Polarity's health form referencing gluten intolerance other than to foods. I recommend that you update her health form to include intolerance to soap."

Mom's pencil lead snapped.

Without a pause, Mrs. Sanchez passed a pen across the table to Mom. "If you would like further action, Mrs. Weeks, on any of the concerns you raised earlier, I will provide you with the procedures and forms to file a formal complaint."

Powerlessness settled over me. The mug shot of Ross Jones from Scooter's Dove Dove wall flashed in my mind—the prisoner's helpless expression. *I'm innocent, but I'm being punished anyway.*

Throughout Mrs. Sanchez's monologue, Mom breathed hard and jerked in her chair from time to time, as if she were about to speak, but she kept stopping herself. Dad reached his arm all the way across my back to hold Mom's shoulder.

"If there are no questions, I will now advise what your options are. The most obvious is to attend the alternative campus for twenty to thirty days. The second option is to appeal my decision to the superintendent of the district. You must give me written notice of your intent within ten business days. A third possibility would be for you to bring me additional information."

Additional information! There has to be something else. I'll talk to Arvey and Ethan. I'll convince Mom to let me continue the Internet searches. We can send written requests to the police to get the status of their lab work and to hurry them up.

"For example, if you can bring a doctor's affidavit stating that exposure to soap can cause Polarity to forget periods of time and behave in an uncharacteristic way, I will reconsider my decision."

"Oh." Mom's voice jarred like a sonic boom. "You can count on it. You'll have a doctor's affidavit immediately."

"Thank you, Mrs. Weeks. Are there other questions?"

Dad spoke for the first time. "We'll appeal your decision. Please schedule it as soon as possible. We want this done before school starts."

"I'll get it on the calendar today. Can you give me your availability times and dates?"

"Every day, any time," Dad said. "Just pick the soonest time that works for the superintendent. We'll be there. Also, what would happen if we move away from Garcia?"

I looked at Dad in surprise. *That could be an easy out—just go home to Houston. But then I might never know the truth. And I'd never see Ethan again.*

Mrs. Sanchez said, "This placement would follow Polarity if you enroll in any public school in Texas. If you enroll her in a private or out-of-state school, I don't know—response would be varied. However, some private schools won't accept students with a pending disciplinary placement."

"What if we homeschool her?" he asked.

"That would work unless you ever enrolled her in a Texas public school again," she answered, as if she heard these kinds of questions all the time. "She could still be required to complete the disciplinary placement. Other questions?" She paused and then slid a folder across the table to us. "Here's an enrollment packet, with the registration procedure and uniform requirements for alternative school."

She scooted her chair back and stood. Numbed and on autopilot, I followed my parents and Mrs. Sanchez out of the conference room.

As we were parting, Mrs. Sanchez offered her hand to Mom and Dad and said more nice things about our supportive family. Mom, after her stiff handshake, rushed out of the reception area with noisy, high-heeled click-clacking. I dreaded the explosion we'd have when we were out of hearing distance from the school.

Mrs. Sanchez took my hand with both of hers, and she gently squeezed for a full second. Dad stood in the doorway, waiting for me. The tender handshake could have been her way of saying good-bye, but when I started to pull away she held on. "I love your poetry. I read the ones you did in your English class. You're a gifted writer."

"Thank you," I said. "That means a lot." I walked out of the office with Dad, and together we went through the main exit and into the parking lot. I was looking down at the ground, thankful there were no students in school yet, when my body tingled in reaction to a deep, clear, distinct voice before my mind could form the name: *Ethan.*

"Mrs. Weeks, could I speak with you?"

Dad whispered to me as we approached his truck. "Who's that?"

There in the visitor's parking lot, empty except for Dad's truck, Ethan and Mom stood. I had memorized his body, but the in-the-flesh solidness of him in the bright sunlight with his sleeveless T-shirt and faded jeans collided with my heart.

Good thing Dad had whispered because a whisper was all I could force out. "A friend from school—he tried to help me."

Mom remembered him from my first day. "Well, hi there, Ethan." Torqued as she was about the hearing, she could instantly switch to an upbeat tone. "Good to see you. How are you?"

Dad approached. "I'm Polarity's dad, Seth Weeks."

Ethan shook his hand. "Ethan Rawls." The sight of them together took my breath away. Both tall, special, and handsome. Of course, Ethan took my breath away, no matter who he was with. "I have some information about what happened to Polarity." He held several sheets of paper with long lists of names in an Excel chart. "Hope this will help."

I made myself speak. "Hi, Ethan."

He glanced my way. He still held the papers in front of him, but whatever he was about to say escaped him because he stood silent, looking at me for too long.

Warmth—too much warmth—crept up my neck toward my face. "How did you know we were here?"

Ethan's broad chest expanded even more as if he planned to speak, but he was still frozen, with his eyes on me.

Mom said, "Oh, I bet I can answer that. Miss Smart told you, right, Ethan?"

He shifted his gaze away from me and smiled at Mom. "Yes, ma'am. I asked her to let me know when Polarity came back."

Mom giggled. "Yes. I could tell that Miss Smart would do anything for Ethan." Giggling. Mom never ceased to amaze me.

Dad reached for the papers. "What have you got here?"

"During the last two weeks of school—after Polarity left, I found out that a lot of students had received texts about the picture. This chart lists the eighty-two students that I know of who have phones."

Ethan moved his hand over the names on the first page. The moment when that same strong hand covered mine own rushed back to me.

"I wanted to see who sent the texts, so I could backtrack to the original person," he said.

Dad frowned as if puzzled. "How did you get this list?"

"I got a list of the entire student body from the office. My friends and I marked through the ones that we thought didn't have a phone. If we weren't sure about a name, we just asked them." He pointed out columns with phone numbers and dates. "Looks like these six students forwarded the text to most of the rest." He pointed to six names highlighted in yellow. Cynthia and sheep, of course.

Dad still frowned. "How did you get the record of their texts?"

"My friends and I borrowed phones and checked out their text history. It took us a couple of weeks, but one by one, we looked at enough of the phones on this list to figure out that Cynthia received the first text from a number that doesn't belong to a student." He pointed to row eighty-three, which had a question mark instead of a name. "And it became clear that Cynthia and her friends forwarded the texts to others."

According to his chart, row eighty-three sent Cynthia a text two weeks before the sixth-period reveal. Queasiness punched my stomach—for two full weeks, the link had floated around to all these students. "How did you find out Cynthia received this text?"

Ethan said, "Same as the others—friend of mine borrowed her phone."

Mom put her hand on Ethan's arm. "Ethan, this is brilliant."

He went on in his same humble tone as if he were talking about mowing the grass or doing a history assignment. "That number could be the originator of the text. I called it but just got a 'no mailbox' automated answer. So I did a reverse lookup, and the number belongs to a company in San Antonio, Technology Integrations Horizons. I called them, but the person I talked to didn't know or wouldn't tell me who the phone belongs to."

"The principal or police don't know about this?" Dad asked.

Dad's and Ethan's gazes locked. "No, sir. I want another couple of weeks back at school to force some questions with these students." He pointed to the six yellow highlighted names. "And get the originator's name. Then I'll turn it all in to Mrs. Sanchez."

Dad nodded but pressed, "I don't like waiting another two weeks. Why didn't you turn this in sooner?"

"I could have done that," Ethan said. "But I had a better chance of getting the rest of the info without any teachers or the principal involved. I gathered this"—he pointed to the list—"pretty low key. Just borrowing people's phones and asking some friends I trust to do the same. I don't think the six were aware of our snooping. But school ended before I could find out who posted the picture." He reminded me of Scooter with his concentrated focus on getting to the truth. "Now that months have passed, it will be easier to get someone to spill—they think they got away with it."

Mom asked, "Why did you do all this?"

She and Dad scrutinized Ethan, waiting for an answer.

"Ethan," I said. Everyone's eyes shifted to me. "He always helps the underdog."

Ethan's expression didn't reveal anything. He looked down at his feet. "I think Danny instigated it all—somehow. He's pulled some low stunts on people in the past. I want to make sure he doesn't get away with it again."

Dad said, "I don't know about waiting. I think this information should be turned in now."

"Dad, Ethan is right. They"—I pointed to the six highlighted in yellow—"will never tell the principal anything. They won't rat out."

Were Mom and Dad thinking, *Yeah, just like you won't rat out?*

Mom took the lists from Dad, and she frowned up at Ethan. "If you start asking these kids hard questions, aren't you afraid you'll become their next target?" A white car pulled into the parking lot and stopped a couple of spaces from us.

Dad and Ethan chuckled at Mom, and Ethan glanced at the white car and waved at the people—an older woman in the front seat and three girls in the back. *Is Shanique in there?*

"Seriously." Mom inched closer to Ethan. She looked as if she were about to stomp her little high-heeled foot. "Ethan, you are setting yourself up."

"Ethan." A little girl about five years old had rolled down a window of the white car. "Can we go to the Dairy Queen now?"

Ethan nodded at her and turned back to us. "My grandmother and sisters. Beginner's license—get to take the crew everywhere I go."

Mom, blurting Ethan's praises, hoofed it over to the car, with Dad trailing her. Ethan and I followed behind, and while we stood back a couple of feet from our families' self-introductions, Ethan's eyes caught mine.

In a low, private voice, he said, "It's good to see you." His gaze piercing mine, he gave my shoulder a warm, gentle squeeze that I could feel in every part of my body.

Mom's social chatter pulled me back to reality. "And this is our daughter, Polarity." The grandmother, with her gray hair back in a bun, and three little girls made polite introductions from inside their car.

But soon, the youngest one, Keisha, asked again, "Ethan, can we go to the Dairy Queen now?" And the visit ended.

We went back to Dad's truck as Ethan's grandmother slowly scooted over to the passenger side of their car. Our back windows were tinted, so I stared, soaking in every move Ethan made. He slid the front seat back and got into the driver's spot. Keisha, with bright red ribbons on two ponytails, bounced up and down in the back seat. Ethan started the car, but he turned around, as if telling the still-bouncing Keisha to buckle up. After she buckled, he reached over the seat and high-fived her. They drove past us on their way out of the parking lot, their car full of smiles. All three girls waved to Mom and Dad.

Dad delayed starting his engine. "I still think we should tell the principal and the police about this now. I know Ethan means well, but I don't like the idea of him continuing to do this on his own. The police might have information about this company."

Mom stopped her scanning of Ethan's papers. "No. We shouldn't let them know yet. We'd be nowhere if we had left it to the principal and the police to handle things. Let's just give him a couple of weeks more—that much time won't hurt." She spent most of the short drive home reviewing Ethan's list. "I can't believe he accomplished this in two weeks—especially since he doesn't have a cell or computer of his own."

"He doesn't?" I asked. *That reduces the chances that he saw my picture.*

"That's what his grandmother said."

Dad eased the truck into the tight parking space by our trailer. "How did he do the reverse lookup without a computer?"

"He must have done it at school," I said.

Mom flashed me a weird, squinty little smirk. "What was that look I spied between you and Ethan?"

"What?" A blast of heat saturated my face. Even my ears blazed.

"You know what. Don't act innocent. There's a little crush going on between you two—right?"

"No, Mom. I'm pretty sure Ethan has a girlfriend—Shanique."

CHAPTER 7

D AD DIDN'T EVEN GET OUT of his truck. He said he had to go to
San Antonio for work. Mom flew into the trailer, grabbed her
laptop, and composed a statement for the pediatrician to sign.

*If Polarity Weeks is exposed to soap containing gluten, she will exhibit
extreme, uncharacteristic behaviors and will have memory lapses.*

Exasperated with her, I blurted, "Why are you lying about that?"
But even before the words were out of my mouth, her eyes narrowed
to slits. Her Ethan-induced good mood collapsed.

She slapped her laptop lid down and slowly raised ice blue eyes to
me. "How dare you ask me that? You, who haven't given us a truthful
answer yet. If I'm not telling the truth, then you tell me what the
truth is."

I didn't bother to talk to her about the performing-for-boys theory.
Every cell in my body screamed about her heartless unfairness, but I
let it go. Why reason with her if she thought I was lying?

She charged forth with her new mission to prove I danced
naked for the camera while in a gluten-soap-induced ecstasy. It was
all the soap's fault. Everything else was forgotten. She called the
pediatrician's office in Houston and demanded that a nurse get the
doctor's signature on her statement.

I tried to ignore Mom's fuming and used the time to work
through Ethan's list, matching the names of the students with

their TeensterBlast posts. I missed having full access to Grandma's computer.

The doctor finally talked with Mom. She furiously went back to work on her statement muttering that he insisted on changes before he would sign it. This tug-of-war went on the rest of the day. Each time Mom made a change, apparently the people on the other end of the line wouldn't accept it. Mom would hang up, make more changes, and call them again. By the pediatrician's closing time, they still weren't in agreement. The day ended with his promise to revise it and have it ready for her by morning.

She stayed up most of the night, researching the latest findings on gluten intolerances. By morning, she was so jittery that poor Gypsy stood tensely and whined at Mom, who was pacing with her car keys in hand and waiting for eight o'clock so she could call the pediatrician's office again to see if the affidavit was ready.

Dad asked where she was going.

She said, "I'm not taking any chances. I am personally driving to Houston to pick up the doctor's original signed document. I want to see that woman's face when I give her the signed original. And I want to be ready if she won't accept a fax or e-mail."

Yes. Go to Houston and stay away all day.

"Hon," Dad said, "let's call the school before you take off on a five-hour drive. They'll probably be happy with a fax from the doctor's office."

"No, I want to personally put it in Mrs. Sanchez's hand, and—"

The phone interrupted, and Mom grabbed it on the first ring. She listened for a moment and rolled her eyes. "Oh, Mrs. Sanchez. Yes, today at one would be fine. We're ready. However, I was going to drive to Houston today to pick up our pediatrician's affidavit. Will you accept a faxed copy or do you require a signed original?"

Apparently, Mrs. Sanchez okayed a faxed copy because Mom said, "We'll see you at one o'clock at the superintendent's office. Dr. George Stone. Got it." She wrote down an address.

"It's at one? Today?" Dad asked.

She nodded.

"Good. That gives me enough time to take care of some business in San Antonio. I'll be back."

I couldn't believe he was leaving me alone with Mom again. I had hoped he'd be there as a buffer. I'd hoped the three of us would talk about Mom's accusation that I was dancing for boys. It didn't seem right for him to leave at a time like this. Mom went back to her computer, muttering about the research articles to take to the hearing. She didn't notice the fax come in a few minutes later.

I picked it up. On the pediatrician's letterhead, it listed my name and date of birth at the top. *Patient has documented history of gluten and soy intolerances that can cause digestive disturbances, rashes, and dizziness. External body lotions, shampoos, soaps, etc., if orally ingested, can cause symptoms.*

Mom read it over my shoulder, snatched it from my hand, and speed-dialed the pediatrician's office. I didn't want to hear her argue again, so I picked up my folder containing Ethan's lists and my reports, leashed Gypsy, and started outside. It was already ninety-plus degrees and getting hotter by the minute, but I'd rather be out there than in the closed, air-conditioned trailer with Mom. On my way out the door, I grabbed my old Emily Dickinson book that someone had left on the counter.

"I can't believe you're going outside to read poems at a time like this. What's wrong with you?" she asked as I walked out the door.

I wished I were back at Grandma's. I sat with Gypsy under a tree far enough away that I couldn't make out what Mom said on the phone. But her angry tone, punctuated with objects being slammed down, stabbed at me like ice picks.

I could see the back of Arvey's trailer. There were about a dozen trailers between hers and ours, but hers stuck out, sprawled near the entry gate. Much larger than the rest of the travel trailers, hers probably wouldn't fit anywhere else in the park. For once her house seemed deserted. *How dismal for her to spend her whole life in this place.* I searched Ethan's list for Arvey's name. It didn't surprise me that it wasn't there. I didn't expect her to have her own phone.

I closed the folder in frustration and picked up the poetry book.

I liked to let the book fall open randomly and read the first poem I saw. A slight breeze settled the pages to a poem I didn't remember reading before, about a shipwrecked person thinking he's seeing the shore over and over but always being wrong.

Was this my story, my trap? I thought I had seen the shore many times since the picture came out, but each time I was wrong. At least I no longer fantasized that I saw land. My hell was nowhere near over, and Zada had nailed it—things kept getting worse. I had believed we were home free when Mom and Dad got cleared, but now I was sentenced to alternative school. I still didn't know how the picture got made. And the school *and* my parents thought I was responsible for it.

I closed the book and let it fall open again. This time, it fell open to a place that had a folded sheet of paper wedged between two pages. On the outside Mom had written in squared, jerky capital letters, TO POLARITY WEEKS FROM JENNIFER WEEKS... FOR YOUR BELOVED EMILY DICKINSON. It was a printout of a biographical article from the Internet. Mom had underlined a sentence in red that claimed the poet said Irish immigrants should be **eradicated so there would be more** space for **Americans.** At the bottom in the same angry capital letters, Mom had written, EVIL. I checked the printout time to see when she'd done it—eleven thirty last night.

Have I been wrong about Emily Dickinson all these years? I slammed the book shut. The words, the ideas, the rhyme and rhythm that I loved—they made sense of the world.

They were all a joke as obscene as my naked picture.

A secretary took us into Dr. Stone's conference room, which had pictures of a man, I guessed Dr. Stone himself, shaking hands with people and holding golf trophies. Mrs. Sanchez, already seated at the table with her hands folded in front of her, greeted us.

The secretary scuttled around, checked the tape player, gave everyone bottles of water, and asked each of us to sign a roster. She buzzed an intercom button. "Dr. Stone, we are ready to proceed."

He entered immediately, short and tan, in a black suit and burgundy tie. His nails shone as if they'd been buffed for an hour. He carried a thick book next to his chest, like a preacher might hold a Bible. But when he set it down, the title flashed in silver letters: The Garcia Education Code. He pointed to the secretary, whose hand hovered above the tape recorder, poised to push Record. The little red Record light came on.

"I'm Dr. George Stone, superintendent of the Garcia Independent School District. We are convened for the appeal hearing of ninth-grade retained student Polarity Weeks…"

I'm still in the ninth grade. On top of all my other problems, they hadn't advanced me. *Sucker punch* flashed in my mind. *I'm as low as I can get, and pow.* I lost the next part of his speech, but I think he gave the same rules we'd had in the first hearing. Mrs. Sanchez explained why she sent me to alternative school.

Mom talked. And talked. But as soon as she started referring to her pages and pages of research, Dr. Stone held up one hand and said, "Stop."

He spoke at the recorder. "Let the record show that the parent is referring to printed documents. Mrs. Weeks, did you bring copies for everyone?"

"No," Mom said calmly.

Back at the recorder, he continued, "We will now call a recess at one thirty-three p.m. to make copies of the documents. The recording will stop while the recess is in session."

The secretary clicked off the recorder and gathered Mom's papers. We sat silently, listening to the whirring of the Xerox machine in the next room.

The interruption didn't impact Mom's confidence. When the secretary returned with four neat stacks of Mom's pages, the recording started again, and Mom lectured about gluten intolerances being related to an array of brain conditions from autism to Alzheimer's. She sounded so convincing that I began to wonder if maybe I did have brain issues. Somewhere in her lecture, she referenced the pediatrician's note, which still had the same two sentences he'd sent

2

that morning. I think Mom hoped they wouldn't notice the lameness of his statement while she wowed them with all the research.

After she exhausted the medical lecture, she launched into a replay of her tirade about all the school's mistakes. Dr. Stone's polite listening shifted. Each of Mom's complaints deepened his frown.

At the end of her final gripe about how poorly the school handled everything, Dr. Stone cleared his throat. "*You* should be grateful that the district is handling this case at all." His accusatory tone matched Mom's as he powered down on the word *you* each time he said it. "You know the police could take over and charge Polarity with collusion to transmit material of a sexual nature via digital means in a public school. They could still charge her, you know. You're just lucky that it's not still a felony offense in Texas. You should be glad that the Garcia County Sheriff's office is leaving this one to the district to solve."

Charges. The police could file charges against me. I had been so worried all summer about the police charging Mom and Dad that I had ignored the reality that they could now charge me.

"Dr. Stone." Dad held his voice low and calm. "Sounds like you're giving us legal advice."

"Oh, no. I'm not doing that. I can't give you legal advice. I'm not going there. I'm just—well, I'm just saying, well. In the best interest of the student, well—"

"I heard what you said," Dad cut in.

Eyes wide, Dr. Stone opened his mouth as if to say something. He closed it. Opened it. Nothing came out.

Dad asked, "What is your decision on our appeal?"

Dr. Stone did the fish-mouth thing a couple of more times before speaking. "I'm not giving a decision today. I'll send you a letter within ten business days."

"What!" Mom slapped the table. "That is ridiculous. School starts on Monday. There's no reason to wait ten days."

Dr. Stone put his hand on his book. "Under the Garcia Code, I have up to ten business days to give a decision. In the meantime, the student will attend the alternative campus as prescribed by Mrs. Sanchez."

Dad reached past me and put one of his hands on Mom's, which she held on the table ready to slap again. "Dr. Stone, doesn't it make sense to postpone the placement until we know the truth? This placement will be a part of her high school permanent record. Shouldn't you finish investigating? There's no proof at this point that she's done anything wrong."

Dr. Stone sat up tall and squared his shoulders. He started bobbing his head up and down as he opened his book and took out a sheet of paper folded in half. He unfolded the paper, not letting us see the front. In a swift move, he slapped the paper face up on the middle of the table.

The naked picture.

He pointed to the picture. "That's all the proof I need." His stiff-armed pointing and head-bobbing continued a few moments after his words stopped.

A black rectangle covered the private parts. But even with the cover, the picture was obscene. The crazy big toothy smile, the wild waving hands. I could have been doing the Lindy Hop in Grandma's Netflix classic, *Hellzapoppin'*.

Everyone, even Mrs. Sanchez, gasped. "This is uncalled for," she said to Dr. Stone as if he were one of her rowdy students. She reached across the table toward me even though the table was too wide for her to touch me. "Polarity, I'm so sorry."

Dr. Stone ignored everyone's reaction. He spoke mechanically as if reciting a memorized speech. "This picture clearly shows a naked student posing for a camera. Joyfully." And he seemed joyful to be giving his own performance. "And as superintendent of the Garcia Independent School District, I go on record that this behavior is not appropriate—"

Dad slammed his briefcase on top of the picture. We all jumped. He calmly snapped the lid latches open.

"Go ahead and finish," he said firmly—using the same tone he used on Mom when she was unreasonable.

Dr. Stone continued, "Ah, well, ah, this behavior is not appropriate at school. We expect our students to behave with decorum, and we cannot let this example go unpunished. If we allow one student to get by with this, we must allow all students to do it."

Dad waited for a moment. "Are you finished?"

Dr. Stone stood and clutched his black book to his chest. "Yes, I will mail my decision within ten days, and you will have the right to appeal to the school board if you don't agree."

Dad lifted some legal documents from his briefcase. Dr. Stone froze in place and watched as, one by one, Dad laid copies in front of Mrs. Sanchez, Dr. Stone, and the secretary. "Please sit down, Dr. Stone."

He sat.

"This affidavit states I want copies of all notes and documents and tape recordings, including the one today, related to this case."

Dr. Stone said, "Oh, no. You don't get that. It is FERPA protected. It has names of—"

"I'm familiar with the Family Education Rights and Privacy Act. The document accounts for your duty to redact information that violates the act. May I continue?"

Dr. Stone nodded. So all morning, Dad had been at an attorney's office. For once Mom remained mute. It was as if she and Dad were on a relay team—the baton rested in his hand now.

"This memo to the principal requests an immediate decision from the campus attendance committee regarding Polarity's promotion to the tenth grade." Dad, always the safety net—thinking ahead—was saving me, just like all the times he'd saved Mom. "I feel that the committee will find that being erroneously removed from her home by the state is extenuating enough to allow her to be excused for missing the end of school." Dad angled his head toward Dr. Stone's black book. "And the Garcia Education Code does allow the committee to make exceptions under extenuating circumstances."

Mrs. Sanchez gave Dad an approving nod. "I've already scheduled the committee to meet on Friday, so we can get it done before school starts. You're welcome to attend."

Mom started to say something, but she sagged back into her chair when Dad lifted another document.

"I'll be there," said Dad. "This memo is my intent to appeal your decision, Dr. Stone, to your board. I understand you have ten days to give your decision, but I'll provide you with my intent today, so that you can get the board meeting scheduled. And note that the memo informs that I will have an attorney present."

Dr. Stone did his fish-mouth routine again.

Dad lifted his case a little and folded over the picture as he slid it out. He dropped it into his case and snapped the lid shut. I had never seen my patient dad so angry. With his jaw clenched, Dad glared at Dr. Stone. "Let the record show that Dr. Stone introduced a copy of a document and let the record further show, that I, the father, have taken possession of the document."

"And," Mom piped in, "let the record show that Dr. Stone failed to provide duplicates of said document for everyone."

For one sickening nanosecond, I envisioned the secretary zipping back to the Xerox machine again with the naked picture. Dad slid his case back down to the side of his chair and dropped it to the floor with a soft click. No one said a word.

Dr. Stone started stammering, "Ah, okay, ah, this concludes the hearing of—"

Mrs. Sanchez said, "Excuse me, Dr. Stone, may I ask Polarity a question before we conclude?"

"Oh, yes, of course, we always like to hear from the student." He peered at his biggest golf picture.

"Polarity. Now that you've had a little more time to think, is there anything else you'd like to share?" Her question comforted me.

I almost said no as all the bummers shot through my mind. *Alternative school. Police charges. Retention. Lawyer fees. The naked picture on the table. No one believing me.*

But I thought about the courage my grandfather had to walk into a fire to save his family—about his commitment to do the right thing even when it cost him his life. In comparison to his nightmare, my mess was nothing. Less than nothing.

113

"I don't know how the picture came into being. I have no reason to lie. Also, I don't care if I go to alternative school. No offense, Mrs. Sanchez, but I don't think it could be any worse than Star. And what is the worst thing that can happen?" A psychologist had trained us to use this line of reasoning with Mom when she got off on a gloom-and-doom scenario. Right now, everyone needed to think about what the worst thing could be before this battle became more destructive than the worst thing. The stress of these hearings battered my family too much. "If it ruins my high school record, I just won't go to college. It's not the end of the world."

I said that last part for Mom and Dad. I didn't want them to feel as if the earth would stop moving if I went to alternative school. *It will be horrible if I can't go to college, but I'll figure that out later. Right now, I want to end the pain for Mom and Dad.*

Mrs. Sanchez said, "Be assured that this one incident will not ruin your high school record or keep you out of college. With your grades and your remarkable writing, you are definitely college bound. And with the supportive parents you have, you'll get through this and do fine."

She sounded a little cheesy, and I hoped she was right. But how much of what she said was just to make us all feel better?

"Yes, you will do just fine," Dr. Stone said, and this time he looked at me. "Do you have anything else you would like to say?"

I wished he'd stop looking at me and focus on his golf pictures again. "No, sir."

Back in our truck, Dad asked, "You okay?"

I nodded. Mom remained rigidly facing forward towards the brick wall in front of the truck.

"Don't worry about police charges. They aren't touching this. Our attorney has been in touch with the district attorney and the sheriff throughout the ordeal. The legal system lost interest in it after your Mom and I were cleared. They aren't going to charge you with anything."

Mom said, "Drive. Let's get out of here."

Dad faced the front and started the engine.

"Thanks, Dad." *Okay, the worst is over. I'll probably get promoted—do some time in alternative school, but I'll get through it.* Dad pulled into the street.

Mom jerked her face toward Dad. "How dare you go into that hearing without telling me I needed duplicate copies? You made me look like a fool. And how dare you keep the legal documents from me."

"I'm sorry about that, Hon. There wasn't time to talk it all through before we went in. I got those documents and this latest legal advice this morning. If we'd had more time, I would have discussed it with you. But it's good that things are moving fast. Maybe we'll get to the bottom of this tomorrow when I go to Technology—"

"And you!" she said, shifting her narrowed eyes to me. "How dare you say you are willing to go to alternative school? That's nothing but an admission of guilt. Why don't you just tell us the truth? You must know something!" Her voice shook with rage.

I covered my ears, but it didn't block her out.

"I'm sick of your lying, and I'm sick of that picture. How do you think I felt when Stone slapped your picture down?" She faced the front again. "You both are doing everything you can to make this worse for me."

We got through the rest of the day walking on eggshells. Mom and Dad each went outside to have private phone conversations several times, they took turns huddled over the computer, and once they went outside together.

Finally, the day ended, but at around one in the morning, I woke up to the sound of their whispering. Their bedroom, at the opposite end of the trailer, was only about thirty feet away, and it sounded as if their door was open.

Dad talked in his patient tone, reasoning with Mom. She started sniffling, and I could make out her saying, "I must be a bad mother for Polarity to do this."

Dad replied something I couldn't understand.

Mom said, "You know, Polarity is right about one thing. It's not the end of the world, to go to alternative school for twenty or thirty days."

His volume rose a little as if he forgot that I wasn't that far away. "I'm not putting my little girl in alternative school. There will be kids there with police records, violent backgrounds, substance abuse offenses. I checked it out—all the worst offenders from six districts are there, and it's twenty miles away."

That sounded bad, but I didn't dread those students nearly as much as I did the mean girls at Star.

Dad sighed. "We won't be nearby if she needs us."

"I checked it out, too," Mom said. "Their website has the rules. Everyone is searched every day before they go in. No one can have drugs, weapons, jewelry, money, phones—anything. She'll be safer there than she would be at a regular campus."

The bed squeaked as if one of them sat up. Dad's voice got louder. "I don't care. I won't have her in a place like that."

"But think about it." From the pleading in her voice, I pictured Mom trying to pull Dad back. "It's not a good idea for her to run away from her punishment. It's best for her to see this through—see what consequences are like in the real world. If we let her run away from this, we're giving her a crutch, setting her up for the same kind of mistakes in the future."

It sounded as if Dad stood and shuffled around the room. "I don't know how you can say we should not let her run away from this mess, when we've moved, time after time, so you could get away from whatever trouble you've gotten yourself into."

Mom shifted into her helpless, trembling whine. "It's different. I had reasons. You must hate me. You must think I'm an evil person to say this to me."

I expected Dad to start the same speech he used over and over to help her relax. Instead, his voice moved closer to their doorway. "I've got to get out of here for a while."

"Don't leave." Her whining ratcheted up—louder, shriller. "Please don't leave me."

He'd have to really be mad to leave her now because her fear of abandonment tormented her.

"I'm just going outside to walk." His voice sounded flat, defeated. "I'll be back."

She gasped as if she weren't getting air. "Please don't leave."

His heavy steps approached my bed. He stood near me a long time. His steady breathing accompanied Mom's crying in the background. I pretended to sleep because their pain would be worse if they knew that I knew.

He stepped away. The chirps of night crickets drifted into the trailer when he opened the front door. As soon as it clicked shut behind him, Mom stopped crying.

CHAPTER 8

THE MOMENT I OPENED MY eyes in the morning, I sensed something was wrong. It was late, and everything was dead quiet except for Gypsy, standing by the door, crying to go out. Gypsy never cried. She had great patience in the morning. She had been waiting too long. I jumped up to grab my long T-shirt and her leash that hung by the door.

I gasped. Mom sat frozen in a chair near the kitchen counter—close enough that I could have touched her. I'd been so focused on Gypsy at the door that I hadn't noticed Mom. Dressed in her tan slacks and red blazer, she stared at me with her hands folded in her lap and her face dead blank. She must have been sitting there, watching me sleep.

"What's wrong?" I asked.

"Nothing. Just waiting for you to wake up."

"Gypsy hasn't been out?" Usually, whoever woke up first took her out. I hooked on Gypsy's leash.

"No, I guess not," she said, as if she hadn't noticed Gypsy. "I guess she's waiting for you to get up. Or are you saying that I'm supposed to take her out?" The sugar-sweet tone coating her bitter words made my stomach churn. "That's another one of my duties? Just like everything else in your life?"

I reached the doorknob. "No, no. I didn't mean you're supposed to take her out. I'll take her. Be right back."

"Take your time," she said. Too calmly.

Dad's truck was gone. I didn't know whether he'd never returned last night or he'd left early this morning for San Antonio. *Breathe, breathe.* With my free arm wrapped around my stomach, I stalled outside as long as I could. Gypsy licked my leg and whined softly.

Once I couldn't make the walk last any longer, I opened the trailer door with dread crawling all over me.

Mom still sat in her chair, hands folded in her lap. "Would you like your breakfast now?"

"Sure, thanks." *The bomb is ticking. How can I defuse it?*

"Good. I'm getting a headache from hunger." She went to the small sink and squirted pine-scented soap carefully on each hand. She flipped on the water. "Will an omelet suit you this morning?" She watched the water trickle over her hands for a while before she lathered.

"Sure, but you didn't have to wait for me to wake up, or you should have woken me. I'm sorry, I didn't know—"

"Oh, I wouldn't dream of invading your sleep." She slowly rubbed her hands together under the water.

"Where's Dad?" I had to know, no matter what explosion the question might cause.

"He left hours ago. Technology. Integrations. Horizons." She patted her hands dry with a paper tower. "Should be interesting to see what the next layer of this saga is."

I folded my bed and went into the bathroom, wishing Dad were here. I reminded myself of all the scripts we'd learned over the years for dealing with Mom's bad times. She was clearly steaming head-on into a big one. Sometimes it helped to distract her, to bring up new subjects. I would tell her about Zada, who still hadn't answered my letter.

When I came back in, she stood at the stove, watching the eggs. She already had the table set.

"Mom, at the protective services house that first night, I met a really special person—"

She slammed the spatula on the stove. A nearby spoon clattered from its saucer. "You dare to tell me about the fun time you had—the special person you met! You dare! While you were enjoying yourself, I was being questioned by the police. I was kept apart from your father half the night. I was accused of every kind of child abuse imaginable. You know what would be fun for me? It would be fun to not have this mess in my life. That would be fun for me."

"Mom, please remember your limits. All this stuff that has happened is making you—"

She picked up the pan of eggs as if she were going to throw them on the floor, but instead she banged them onto the stove next to the burner. She snapped off the burner. "Don't tell me what to remember. Here's what I remember: I had a happy life. I had people who told me the truth. I was safe from invasive investigators. I had a husband who respected me and a mother who loved me and wasn't irrationally in love with her lying, evil granddaughter."

I stood frozen. "Your limits." I started to raise my hands to calm her but stopped—any movement might trigger something worse. I stood a few feet from the front door. *Should I lurch for it? Or ride this out?* "You are crossing boundaries. This is your borderline—"

"No, you crossed the boundary when you dragged us into this mess, and you have exceeded the limits of common decency with your continued lying. You are evil. Evil." Her eyes were cold and hateful as if viewing a despicable reptile instead of me. "And I wish you had never been born."

"No, Mom." I tried to make my tears stop and keep my voice even. "You don't mean that. Remember this is like a storm. It will pass, and you'll feel better in the aftermath. Remember what we learned: let the storm pass—don't fight it." I slowed my voice to sound calm and patient as Dad and many counselors had done. "I'm sorry that you're stressed. I'm sorry for all that has happened, but you don't mean…"

I couldn't repeat what she had just said. I wasn't ready to deal with the pain her wish had carved inside me.

"Don't mean that I wish you'd never been born? Let me be more precise. I wish I had no child. I wish I could cancel you." Her voice took on a gruff, gravelly quality, and she sucked in a loud breath between each of the next three words. "I. Hate. You. I hate everything about you."

The whites of her eyes were red and watery. Her beautiful face morphed into a splotchy, swollen thing—flushed from her anger. She didn't look like my mother. "You've ruined my life."

"When will Dad be home?"

She threw the spatula to the floor. It clattered against my foot. She jerked forward and grabbed my shoulders, her hands squeezing me like iron clamps. Inches from my face, she screamed, "Who knows?"

I could feel her breath and saliva. For a curious moment, I thought about how nice and familiar her face was to be saying such disgusting things. And the mix of familiar with disgusting curdled inside me.

"Maybe he'll be gone forever, trying to solve your mystery. Hiring more lawyers."

With each syllable, Mom shook me harder and screamed louder. Gypsy cried and barked in alarm.

I worried that neighbors would hear, would call the police. As scared as I was of her, I didn't want the police to come.

"But it won't matter when he comes. He can't change what you've done. You've completely ruined my life. Completely."

I tilted my face downward so I wouldn't see her anymore. Slick, salty tears splotched onto my T-shirt. I didn't know what to say. I had no script. I wished I could make this scene disappear. I could break out and away from her if I forced it—I was close enough to the door—but running out wouldn't solve anything or take away what she had said.

From somewhere inside me, a place I hadn't found before, came one soft sentence, "My name is Polarity."

She paused in surprise. At first, her blank gaze said it made no sense to her why I would utter my name in the middle of this argument.

I said it again, a little louder, looking straight into her eyes. "My name is Polarity. My mother gave me my name, Polarity." I sucked in air and stretched myself taller, but I didn't try to pull away from her. I hoped that my name and her memory of choosing it for me would take her to the place that the counseling scripts couldn't reach.

With our eyes connected, a change came over her face, and a curtain opened. A trace of understanding flashed in her eyes and shifted into sorrow. With a new, small voice that I could barely hear, she said, "Oh, my God, what have I done?"

We stood still—our eyes locked—her hands still gripping my shoulders. She began to tremble. Or maybe I was trembling. Or maybe we both were.

"Mom, it's okay. Everything is okay. I love you. You love me. We're okay."

As far as I knew, this was the most intense scene Mom had ever had. She pulled me to her, wrapped her arms around me, and rocked me from side to side like a baby. Sobs deep from within her filled the trailer. "Oh, my child, my Polarity. Oh, I love you with all my heart. I'm so sorry, so sorry."

"I love you, too, Mom. I love you." Her words should have relieved me—and in a way, they did—but years of experience and therapy had taught Dad and me that this was a part of the pattern.

Even as she said she loved me now, a sick feeling whispered that in time, she'd forget again. But today as she held me and wept, the little girl who suffered so much horror during the fire and for the long months afterwards was still inside my mother. I had a mother who loved me and struggled with this curtain that sometimes smothered, confused, and twisted her emotions. But under the curtain was the beautiful, loving woman who named me Polarity.

"I love you, Mom."

"I promise this will never happen again. You are my Polarity. I love you, and I will never do this again. I promise. I promise."

"Good—that's good," I said, knowing that even though she meant what she said, she wouldn't be able to live up to it.

Gypsy jumped up and barked at us. We both laughed and started petting her. The crisis ended.

Mom picked up her spatula. "Well, let's have a good breakfast and go shopping."

"Shopping?"

"Yes. We have to get your uniforms for the alternative center."

We had entered the aftermath, and I hoped it lasted a long, long time.

After we finished at Walmart, the only place to shop near Garcia, I had three pairs of khaki slacks, three white polo-type shirts, one pair of canvas tennis shoes, and a black belt. Everything I bought, except the shoes, was two full sizes larger than my last shopping trip with Mom. Grandma had been right when she predicted I had my height and now was filling out.

Mom and I always had our best talks while riding in the car—especially after shopping. I told her about Zada and how I wanted to find her. She had never answered the letter I sent her. Each time I talked with Grandma on the phone, she said, "No letter yet."

Mom asked, "Do you know what town that safe house is in?"

"No, but it was in Baker County because the next morning, we went to the Baker County Sherriff's office, and it wasn't very far away."

"Find the Baker County Sherriff's office." She nodded toward her GPS screen mounted on the dash.

After a quick search, I said, "It's about fifty miles from where we are."

"Which direction?"

I flipped the screen so she could see. "We're headed toward it now."

"Well, let's just go to the Baker County Sherriff's office and see what we can find out about Zada."

This was an amazing thing about Mom. She could hear a story about a stranger and feel compassion. The last Thanksgiving that we were at our home in Houston, Mom invited a homeless family of seven to have dinner at our house. And she helped the mother of the family find a job and temporary housing the next week. When another family, from my previous school, lost their house in a freak flood, Mom led a fundraiser that helped them get into a new home.

But with people in her own family, sometimes her ego got mixed into her emotions, and her compassion got lost.

The sheriff's office reception area slammed me into the memory of leaving for the airport with Deputy Gonzalez and Tammy. I hadn't paid much attention to this room back in May—brown plastic furniture, dust-coated ivy plant.

Mom walked up to the reception counter as if she owned the place. "I need to see Deputy Gonzales, please."

I didn't recognize the receptionist.

"Sorry, ma'am," the lady said. "He's off today. Can someone else help you?"

"Is Tammy here?" Mom asked.

"Yes. Who can I say wants to see her?"

"Jennifer Weeks."

A few minutes later, Tammy, wearing another flower-bordered shirt with black slacks, came from down the hall. She tilted her head, looking puzzled as if she didn't recognize me, and she'd never seen Mom. I reminded her who I was and told her I wanted to find Zada. She asked us to come back to her desk in its same little nook—not a closed office but more of a widened place in the hallway. The adjoining, bare-walled, glassed-in room reminded me of my morning with Nelda Sims's questions. It gave me chills to think about all the misery that had been shared in that room, including my own. And it made me thankful to be back with my parents.

"I wish I could help you," Tammy said. "But even if I knew where Zada is, I can't give out information on minors—no one can."

"I want to know how she is, if she had her baby, if her grandmother got better." I couldn't forget about Zada. We spent only minutes together, but she illuminated a faint streak of light into the darkest place of my life.

Mom said, "There must be some way we can find her. We'd like to help her and thank her for being a friend to Polarity."

Tammy chewed on her lip and tapped a pencil on her metal

desktop. "Well, I guess there is one thing I can do." She started typing on her computer. "Have you Googled her?"

"Yes," I said. "At Grandma's, but I didn't know her last name. I didn't find anything."

"This is public information, so I'm not violating anybody's privacy." Tammy rotated her computer screen, so we could see the page she'd pulled up—Missing Children in Texas. She scrolled down to Zada's picture. Zada Lynette James.

My heart sank to see that Zada could be lost or kidnapped or dead. The missing date was two weeks after I met her. *She might have received my letter before she disappeared.*

We stared at her smiling, hopeful face. She wore a white shirt, like a school uniform. The picture, clearly from years earlier, already portrayed Zada's sweet expression that made me connect to her. She even wore the same black braids coiled around her head.

"Oh my God," Mom said. "She was born the same year as you. She's just a child."

"What happened?" My voice trembled. "Did someone take her from the safe house?"

"No. Oh no, that couldn't happen—the security is good there. This happened after her release. But I can't give you any details. If you want to find her, your best bet is to post on TeensterBlast or something like that."

Mom gasped, and her mouth fell open. "TeensterBlast! A child has vanished, and we're supposed to look on TeensterBlast! Why wasn't this on the news? Why weren't there statewide bulletins everywhere? I never heard about her."

"I know." Tammy nodded and said, sounding sad, resigned, "It wasn't in the news. I don't know why some cases are headlines and others are forgotten."

On the quiet ride home, I couldn't believe Zada was gone. Just gone.

For the rest of the day, Mom helped me search the Internet, but there was nothing about Zada anywhere except for the one picture on Missing Children in Texas. *Did she go away with her baby's father? Was she abducted? What happened to her grandmother? Zada's probably a mother by now. How does a fifteen-year-old girl with a baby make it?* Zada had come into my room that night and comforted me, a stranger. Despite all her own problems, she cared. I wanted to help her in that same way.

Mom let me continue to use her computer while she fixed dinner. I scanned the TeensterBlast posts to see if the Star students had added anything else since I left Grandma's. "Mom, I have an idea. What if I set up a TeensterBlast account in Zada's name? Maybe someone who knows her will see it and help us find her. Or maybe even Zada will see it and message me."

Mom, high in her aftermath, was in a great mood and told me to go for it. I set up an e-mail account, *plweeks@gmail.com*, careful not to use my now-notorious-first name, and I set up a TeensterBlast page for Zada Lynette James, using her picture from the Missing Children in Texas website. I posted a message: *Zada, you helped me when we met at Hannah's, and I would like to reach you. Please respond or message me. Your Friend, P.*

"What do you think?" I asked Mom when she looked over my shoulder.

"Hmmm. Needs one more thing." She sat next to me and slid the laptop in front of herself. She did some searches about missing children and found a quotation she liked and posted it below my message:

According to the National Center for Missing and Exploited Children (NCMEC), nearly 800,000 children under the age of 18 are reported missing each year in the United States. Of that number, 33 percent are African-American.

With the rare exception, the unprecedented number of African-American girls who disappear from their classrooms, communities, and churches... end up exploited uncounted.

Invisible.

Forgotten.

"Mom, I know that's important stuff." I treaded on thin ice to object to Mom's quote. "But I don't think Zada will like that—I don't think it will help."

"Leave it," she said curtly. "You'll understand as you mature that being silent equates to being negligent. There are too many Zadas—voiceless, undefended. They—"

She probably would have lectured for an hour, but Dad came home. His and Mom's faces gave no hint of their argument the night before. They kissed just as they always did. Who knew? They were either great actors or a couple who had made up. Dad placed an odd-looking cell phone on the table next to the laptop.

I picked it up. It was more like a camera than a phone—it even had a retractable lens. "What's this?"

Mom moved closer. I clicked on the video app, and a dozen options lit up. You could freeze frames, crop pictures, add in art, and send with a few quick commands. And there were other functions I didn't recognize. My heart sped up. *This could be it—the monster that can distort faces and make people naked.*

"It's a phone like the one that took the picture." He waited while I continued to fiddle with it. "Have you seen it before?"

"No." There were so many apps on it.

Mom grabbed it. "So who has the one that texted Polarity's picture?" She flipped the phone over and over, as if she might find an answer.

Dad sighed and sat down. "They don't know. The owner of Technology Integrations Horizons died about a year ago, and there's been a lot of turnover in the company. After I called them yesterday, they searched their inventory. Today by the time I got there, they'd figured out five phones are missing. According to their bills, those phones haven't been used in a year. Except for the one text that Ethan already figured out went to the Cynthia girl."

I itched to get my hands on the phone again. "That doesn't make sense. No one used the phone except once—to send a message to Cynthia?"

Dad nodded.

"Well, how could the company be getting bills all this time for five phones they've lost?"

"They've got dozens of these phones. They use them with various clients, sometimes letting people keep them for a while. Five just got lost in the mix."

Mom continued to push buttons. "It's kind of old."

"Yeah," Dad said. "They're phasing them out."

My heart sank. I had been hoping for secret-cutting-edge capacity. "Well, phones have GPS mechanisms in them. Why can't we find the person that way?"

Dad shook his head as if he was defeated. "That's what I thought, too, but these phones were custom made, loaded with extra photography stuff. They left out a lot of standard features."

Mom set the phone on the table.

I picked it up again. "So, what's next?"

"We wait," Dad said. "While I was there, we called the sheriff's office and gave them this information. They think that the phone somehow fell into a kid's hands. Just a matter of time until kids use it again. The company is going to leave the phone activated and hope that someone sends another text or makes another call."

"I bet Ethan figures it out next week—unless the police tell Mrs. Sanchez and she interferes." I wished Dad had waited to give Ethan the time he wanted. "Can I take pictures with it?"

"Sure," Dad said.

CHAPTER 9

O N ALL STUDENTS' FIRST DAY of school at the Alternative
Learning Center in Beauty, Texas, they were required to attend
a morning orientation for students and parents. We arrived in the
town of Beauty too early, so Dad drove around. The rundown main
street consisted of a post office, gas station, a few cafés, a grocery
store, three small churches, and a large, two-story red brick building,
which was the destination for kicked-out students like me. Mom read
on the Internet that the alternative center had once been the town's
school, but now all the regular students were bused to larger nearby
towns.

We drove up to the school. There were one or two entrances on
each side of the rectangular building, and we couldn't tell which
one to use. A few oak trees and old, wooden picnic tables dotted
the grounds around the building, and there were no fences. Other
than the modern security cameras mounted at each corner, no obvious
upgrades had been added to convert this old school into a disciplinary
placement center.

Mom said, "Stop here and let me go up to the door and ask
someone if this is where we're supposed to enter."

About the time she reached the doorway, a big yellow bus pulled
up, and boys started piling off—big, old-looking boys. Most of them
had long black hair. Even though they wore the exact uniform I did, a
few them had their pants hanging low and baggy, and all the boys had

their shirttails out. Some of the boys started checking out Mom—staring, strutting, and looking her up and down. Mom was pretty, but this uncensored view of their reactions reminded me that her small size and long blond hair made her appear young. Mom approached one boy and started talking to him as she pointed to the nearest door.

Bam! The whole truck rocked from Dad slamming his door. A few fast steps with his long legs put him next to Mom. The boys' demeanor flipped from chill to tense. Their sneers vanished, and the strutting stopped. A man came out of the building, and magically, shirts were tucked, baggy pants were up, and the boys formed a single file line with their pockets turned inside out and their hands clasped behind their backs. The man addressed Mom and Dad and pointed around to another entrance.

By the time Mom and Dad got back into the truck, a second bus had pulled up, and another group of mostly boys, this time with three girls, got off and formed a line, pockets out and hands clasped behind their backs. The students—it looked as if only one boy was white—waited in their line, and as odd as it might seem, I felt ready to be a part of this place for twenty to thirty days. Everyone here had one huge thing in common: all were outcasts. It would be easier to go through enrollment and the first-day adjustment here than it had been at all the other schools I'd attended in the past two years. Plus everything was so structured, with the lineup and the strict dress code, that I wouldn't have to worry about socializing.

More staff came out and started inspecting the students as we drove around toward the other entrance.

But instead of parking, Dad kept driving.

"Where are you going?" Mom asked.

"We're not leaving our daughter in that place."

For once, Mom didn't argue, but I did. "Dad, please. Let's at least go through the orientation. You can be with me the whole time." I understood his reaction to the boys strutting their stuff for Mom—that was seriously juvenile—but I did not want to go home and deal with more debate on what to do with my life's problems. "Let's at least do that much, and then you can decide."

He kept driving away, heading toward the edge of Beauty, where the main street connected to the highway back to Garcia. "No, I'm not leaving you there. I used to think schools were logical, safe places. That they'd sort out this mess, do the right thing. But after everything that's happened, I don't trust schools anymore." He gripped the steering wheel with both hands. "Those boys back there look… They look… hardened. If Star can't manage regular kids, how can we expect this school to manage these kids?"

"Dad, I know you want to protect me, but it will be easier for me to go to this school for a few weeks than it has been to go to all the other schools. I won't have to talk with anyone. I'll just do my work and mind my own business. None of those kids will talk to me or bother me. They all behaved as soon as the teachers came out."

Mom's phone rang. "It's Mrs. Sanchez." She listened for a minute, thanked her, and hung up. "She said Polarity's finals have been faxed to Beauty, with instructions for the staff to let her take each one as she's ready."

Because I missed the last two weeks of ninth grade, I would not be promoted until I fulfilled the attendance committee's requirements: I had to complete my English and history reports from last year and pass four finals. That would be easy. I just needed to get it done ASAP so I could delete retention from my list of problems. "Please, let me go until I take my finals and get the reports turned in. I'm still a freshman."

Dad stopped the truck and pulled over to the side. We were about a mile away from the school.

I put my hand on his shoulder. "Dad, I'll be fine."

It hurt to see the pain in his face. He sighed and rolled his shoulders. "Okay, we'll go back, at least for the orientation."

The first hour took place in a small, old-fashioned auditorium with about twenty other new students. I was the only white one and the only one with two parents. In fact, one Hispanic boy with a black lightning tattoo on his neck had no adult with him.

The principal, standing center stage with a clipboard, peered out over the audience and did a head count. He cleared his throat into a little mic clipped to his white shirt. "Sir." He pointed to the parentless boy.

The boy stayed slouched back in his chair and gave the principal a single, chin-thrusting, backwards nod. "Yo."

"Are you in attendance without a parent or guardian?"

"That's right."

"If you read the orientation form, you would know that you won't get credit for attendance until a parent or guardian comes."

The boy unbent his slumped back and heaved himself up taller in his seat. "Sir, why can't you just orient me by myself? My mom can't take off work for this."

"I'm sorry. It's required. You can continue to attend, but your days won't count until a parent or legal guardian comes with you for orientation."

"Aw, man," the boy said. "How about her?" He pointed to a pretty Hispanic girl near the back, who was also alone. "How come she don't have a parent or guardian? Do her days don't count?"

The girl rolled her eyes. "I am an emancipated minor. I don't need a parent or guardian."

"Well, I want to be a 'mancipated minor, too."

"You dumbass," she said. "I have a kid. That's why I'm emancipated."

"Well, I probably have..."

A security guard, after getting a nod from the principal, approached the arguing boy, who stood and shrugged with both arms widespread. "Aw, man. Now what?" The guard motioned toward the door. The boy, still waving his arms and muttering, left.

The principal cleared his throat again. "Pardon that interruption. Sometimes it takes students a few days to become acclimated to our climate of respect in this school." He tapped on his little mic and scanned the audience as if he wanted to make sure all eyes were on him. "Why do you think there are so many of you here today?"

He paused and strolled across the stage, peering into the audience as if the answer were somewhere on a sign among us. "Students, look at the student to your left." He swung his head to his left, his eyes wide and still staring ahead. "Look at the student to your right." He looked right. "Look at the one behind you and the one in front."

Mom's eyes rolled at his theatrics.

"Now, look at yourself." He pointed toward himself with both hands.

Please don't say anything Mom. Even Dad shook his head.

"Each and every one of you committed an infraction that landed you here. Now, think about how much smarter it would have been to have behaved yourself. Today you would be with your classmates..." He went on for half an hour and reviewed every rule in the student code of conduct—annoying but predictable. After the past four dicey months, I could tolerate predictability. At the end of his lecture, there were lots of questions about schedules and rules. *Mom, please don't ask anything.*

"Sir." A tall black boy sitting next to Dad raised his hand. "Why do we have to wear these canvas shoes? Why can't we wear athletic shoes here?"

"Two reasons. One, as you well know, certain brands have gang significance. And two, athletic shoes are too hard to search for drugs or blades. These canvas shoes cut down on our search time and give us more time to spend on academics." The principal couldn't see the boy's smirk because he covered his mouth with his hand.

Dad raised his hand. Everyone looked at us. I wanted to melt under the seat.

Dad asked, "Why are all the students required to ride the bus?"

"Great question. Thank you, sir," the principal said.

He hadn't thanked anyone else for their questions, only Dad. That irked me.

"We can't have late or staggered arrivals because the staff does a scheduled check-in and search of all the students as soon as they arrive. Group arrivals allow us to utilize staff time better and insure consistent, thorough inspections. Does that answer your question?"

Dad nodded. Once. To the principal this short head movement

probably said Dad was okay with the answer. But Dad meant, "I hear you, but it's not going to happen your way."

Next, they took us on a tour. It was weird to see middle and high school students in the same school, and it was the quietest school I'd ever been in. There were guards standing in each hallway. And there were only about ten students in each class. No group work or class discussions were going on. No cafeteria. Everyone ate in the classrooms—lunches, they explained, were delivered on carts. No gym. More studying and reading went on here than in any other school I'd attended.

It must have impressed even Dad. His jaw, which had been clenched since he slammed out of his truck, began to relax.

After the tour, everyone splintered off to do paperwork, get their photo ID badges made, consult individually with a counselor, and meet their homeroom teacher. When Mom, Dad, and I got our turn with the counselor, she left us waiting in her tiny office for a few minutes. It was the first time the three of us had been alone since we got there. A nice feature of this old school was its tall ceilings and large windows in every room. From this office, you could see an oak tree and a picnic table.

"There are hardly any other white students here," Mom said.

Dad—sitting with his elbows on his knees, his hands clasped together, and his head downward—shook his head without looking up.

"Whites don't get into the system as much," I said, echoing the girls in the safe house, thinking that the discipline system was like the protective one. It would be weird if I were the only white student in my classes, but as a gluten-intolerant, poetic, transient, trailer trash, borderline's child with a nude picture on the Internet, I was used to being the odd one in the class. Different reasons but still odd.

"It bothers me," Mom said. "There are very few black people living in the towns that feed into this center, yet most of the kids here are black and the rest look Hispanic. In these counties, at least half the local population is white, so half the kids here should be white."

The counselor, wearing a large pendant with praying hands, came in, reviewed my schedule for tenth grade, and recommended I take one final a day until finished. I could go ahead and start doing my sophomore work at the same time. I wanted to get the tests started, so I asked her to schedule my science for that afternoon. Because of my school transfers last year, I'd covered the second semester material twice. Also, with a final on the schedule for the afternoon, Dad might be more inclined to let me stay for the day.

After she dismissed us, we went into the hallway.

"Bye, Mom and Dad. Wish me luck on my test." *Dad, please don't balk like you did this morning.*

He said, "Go ahead. I'm going to the office to talk about the bus arrangements."

I let out an exhale in relief and headed to the lineup of students going to the same area I was. "Bye."

Mom said, "I'm going with Polarity to check the food. I listed her intolerances, but I want to check it out myself."

"It's okay, Mom. If anything is suspicious, I won't eat it. I'm not hungry, anyway."

What a waste of breath! Mom, the world's champion food sheriff, marched right along with me to my room—only she didn't put her hands behind her back as the rest of us were required to do. As if I didn't already stand out as a white girl, now I'd be the only person with her mother tagging along.

There were about ten other students in the room, and the desks were spread apart. No one could touch each other.

Mom immediately said, "There must be a mistake in Polarity's schedule. This doesn't look like a ninth- or tenth-grade class."

Students raised their heads from their work and peered at us with interest—as if relieved to have a bit of distraction. Most of them looked old and big, a different world from my classes at Star Ninth Grade Center.

The thin, young teacher stood and scanned my paperwork. He said, "Her schedule is correct, ma'am. On this campus, since everyone works on individualized learning packets, we group by content area rather than by grade level."

I guess Mom's firmly planted feet told him she wasn't leaving because he grabbed a folding chair from the corner.

"This is her science class." He set the chair next to my assigned desk.

Before Mom could comment, a lady wearing a hairnet rolled in a cart with lunches in bags. She consulted a clipboard as she handed out the bags. When she came to me, she checked my new ID badge, and said, "Polarity, gluten- and soy-free?"

I took the lunch, and Mom immediately relieved me of it, pulling out the sandwich, banana, yogurt, cookie, and chips. Of course, none of it passed her inspection.

"Excuse me, but we specifically ordered gluten- and soy-free food for my daughter," Mom said to the teacher. "This, in fact, is a gluten-full lunch!"

All the students watched us as they quietly started on their meals. Mom and I were their TV, broadcasting a mindless but distracting channel—sort of interesting, but nothing to get passionate about.

The poor teacher—I could tell by his worried frown and hesitant voice that Mom made him nervous. "Oh, let me call someone from the office." He picked up his phone.

"Mom," I whispered in spite of the no-talking rule. "Please—just go. I'll eat the banana. It isn't right for you to be in here." She ignored me as she squinted at the ingredients listed on the condiments.

The assistant principal, a young black man, who came in to resolve the issue, was no match for Mom. He tried his best anyway. "Ma'am—this lunch is labeled just as you ordered it. See?" He pointed to the red label on the bag: *gluten and soy free*.

"So, you will certify in writing that this food is gluten and soy free?" Mom asked. "And you will certify in writing that my daughter will not be harmed from eating it?"

Aside from the crackle of chip bags, no one in the room made a sound as they ate and kept their eyes on us. We provided the best entertainment of the day.

"Well, ma'am, that's what the label says."

"You didn't answer my question because you obviously have no confidence in the provider of this..." She glared and gestured toward the lunches. "For your information,"—she squinted at his badge—"Mr. Assistant Principal, this product"—she picked up a mayonnaise packet—"contains both gluten and soy. Furthermore, this bread is made of white rice flour, which is totally inappropriate for anyone with food intolerances."

"Mom, I'll just eat the banana," I said again.

She ignored me. "Children such as Polarity must have whole grain products to compensate for the nutrients their intolerances deprive them of."

I gritted my teeth.

"And given this blatant example of the incompetence of your provider, I want written certification that there is no cross-contamination in the food preparation."

This assistant principal knew when to fold. "Ma'am, what would you like for me to do?"

"Allow my daughter to bring her own food, starting today. I always carry appropriate nutrition for her in my purse." Mom pulled out four plastic containers and utensils, and she gave little lectures about the contents and preparation as she opened them and set them on my desk. I expected the other students to be eye-rolling and smirking, but they still just seemed mildly entertained. *Maybe they think this is the white normal in alternative school.*

The assistant principal started backing away. "I'll have to check with the principal. Students are not allowed to bring anything with them. We'd have to search her food every day."

Mom folded her arms. "Either she brings her own food, or I bring her food daily, or you come up with an alternative. But this"—she gestured to the sacked lunch items—"will not do."

"Okay, Mrs. Weeks, I'll check with the principal," he said on his way out.

It was embarrassing that Mom sat beside me while I ate, but pre-picture it would have been mortifying. After having been naked on the Internet, this situation was not planet-shattering. She didn't talk anymore but continued her disapproving dissection of the lunch the school had offered. It was a relief when she dropped it in the trash and stopped muttering to herself.

I'd never had such a quiet lunch at school. As students finished eating, they took restroom breaks, only one person out at a time.

The teacher handed out learning packets to everyone else and said, "I have a final exam for Polarity." Frowning nervously, he glanced from the exam in his hand to Mom and back again.

I was afraid Mom wouldn't take the hint that she needed to leave while I took the test, but she gathered all her little containers and utensils. "I'll wait outside for you."

There were three hours left until dismissal. I didn't want to open a conversation with her in front of our viewing audience, but I hoped that she didn't intend to stay around the rest of the day. Surely the school wouldn't allow that.

I didn't see Mom or Dad in the classroom again, but Dad's truck was still in the parking lot. And during a restroom break, I passed by the office and spotted them through the windows. Mom and Dad were standing in front of the principal. Dad was talking and nodding in the clear, strong way he does when he gives directions to his construction crews. Mom, with a pad and pen, was furiously writing something, no doubt taking notes on the conversation.

All the office workers were watching my parents. I wished they had gone home like all the other parents. *Mom and Dad, please don't get me kicked out of here.*

After the regular classes were over for the day, everyone went to a twenty-minute period called Debrief. According to our orientation, this was the time to go to homeroom and talk about whether we met our goals for the day and whether we got demerits on the point system. There were eight other students in my Debrief, seated in a circle, led by the praying-hands counselor. "Unwind. Four minutes."

Everyone, even the counselor, stretched and, for the first time all day, talked freely. A tiny Hispanic girl, maybe even shorter than Mom, sitting next to me scrunched closer and asked, "What you in for?"

"Nude picture on the Internet, but I didn't do it." Amazing how easy it rolled out in this environment. "You?"

"Weed at school, but I didn't do it, either."

An eavesdropping boy next to her said something in Spanish. He snickered and said in English, "I didn't do it either."

A black girl smirked at me. "Nobody here did anything."

The counselor interrupted the circle-wide conversation about everyone's innocence and asked for demerit summaries. We listened to complaints about undeserved demerits until she asked us to state our goals for tomorrow.

Finally released, I fell into the line to await the Garcia bus, but when our line marched outside, Dad, standing next to his truck, stepped forward and motioned for me to come to him. Mom sat inside the truck, waiting.

Oh, no. He was making me break the bus-riding requirement. I still had three finals and two reports left to do. I opened my mouth to start my plea, but his stern, hard expression shut me down.

The girl behind me sighed. "Guess white girl doesn't have to ride the bus."

I tried to make eye contact with Mom as I climbed into the backseat, but she sat stiffly, faced forward and hidden behind her sunglasses.

The whole line of students watched us as we pulled out of the parking lot. We drove about five seconds in silence. Then, as if there had been some secret signal between them, Mom and Dad turned their heads toward each other, still frowning.

What now?

They both burst out laughing. High-fived each other. Laughed some more.

"Did you see the principal's face," Mom asked Dad, "when you gave him your lawyer's name after your sexual harassment spiel?" She giggled.

Dad said, "Yeah, and did you see how panicked everyone in the office got when you didn't even let them respond before you started dressing down the principal for the food?"

Sexual harassment? "Time out," I said. "What are you talking about?"

Mom turned around beaming like a kid at Christmas. "Dad

told the principal about the boys before school this morning saying sexually harassing things when I asked them which door to enter for orientation. And it's all on the surveillance tape—which also shows the absence of supervision. After we got through with that principal, he decided that you don't have to ride the bus. Yay, Seth!" She and Dad high-fived each other again.

"And your mom lit into them about the food, so you don't have to eat their food—you can bring your own." Another high-five.

Seriously, they were enjoying this after-school-special moment too much. I hated to burst their bubble, but I punctured it anyway. "Four hours ago, you said it bothered you that there are more black and Hispanic students in this school than whites. Then you bullied the school into breaking rules for me. I'd rather ride the bus and eat the food than stand out as the privileged white girl who doesn't have to follow the rules."

Mom slowly pivoted her body around to face me. I held my breath. I'd set something off in her. Dad kept his eyes on the road.

Mom's face went blank, signaling a looming tirade. "You know, Seth. Polarity is right."

I didn't move. *Does she mean this? Or is this a twisted attack?* Dad didn't respond—almost as if he didn't hear her.

Mom held onto the back of her seat like an excited child, her face bright and animated. "You're probably the only student in that school who has two parents with the time and means to spend the day at school advocating for their child. And we did pressure them into changing the rules for you." Now into her planetary-marshal-of-equity-and-justice-for-all mode, she could give speeches for hours. "We totally bought into the abuse of power over the underserved. We used the structure to serve our family's needs without—"

"That's right," Dad interrupted, with a single nod. "We did. But my daughter is not riding that bus."

My frustration bubbled over. "I feel like a hypocrite." What I really wanted to shout was that my parents were hypocrites. "I'm not following the same rules as everyone else. It's like I'm getting privileges for being white."

"Oh my gosh," Mom said. "This is such a teachable moment. Don't you see?" She raised her index finger like a scientist announcing a great discovery. "We, the privileged majority, talk about equality until it comes to our own family having to give up something." Mom had elevated herself into a lofty mission—the bus-riding issue no longer interested her. "You see, Seth, you're saying that you choose to feed into the systemic abuse of—"

"No. I'm saying my daughter is not riding that bus. Call it whatever you want, but it's final."

CHAPTER 10

WEEKS WENT BY FAST AT Beauty. I finished my ninth-grade work, got ahead on my tenth-grade assignments, and even had time to journal. After we all got adjusted to the routine, two things started to weigh on me.

First, when my Beauty time ended, I would be back in school in the Garcia district. Even though I would be at the high school, all the ninth-graders who saw the naked picture would be there, too.

Second, at Beauty I was invisible. At first I liked it when I walked down the hall and the other students cast their eyes away. I liked that no one except the teacher looked at me in class. It was a nice break after being singled out as weird at other schools. But at Beauty, other students did look at each other—grin, give little shoulder bumps when they were out of sight of the cameras or teachers.

At Beauty I felt invisible. Less than human. Lonely. I missed being seen.

During the students' final week at Beauty, they became Exiters and were entitled to special privileges, probably to encourage the newcomers to hang in there and also to get Exiters ready to go back to regular school. For example, when there were three days left, Exiters could start walking around without their hands behind their back. And on the last day, the soon-to-be-liberated student could choose someone without demerits to eat lunch with, either in the auditorium or, if the weather was good, outside at picnic tables. The two students got thirty-two minutes of talk time while eating away from the classroom.

When my last day came, I figured, instead of taking the privilege to eat and talk with someone, I'd have lunch in the silent classroom as usual. I didn't know anyone to talk to, and nausea gagged me as I envisioned enrolling in a regular school on Monday. Coming to Beauty, where I didn't know anyone and where everyone else was in trouble, too, had been easy. Going back to a regular school where I'd stand out as a girl with a disciplinary removal was going to be bad enough. But the reality that most of the students had seen the naked picture was hell. There would be unending stares and remarks, worse by far than the old poetic-skinny-trailer taunts.

To make matters worse, Mom and Dad couldn't agree on which school I should attend. Dad wanted to move back to Houston immediately, but Mom wanted me to go to United High School in Garcia for a semester and then transfer to Houston, so no one in Houston would know—unless they really probed my records—that I'd been in trouble. It was already twenty days into the semester, so I'd stand out as a new student in Houston whether I enrolled at the semester break or now. But Mom said people in the Houston office wouldn't be as likely to notice Beauty on my record if my sending school were United High School. If Mom got her way, I'd have to face the Star students who might still have copies of the picture. Even with the possibility of talking with Ethan again, I just couldn't go to school in Garcia.

Right before lunch, a new boy came in from orientation, and the teacher placed him in the desk next to mine. Accustomed to my isolation, I kept my eyes on my work. But that feeling of being watched crept over me. A girl across the room asked for the teacher's help, so I glanced at the new boy.

He looked right at me and smiled.

Ethan!

The magic of all our moments whooshed over me—that first day in the office when he tended to the aquarium, his angry reaction to Danny in the history class, his well-plotted visit with me in Mrs.

Sanchez's office, his warm hand on mine, his text-tracking spreadsheet, his hand on my shoulder while our families talked. Now, sitting next to me, his eyes connected with mine and launched a buzzing inside me. *Shanique,* I reminded myself. *He has a girlfriend.* But I couldn't help noticing that on his muscular body, the boring white polo shirt and khaki slacks that we all had to wear looked seriously hot. And next to that shirt, his rich, dark skin on his strong arms called out to be touched.

I made myself breathe. What could he possibly have done? He had always acted more mature than the other boys. Never clowned around, never said bad words.

I smiled at him and mouthed, "Ethan. Hi."

He mouthed, "Polarity."

I forced my eyes back to my work. But the page could have been Martian because one incredible thought Surround-Sounded in my brain. *Ethan. Ethan sitting next to me, breathing the same air.*

A few minutes later, when the teacher came and asked who I wanted to request for my reward lunch, I didn't miss a beat. "Ethan."

"Oh. Well, that's easy. I won't have to check his demerit record since he just started this morning. Ethan, would you like to have lunch with Polarity?"

Ouch. It sounded like a date when she said it that way. All the other students lazily raised their heads and observed. I provided another bit of entertainment in a routine day.

"Sure." Ethan's pleased eyes were too beautiful to look at and yet too beautiful to pull away from. He didn't pay attention to our audience staring at the new guy, going to lunch with the Exiter.

Moments later, the cart lady rolled in. It took forever for her to give Ethan his food. My heart hammered. I couldn't believe I was about to have lunch alone with him.

A security guard, smiling at us as if he thought we were cute, walked us to an exit door. He pointed to a picnic table. "That's your spot. I'll be back for you in thirty-two minutes." He pointed to the camera. "No going anywhere else. Got it?"

"Yes, sir," Ethan said.

The guard walked back inside.

Now we were alone. We were quiet as we maneuvered onto the bench, side by side. The other bench lay on the ground, broken. I could have leaned slightly and closed the five and a half inches between us, and my shoulder would have pressed into the side of his arm. My insides quivered.

He rubbed the top of his lunch bag with his thumb. I glanced down at my bag, and my own thumb was doing the same thing.

I said, "Better eat, I guess. Thirty-two minutes will zip by. Probably twenty-nine by now."

"Thanks for picking me for lunch." He always looked directly at me when he spoke. His warm brown eyes had a voice of their own.

"I'm glad you were here for me to pick." I gasped and placed my hand over my mouth. "Oh, I didn't mean I'm glad you got sent here! I meant—I meant…" What did I mean? "I meant I'm happy to see you."

He nodded, still smiling at me. "Me, too."

We both went silent and turned to face our bags.

I rolled my apple in my hand—couldn't bring myself to eat. He arranged his sandwich, bag of chips, yogurt, cookie, and orange. He wasn't eating, either.

Silence. We both started speaking at the same time. We laughed. We both said, "You first." We laughed again.

He said, "Ladies first."

"Okay. Why are you here?"

A flash of anger furrowed his eyebrows. "The drug dog alerted on my backpack, and when they searched it, there was a bag of weed in it—a large bag."

His fists clenched just for a moment. His anger faded, and a resigned expression took its place—as if he'd said this next part over and over and didn't expect to be believed. "Someone planted it. I don't have anything to do with drugs. I think some students get a tip when the drug dog is on the way, and they stash their stuff wherever they can to keep from getting caught. But I can't prove it—yet." A muscle flexed in his jaw. "I'll get whoever did it. It may take some time, but I'll get him."

"Ethan, that's terrible. Are you appealing? You have ten days. Or you can get a lawyer or request copies of the—"

He shook his head and looked down, cutting off our eye contact. He glanced at me as if I had a shirt on inside out and didn't know it.

"What?" I asked.

He rearranged his food again. "No one would tell me who Cynthia got the text from, so I gave the spreadsheet to Mrs. Sanchez last week."

He had changed the subject too abruptly. *Why doesn't he want to talk about appealing his case?*

He continued, "At least now she knows who the six are that forwarded the text to all the others. Rumor is she's having all six sent here."

"They admitted to sending the link?" I never expected this.

"Not at first. But Mrs. Sanchez told their parents she'd get a court order for their phone records if the girls didn't tell the truth. Guess it worked. One girl caved, and the others followed."

I started to ask if anyone admitted to taking and distorting the picture, but he must have sensed my question.

"So far no one is telling who made the picture or who posted it." Disappointment flickered in his eyes. "And I couldn't show that Danny was involved—yet. But I'm not finished."

His determination to find these people impressed me, but at the same time, the threatening edge in his voice alarmed me. "Thank you, Ethan. You did more for my case than anyone else. It's amazing what you accomplished. Who all helped you? Shanique?" The question nipped at me. I wanted to know how close they were and how she fit into everything.

He nodded. "And a couple of other people. It wasn't as hard as you think. There's a lot of phone borrowing at school—looking at pictures and things like that. I just made a list, and we started checking them off."

Is Shanique your girlfriend? I couldn't make myself ask the question yet. "You should eat. We'll run out of time, and they won't let you carry food around for later."

While he ate, I told him what we had learned about Technology Integrations Horizons. Up close, he was bigger than I remembered— several inches taller than me, muscular arms and neck. His large brown hand dwarfed his sandwich. I wanted to touch his skin, starting on the back of his hand and up the defined muscles of his arm. He ate his sandwich in four bites. His color, muscle tone, and strong features made me think of art. If I could, I would have painted him.

I sensed his gaze on my face and stopped staring at his arm.

He said, "You've been through a lot." The tenderness in his voice contrasted with the dangerous edge he'd shown earlier.

I shrugged and pulled at the stem of my apple.

"But good thing it happened back then instead of now." For the briefest smidgen of a nanosecond, I think his eyes dropped to my chest, but he instantly jerked his face back down to examine the rest of his lunch.

"Why?" I asked.

His skin color deepened to dark chocolate with a deep burgundy flush. "Well, if the picture ever shows up again…" After a long pause, he said fast, "People won't recognize it as you." He rolled his orange around in one hand and studied it as if he'd never seen one before.

Oh. *Boobs? Is he thinking about my boobs?* Something new hummed through my body. An energy that made me feel breathless and energized all at the same time. I gave a chatty overview, sort of as Mom always did, of all I'd learned about appeals, school law, and alternative school.

I was working my way back around to suggesting that he could take some action when he said, "Thank you for telling me this, but I won't appeal. I'm going to take care of it on my own." That threatening undercurrent had crept into his voice again. "And I won't put my family through that."

"My mom and dad haven't minded—they wanted to."

Something sad and serious shadowed his eyes. I could feel his pain even before he spoke.

"My dad died in Afghanistan, and—"

"I'm so sorry, Ethan." Unable to help myself, I put my hand on his arm.

He nodded. "Thanks. My mom is in nursing school in San Antonio, and I don't want her to know anything about this. My sisters and I live with my grandmother."

"Your grandmother could appeal." But even before the words were out, I thought about my parents—their hours of preparation, the money on lawyers, the tense meetings with the principal and superintendent. Too much for most grandmothers, especially with other children to take care of.

We both looked down at our lunches.

"Polarity," he said, huddling closer. I breathed in his words. "No matter what happens, I want you to know that I believe you are innocent."

My heart filled my throat. I wanted to say the same to him. I wanted to say that I believed in his innocence. I wanted to put both my hands on his beautiful face and tell him how much his words meant. I wanted to breathe in more of his breath.

The security guard strolling past asked, "Doing okay?"

"Yes, sir," Ethan said without taking his eyes away from mine.

"You got seven minutes left."

"Thanks," Ethan said.

I was trying to find the words to get us back to the pre-guard moment when Ethan asked, "Hey, you gonna eat that apple?"

I still held it with both hands, my fingers stroking the smooth peel. "No. Guess not."

"Trade?" He offered his orange.

I held the apple up, and he put his hand on top of mine for a moment. The warmth and solid pressure of his hand sent reverberations all over me. He took the apple to his mouth, and I had an excuse to watch his beautiful, full lips again.

"You haven't eaten anything," he said.

Somehow the orange had gotten in front of me. I started peeling it, releasing the tangy citrus aroma. "You don't like oranges?"

"Love oranges. Just don't like peeling and segmenting."

I laughed, broke off a segment, and offered it to him. Instead of taking it from my hand, he lowered his head and took it from my fingers with his mouth. I think my mouth dropped open. The touch of his lips on my fingers forced an exhale from me and kept me frozen until he raised his head. Every fiber of my body pulled toward him.

Together we ate the whole orange. I could have sat there with him forever.

The guard stepped out from the doorway and gave us a sharp wave.

"Yes, sir," Ethan called as we stood up. He gave a soft huff, as if laughing at a joke.

"What?" I asked.

"Last thing my grandmother said to me before she left me here this morning. 'When a bad thing happens, find the good in it. Look for the silver lining.'" He drew closer as he reached across the table to scoop up some litter that had drifted away from us. Centimeters—not more than two—from my face, he said, "Didn't think I'd find it this quick."

I bit my bottom lip, and for the briefest flickering smidgen of a nanosecond, my eyes dropped to his mouth. I floated back into the classroom and spent most of the afternoon gathering my scattered thoughts and stealing glimpses of Ethan.

Lunch with him gave me the courage to face returning to United High School and the resolution to find out who planted the baggie. I would get Mom and Dad to help Ethan's grandmother do an appeal. I would prove Ethan's innocence.

And at the same time, now that Ethan believed me, I would figure out who made the picture. I would beg Mom to let me ride the bus to Garcia on this last day, so I could talk with Ethan some more. And this time I'd be blunt and ask whether or not Shanique was his girlfriend.

About thirty minutes before dismissal time, the teacher received a phone call, instructing that I report to the office.

Mrs. Sanchez was waiting for me, and we went into a private room. "Are your parents here yet to check you out?"

"Not yet."

She nodded. "I just wanted to touch base—see how you are doing—and let you know where we are with the investigation."

"Have you found anything?"

"I'm afraid not much that you don't already know. I interviewed every girl in your gym class. And thanks to your very persistent friend"—she grinned—"I have the phone numbers of all the girls who owned cells then."

"But the first cell—the one that sent the link to Cynthia?"

"Nothing. She says she doesn't know who has that number. But at least now the company that owns the cell is sending me a copy of their monthly bill, so we can check to see if any students' numbers are showing up on calls. Thanks to your father, the company is keeping the phone on, so maybe someone will use it again, and we can figure out who it is."

"Do any of the students' parents work at that company?" Dad had already gone through the company employee directory checking for connections to Garcia, but I wanted to see if Mrs. Sanchez knew anything.

"No. I can't find any connection. I wish I had more news, but that's it."

I nodded. "Well, thanks for letting me know." Why did she come all the way out here just for this? It wasn't much of an update. And even if they found the mysterious cell phone, that still might not explain who made and posted the picture.

As if she read my mind, she said, "I also came today to see how you are."

"It hasn't been bad at all." *Especially this last day with Ethan here.*

"I'm glad to hear that, but sometimes it's harder for students to go back to their home school than it is to come to Beauty." She didn't know that we were thinking of moving back to Houston. "I know you're going to do well, but it may not be easy at first. There'll be questions, jokes. I talked with Mrs. Gamez, the guidance counselor at United, asked her to be a support for you in case you need it. Here's her contact information." She handed me a card. "Just remember, if it's bad when you go back, it will be temporary. Soon enough there'll be a new drama at school. Your story will be old news."

She was right about school drama becoming old news, but in truth, no one who saw the naked picture would ever forget it.

"Do you have any other questions?"

I thought for a moment. "When you talked to the girls in my gym class, what did Arvey say?"

Mrs. Sanchez angled her face with a puzzled expression, as if she hadn't heard me correctly.

"Arvey," I said again. "She tried to let me know about the picture that day in class."

Before she could respond, the door flew open with a sharp bang.

Mom burst in. "Mrs. Sanchez, you should not be here. You are no longer my daughter's principal. How dare you talk to Polarity without my consent?"

I rose instantly, my hands outstretched to block Mom, with her red face and her shrill, out-of-control voice. I scrambled to think of a way to muzzle her or to at least guide her out of the room and calm her.

Mrs. Sanchez caught my eye and slowly shook her head. She seemed to have an intuitive understanding of Mom's issues. "It's my practice to meet with my students before they transition out of alternative school." Mom bristled, but Mrs. Sanchez calmly continued, "Polarity is no longer a student on my campus, but I did send her here. I think it is in her best interest that we assess what challenges are next for her."

"Since when do you have the skill to determine what is in Polarity's best interest? You've not done one thing right from the beginning of this fiasco." Mom, sparking electric currents that stung me, pointed to the doorway. "I want you out. Now."

I wanted Mom out now. And shame to be ashamed of my mother filled me.

Mrs. Sanchez stood and stepped quietly to the door. From the doorway she faced us again. "I think you already know this, but of all the students who received the text, only the six girls forwarded it. I hope it helps you to know that most of my students want nothing to do with this type of thing. Those six students who sent it to multiple recipients will begin their term here at Beauty Monday. I'm delaying their placements until after Polarity—"

"That doesn't make us feel better at all," Mom snapped, glaring at her. "And that should make you feel worse. Over eighty of your students had proof of this in their hands. Proof. And not one of them showed it to you. For two solid weeks, the picture was out there, and not one student let you know. And not one of them has told you the source of the picture. Mrs. Sanchez, that fact screams louder than anything I can say. It screams, 'They don't trust you.'"

"I agree," Mrs. Sanchez said.

"You… agree?" Mom's face went blank.

"I have failed all of my students, especially Polarity, by not being approachable enough and by not preparing them for this type of crime. I've also been saddened to learn that some of my students routinely receive or send inappropriate messages. Students I've talked to say they usually just ignore or delete. I'll work harder to be sure they understand they should report to us rather than delete. I know that doesn't help you." Her tired voice made her seem older. "But as a result of your experience, I'll do better for my students in the future."

"Thanks," I said. "But don't take it all on yourself. I don't have a phone, other than a 911 cell, but if I did, I'd probably just delete junk that I didn't recognize." I sincerely meant this, but I also wanted to undo some of Mom's lashing. "Until now, I wouldn't have thought about taking it to the principal."

Mom said, "Polarity, that's generous for you to say, but you are a child. Mrs. Sanchez is the professional in charge, and eighty kids not telling is symptomatic of a larger problem."

"Your mother is correct," Mrs. Sanchez said as she left.

After Mom and I filled out the Beauty withdrawal paperwork and started toward the exit, I shook off the weariness from Mom's tantrum and said, "Mom, please let me ride the Garcia bus today."

"Of course you are not riding the bus. We are finally getting you out of this place and you want to spend more time with, with... No, absolutely not."

"Please, it's important. I'll explain everything when we get home." I tried to convince her as we walked outside. "I need to talk with—"

"Look around you. The buses have already left."

Ethan was gone. I still didn't have a phone number or any way to get in touch with him. If my parents decided to move to Houston, I would never see him again.

The heavenly high from lunch crashed like a huge, heavy meteorite in the pit of my stomach.

She popped the lock open on her car. "Besides, you'll want to check out TeensterBlast—there's activity on Zada's page."

Her laptop sat open on the front seat. On Zada's wall were three likes by my message and seven by Mom's.

"See?" Mom said, "My post will attract more attention."

None of the names of the likes were familiar, but that evening, I searched their pages for Zada connections, and I sent each liker a private message: "If you know Zada, please let her know I'm searching for her." I started a log just like Scooter had taught me.

That night as I lay in bed, replaying every moment of the day's thirty-two-minute lunch, it hit me. Ethan and I had been almost-kissable close and certainly breath-smelling close, and I hadn't even worried about bad breath. But now I had new worries. *Was what happened between us flirting? Is Shanique his girlfriend? Was he flirting with me even though he has a girlfriend, or was he just being a normal, friendly boy? Maybe the flirting is all in my head.*

CHAPTER 11

SATURDAY MORNING, WHILE WE SAT in the breakfast nook of our trailer having egg tacos, Dad said, "Let's seal the cabinets and box up our loose stuff. I'll settle at the office and get the trailer travel ready. We'll be home by tonight."

"Seth, no. Have you forgotten everything I said? I don't want to transfer Polarity to Houston now. When her Houston campus contacts the sending school, Beauty Disciplinary Alternative, they'll instantly see that she's been kicked out of school. She'll be labeled as a troublemaker. If we wait until the end of the semester, Houston probably won't notice Beauty in the record. They'll just see United High School."

"Jennifer, it wouldn't be any different at United on Monday. Polarity would be labeled at United just like she would in Houston."

"I don't care what the people in this pathetic school district think." Mom shuddered, as if disgusted. "After we leave here in December, we'll never see them again."

Dad uncharacteristically pushed, "What's going to stop Houston from reviewing her record in December and seeing Beauty listed?"

"Nothing." Mom's voice took on its sharp, angry edge. "But it will be old news by then. And most of the front office staff people who enroll kids just do the minimum. They don't usually review anything they don't have to. Polarity's got so many schools in her record that Beauty will just be the name of one more school. Believe me, I've enrolled her plenty of times. No one will notice. They'll get what they need from the sending school to transfer her in."

I swallowed the gut-wrenching dread of seeing Garcia students. Still, I couldn't bear not seeing Ethan again. He said he believed in me, and I wanted to prove him right. And more than anything, I wanted to prove that someone planted the baggie on him. Maybe I'd find that the same person who did the picture planted the baggie. "Mom and Dad, I need to go to United High. It's the right thing to do."

They both gaped at me as if I'd spoken a foreign language.

"Maybe there's a chance I can still find out the truth. If we leave we may never know how the picture was done. And now Ethan's got a bad rap." I told them Ethan's story.

Dad squeezed my shoulder. "I'm sorry about Ethan, sorry he lost his dad. But I don't want you in that school with people who were in on that picture."

"Seth," Mom said, "Mrs. Sanchez is sending the six girls who forwarded the text to Beauty Monday morning. It will be safer for Polarity at United than anywhere. No kid in his right mind would even think about doing anything with that picture right now. Not with all those removals."

"And Mrs. Sanchez has already talked to the counselor at the high school about me, so if I need help, I can get it." I didn't see myself ever going to a counselor for help, but the info might make Dad feel better about my safety.

Dad shook his head, but then he shrugged and sighed. "Okay, okay, we'll give it a chance."

Monday morning my tightly wound nerves about going to United High School jerked me awake at four a.m., sweating with fear. I still wanted to prove Ethan innocent and find out who did my picture, but a cowardly core deep inside wished that I'd sided with Dad. I'd be in Houston now, going to a school where no one had seen the picture.

Mrs. Sanchez's warning about going back to regular school was right on. Walking into United High School was the hardest thing I'd ever done. I avoided eye contact with everyone, thinking that each person we passed in the hallway leading to the office had seen the picture. Most of the faces were strangers, since I knew only the students in the tenth-grade class. I caught the usual ogling that any new girl gets, but there were faces in my peripheral vision that I thought were nodding with recognition.

The receptionist, a gray-haired lady with thick glasses at the front counter of the office, read over my transcript. Her eyebrows shot up above her brown frames. With her eyes riveted on me, she cleared her throat and blasted as if on a megaphone. "Your former school is Beauty."

Heads up and down the counter, in the waiting area, and at two secretary desks behind the counter bobbed up together as if they were all puppets controlled by the same string. *Hello, United High School.*

Mom blasted right back at her, "You are an excellent reader. Congratulations."

If there'd been any chance of keeping my time in Beauty off everyone's radar, it just died. It occurred to me that there was nothing I could do to get out of this spotlight, so I may as well flow with it. Plus it could be an advantage if students labeled me as a bad girl. They would be more open about the drug dog and the baggie.

I took a deep breath, unclenched my hands, and let Mom spar with the staff. I followed her as we were directed to sit at a secretary's desk behind the counter.

While we went through the office processes, I sat up tall and squared my shoulders. Office staff lowered their heads, one by one, as I met their stares. The occasional student, passing through and peeking at the new girl, seemed silly and immature after my time at Beauty. I didn't even bother to stare them down. I was ready to take on this school.

It helped that Mom, still in the aftermath high of our big argument, had given me a super weekend of preparation in San Antonio. Highlight touch-up, new makeup, lots of new clothes. I never looked better. My tapered haircut hung past my shoulders, and shorter layers framed my face. Black leggings tucked into black, two-inch heeled ankle boots. My legs, which used to be stick-skinny, were now, according to Mom and the sales clerk, just right for this fashion. And I wore the first shirt I made with Grandma. She had been right. The loose, creamy layered top had a classic but trendy style that turned heads.

"Pohlee. Pohlee." Tilly's sweet voice rang out.

I looked up from a form to her happy face framed by two pigtails with big blue bows. She stood at the front counter, delivering papers to the receptionist.

I ran around the counter and gave her a big hug. Her baby-soft hair cushioned my cheek when I put my face against the top of her head. She squeezed me with both arms and laid her face against my shoulder. "Tilly, I'm so happy to see you. How are you? Do you like United High School?"

"Pohlee. Pohlee. Pretty, pretty, pretty." She gave me her fullest, squinty-eyed smile. I was glad she didn't say, "Mean girls."

"Hi," Mom said. She had followed me around, leaving the secretary at her desk with forms unfinished. "I'm Polarity's mother. You must be Tilly. I'm so happy to meet you."

We chatted until an aide came and took Tilly away, and then we returned to the secretary's desk to complete the paperwork.

"What a stunning beauty," Mom said, gazing past my face at someone behind me.

I followed her eyes to a small waiting area on the opposite side of the office suite, labeled Counselor's Corner. Shanique, wearing straight-leg jeans and a long, red knit tunic with a tiny white belt cinching her waist, stood in front of a receptionist's desk talking quietly.

"She stands like a classic ballerina. Do you know her?" Mom asked.

"Shanique." This close, she was even more beautiful—her dark amber skin, the angular haircut, and her elegant neck combined to give her an exotic air. Maybe she sensed that she was being watched. She met my eyes as if I had called out to her. Her almond, thick-lashed eyes reflected deep pain and sadness—a contrast to her usual upbeat expression.

The counselor's door opened, and an older lady—I assumed the counselor—stepped out and touched Shanique's shoulder. "Shanique?"

Shanique wrapped her arms around the counselor. I couldn't hear crying, but Shanique's shoulders shook as she buried her face on the counselor's shoulder.

The counselor patted her back, and in a low voice she said, "Shanique, what happened? Are you okay?"

Shanique raised her head, and between gasps, she said, "Ethan. It's Ethan. He got sent to Beauty. It isn't fair." She lowered her face into her hands.

Quickly they went into the office and shut the door. *Don't worry, Shanique. I'm going to figure out who framed Ethan. I'm going to help him just as he helped me.*

The registrar approached the desk where we were sitting. "Polarity, here's your schedule. It's getting late, so you'll miss first period today, but I'll let your teacher know to expect you tomorrow." As in most schools I'd attended, the office area was glassed in and looked out onto a major hallway. When the bell rang for second period, it was clear that the news had spread. A new girl checking in was a big deal in a small town. Every student that passed by looked toward us. The crowd reminded me that this was a high school, not just a ninth-grade center, and there were students as old as eighteen out there. Happily, I no longer looked like a little girl.

After we finished in the office and Mom left, I went to second-period English and got sucked backwards in time. All the courage I'd mustered in the office was pouring away through a sieve. A lot of the faces were familiar, and most of them hadn't changed that much since last year. Not everyone had a growth spurt over the summer. They stared openly, but no one cranked up the courage to say anything to me.

I made myself stand tall and walk right up to the teacher's desk. I showed her my schedule to initial, gave her my best smile, and said in a strong, clear voice, "Hello, Mrs. Dougherty. I'm Polarity Weeks." I had learned a lot recently, watching Mom and Dad stroll into official settings.

My teacher was young and blonde and dressed in a severe navy jacket and skirt. She stood and waved toward a metal file cabinet a few steps away from her desk. "Thank you, Polarity, and welcome to English II. Let me just find you a syllabus." When she walked to the cabinet, I could see that she wore pink and green neon sneakers. They made me like her immediately.

While she tugged a squeaky file drawer open and shuffled through files, I—instead of trying to be invisible or studying her wall posters—faced the class. I scanned the rows, sizing up each person, weighing their possible value in my pursuit of information to help Ethan and me. I wasn't trying to intimidate them, but instead of continuing to check out the new girl, most of them lowered their heads. A few gave a half-wave. I responded with a single nod, just as I'd seen Dad do many times. But even as I did this, a corner of my mind assessed which students had seen the picture.

The morning went smoothly, but no drug dealers jumped out and introduced themselves. At lunch, instead of trying to disappear, I strolled through the cafeteria. It was the typical noisy, over-warm swarm of mostly boys for the first few minutes. They stood impatiently in line, emerged from the serving area with loaded trays, and dived to the first open table.

I sat at the corner of one of the long tables with my brown bag for a few minutes and observed. These boys were all tenth-graders. Danny parked himself in the middle of a large group and gabbed energetically, swiveling his head as if trying to suck attention from everyone at once—just like last year. My stomach clenched. I so wanted to be unaffected by him, but I couldn't blunt the sickening dread he triggered in me. I prayed he wouldn't notice me.

Minutes later, girls started wandering in, having finished their pre-lunch primp and chat sessions. I watched for Shanique. I wanted to thank her for helping Ethan search out the texts about me, and I wanted to see if she had any ideas on how Ethan might have been set up. And maybe she'd mention if she was his girlfriend. Two girls with chips and sodas sat across the table from me. Blond crimps were clearly still in style here. I asked them where Shanique ate.

"Shanique?" One of the girls lifted her sunshades off her eyes and slid them onto her head, carefully settling them among the crimps. "She eats at her other school."

What other school?

"Yeah," said the second girl, who was wearing a silver *Sue* pendant. "She's one of the brainiacs. They get bused to some school for nerds in Vuelta. She'll be back in time for athletics after school."

Wow. Shanique is gorgeous, athletic, and brilliant as well. A mean little streak of jealously nipped at me. But I told myself Ethan deserved a super-girl like her.

There were still no older students in the cafeteria, and Sue and super-crimp perched forehead to forehead, deep in a whispering session. I wandered out toward the student parking lot. It was deserted except for a pickup truck where a bunch of boys congregated, listening to rap pounding from inside. They didn't notice me. The school had open lunch for juniors and seniors, but I hadn't anticipated that so many people would leave the campus at lunch. The druggies probably did their trades and using off campus at lunch.

In an adjacent picnic area, three girls sat at one table—not talking, not eating. At first glance, one of them resembled Arvey, but it was someone else. The three didn't seem to be together. They were solitary people, just waiting for the lunch break to pass. All three scrutinized me as I walked by.

A boy and girl were almost making out at another table. He straddled the bench as close to her as he could get. He had one hand on her back and the other on her knee. They scrutinized no one but each other.

Arvey was nowhere. In fact, I hadn't seen her since the day the picture came out and I left Garcia. We drove past her sprawling trailer every day. Often there were people around—even children—but never Arvey. Once when I was walking Gypsy, an aluminum foil window covering rose at the corner, but it was only for a moment. *Maybe she moved away.*

Next to the picnic area, a curving sidewalk meandered down a passage between two wings. I'd seen the narrow stretch, with a single sparse tree in it, earlier, when I crossed from one wing to the other, between classes. I almost headed back toward the entry of the cafeteria but decided I may as well stroll down that passage.

At first it seemed empty, but the tree appeared wider in the middle than it should be. Someone was propped against the other side of the trunk, standing perfectly still. The sun was shining, and there were students at the nearby picnic tables, but apprehension about walking toward that tree snaked through me. I glanced back at the three girls and the making-out couple, who were being directed to spread apart by a teacher. I would be out of their line of vision, but they'd be able to hear me if I shouted.

I walked toward the tree. The landscape gravel crunched with each step. Anyone could have heard me approach, but the person by the tree remained still. He or she was small, like Arvey. With only a few feet left, I stopped and cleared my throat, to be sure that I wouldn't shock the person—who I could now see wore jeans. Still no movement.

With two more crunching steps, I was even with the tree and met one of Arvey's brown, dull eyes. Her curtain of dark hair hid the other side of her face. She faced me with the same tight-lipped little smile she wore that day she tried to let me know about Danny's screen.

Her expression, as if she had been waiting patiently for me to see her, jarred me. I gasped. "Arvey."

She didn't seem to move a muscle, but the little smile morphed into a sneer.

The bell ending lunch period blasted, echoing too loud in the passage. I gasped again. She didn't move. Didn't blink.

I retreated. When I reached the edge of the building, I looked back before I rounded the corner. She still hadn't moved.

I watched for her the rest of the day, but she wasn't in any of my classes. However, I came face to face with Danny in last-period world history class. I was standing at the teacher's desk, going through my introduction and gazing over the students, when Danny came in the room. The whole picture nightmare sprang to life.

"Yo, Polarity. Heard you came back." His tone and volume hadn't been reduced by high school. His hair was in the same straw-colored spikes.

I hadn't realized it last year, but I was taller than Danny. In ninth grade, I slumped and kept my head down, trying to go unnoticed. Today, despite my quaking stomach, I stepped forward. "You have been well informed, Danny. Congratulations."

I sounded just like Mom. *Groan.* But I didn't act embarrassed. I guess there are some advantages to having a borderline parent.

He lost his smirk. Lost his focus. Lost his voice. His eyes briefly drifted down my body and jerked back up to my face. His pale, acne-punctured skin glowed pink. Even his scalp pinked through his thin hair.

I held eye contact. "So you made it to high school. I hope it's working for you."

He gave me the same wide-eyed jerking nod he dished out to teachers when he was caught off-task. I almost expected him to *yes, ma'am* me. He backed away and slithered to a desk. I stilled my inner trembling and exhaled with relief. *Yes. I've conquered Danny.* I waited at the teacher's desk for the syllabus.

Danny sagged into a seat about four feet away. He snorted and hissed something I couldn't hear to the students around him. Tittering rang out, followed by silence. My face went hot as reality seeped in— the group around him was staring at me. He snorted again, checking out the other students' reactions. His voice grew louder. "Yeah, she should give us an updated picture now that she's got—" He lounged back and put his widespread hands over his breast area.

I froze.

A girl's voice from the group around him rose over the giggles. "Sick, Danny."

The teacher looked up from his papers. "What's going on?"

Heads lowered. Smirks disappeared. But eyes kept targeting me.

"Danny, what are you doing?"

Danny instantly switched to wide-eyed nodding. "Ah, sir, I'm getting out my project. Ah, need to update the picture—I mean diagram—today, sir."

The teacher frowned and glanced over the other students. He said to me, "Here you go, Polarity. This is the background for the project we're doing. Let's see." He quickly checked the room and pointed to an empty desk in the first row—fortunately on the other side of the room from Danny. "You can sit there. Why don't you just read through the material today, and we'll put you in a group tomorrow?"

I took the papers to my desk and slumped over the handouts for the rest of the period. I lost this battle, but the war wasn't over. I'd nail Danny somehow.

That night at dinner, I gave Mom and Dad a pretty thorough description of the day—leaving out the nightmare with Danny. They were quiet about it. In the past, my school day descriptions had been limited to *just fine* or *okay* or *boring*. All this detail probably bewildered them.

Dad said, "Polarity, I know you want to help Ethan."

I nodded.

"But I don't want you sleuthing around the school for kids who have dope."

"Dad, I have to. And it won't be risky. Once I get an idea who they are, I'll just hang with them until they mention stuff—like how to get rid of marijuana when the drug dog comes. I won't even see any drugs. Besides, since Ethan just got busted, no one will be stupid enough to bring it again—at least, not right away."

"I don't care. I don't want you hanging around kids like that." He turned to Mom. "I think it's time to go back to Houston."

"Dad, you don't think there are druggies in Houston schools?" I tried not to be sarcastic.

"I know there are drugs in schools—all schools." He sounded sad. "But I don't think in Houston you'll be seeking them out."

"But we agreed I'd at least do a semester in Garcia. If we move after one day at United, Beauty will still be in my recent transfer notes. I don't want to go to a new school and have to explain that to a new staff." I would say anything to sway Dad.

Mom said, "Seth, the boy seems like a nice young man, and with his dad killed and his mom trying to get her nursing degree, I wish we could help."

"Hon, I would like to help, too. But you and I can't interfere with kids who aren't our own. You know that. And we can't even figure out Polarity's case. How can we expect to solve Ethan's?"

Mom smiled at Dad. "Yeah, that's right." But instead of continuing to discuss what they could or couldn't do, she switched lanes. She was good at diverting a conversation to get her way. "You know, Polarity, I bet a tenth-grader brought the baggie in. The older kids probably don't need to risk dealing or using at school because they can leave at lunch. I wish we had Ethan's schedule. Maybe you could narrow down when and where the baggie showed up in his backpack. Did he tell you what time of day it was found or where he was when the dog alerted?"

Dad pushed away from the table and dropped his plate into the sink with a clatter. "You two are not going to let this go, are you?" Even though he was aggravated and worried, I think he liked that Mom and I both cared about something enough to work on it together.

"I won't let it go," I said. "I know Ethan is innocent."

"You may be right, but the principal at Beauty told me that almost every kid he has ever enrolled claims to be innocent."

A weight filled the room.

Just like me, I bet Dad's thinking. I'll prove Ethan is innocent even if I can't clear myself. The principal is wrong about everybody lying.

Dad ruffled my hair. "Just be careful, and don't be disappointed if you find out that he really did it."

I didn't know what else to say, but Mom said, "No. Ethan is innocent. There's no doubt."

I reminded myself that it was easier for her—maybe because of her borderline—to have empathy for someone she didn't know well. But I still got a lump in my throat, wishing she could have the same faith in me she had in Ethan.

After they went to bed, I started figuring out Ethan's schedule. I already knew that he had been in three of the same classes I had because people mentioned it. In fact, in geometry class, the teacher had pointed me to a desk and said, "You can sit there in Ethan's seat."

A girl across the aisle asked, "Hey, where will Ethan sit when he comes back?"

The teacher said, "Oh, he probably won't come back. If he does, we'll figure that out then."

By the end of the first week, I had asked other students enough questions to figure out Ethan's schedule, including the four classes that we didn't share. I agreed with Mom's logic that the baggie probably came from a tenth-grader, so I ate my lunch each day in the cafeteria. I didn't know for sure Ethan ate there, but he liked lots of food, and the school let anyone come back for seconds.

Most of the time when I sat near a group of girls, they stopped talking or changed the subject to some safe thing like homework. One day as I left a group, one of them whispered, "I don't know why boys think she is so hot. Her clothes are cute, but I don't see what the big deal about her is."

Flabbergasted, I spun around to face her, thinking they were talking about someone else. The girl next to her elbowed her to shut up.

And all this time, I'd thought the naked picture was behind the stares and whispers.

I turned my back on their embarrassed faces and smiled to myself until one of them said, "You haven't heard? They all know she'll dance and get naked for them."

Another one squealed and gasped. "OMG! That's who she is?"

I wanted to shout the truth, but it would just call more attention to me. And they wouldn't believe me anyway. I kept walking and telling myself someday, somehow, I'd prove to the world that I didn't pose for that picture.

I never went back to the passage where I'd found Arvey, and I rarely crossed paths with her during the school day. But every day, she lingered, statue-like, near the parent pickup area after school. Unlike

Star campus, which was two blocks from home, United was a couple of miles away, so Mom picked me up. Most days, Tilly sat with me until her mom came, and every afternoon, Arvey stood apart from the other students. She didn't look my way and didn't move much. I always got picked up before she did, so I never saw who she waited for.

Because I'd attended so many schools during the last few years, I was often an outsider, but Arvey took it to a new level. She created a purposeful barrier around herself that kept everyone away. And that haunting little smile sent the vibe that she enjoyed watching others navigate around her invisible wall.

More than that, her expression took me back to the day she tried to shift my attention to Danny's computer screen. *Does she know something about the picture? Is she somehow involved?*

One day, when there were only a handful of students still waiting and Tilly, who usually sat with me on the bench, had already been picked up, I decided to try to puncture the barrier. I walked to her and stood directly in front of her. "Hi, Arvey."

She kept staring forward as if she didn't hear me.

"How do you like high school?" I waited a moment. "I've wanted to thank you for trying to let me know about Danny's screen last year. I wish I had paid attention to you."

A tight-lipped little smile crept onto her face, but she kept staring at an invisible point in front of her.

"Do you know who made that picture of me? Do you know who posted it on the Internet?"

For the first time, she turned her face, with its frozen smile, toward me. She lowered her lids.

Arvey could talk. I had heard her last year in class. She had a low, brittle voice, but she did speak. Why wouldn't she speak to me?

Toward the end of the third week of eavesdropping for clues about the baggie, I got lucky at lunch. I edged up to a long table with about a dozen tenth-grade boys. Three were wearing United athletic

T-shirts, one boy hid under a black hoody, and several others played with game devices while they shoveled in food. I pulled out an empty chair next to an athlete with Brad printed on his shirt as he was saying, "Who would think the dog would come two days in a row—at the same period? No wonder Ethan got busted. He probably thought there wouldn't be another search for a long time."

Danny, sitting on the opposite side of the table between two gamers, said, "Dumbass nigger."

No one responded to the ugly word. Everyone's eyes dropped, as if sucked down by magnets, to study a tray of food or game on the table. They were cowards, acting as if they didn't hear the word.

Danny, bouncing his head in self-approving nods, continued, "He's so dumb, he got a whole year, and he ain't even appealing it."

Ethan got a year. I couldn't believe it. I had assumed he got a few weeks like I did. Why didn't he say anything to me about a year? Was he being noble? Prideful? Not wanting me to know the harshness of his situation?

"Crap," one of the gamers said without even looking up. "Why so long?"

Brad shrugged. "Guess he'll think twice about keeping weed in his backpack—especially when everyone knows the dogs ain't allowed to sniff your body. He could've had it in his pocket and never gotten caught."

Danny bounced his head with his words. "What can I tell you? Dumbass nigger."

Part of me wanted to stay quiet so they'd keep talking and maybe say something that could help me clear Ethan. But the second time Danny mouthed off, anger welled up. That word slurred at Ethan, my kind, strong, ethical Ethan, made me sick. My breath quickened, and my eyes watered. "Danny, I don't like that word."

My loud voice stilled everyone at the table. Even the gamers cut their eyes up at me.

Danny's eyebrows shot up. "Which word is that?"

His mouth hung open while he waited for my answer. The hush at our table spread to the next table. Curious stares targeted our silent zone in the noisy cafeteria. The boys at our table looked back and forth between Danny and me.

"You know which word." My voice trembled.

"Well…" He was serious until he glanced around at his audience.

At least a dozen curious faces watched him expectantly. The game punching and food shoveling stopped.

Danny's face took on a pink glow, and he sneered. "I believe, Polarity, that I said three words." He held up three fingers and looked to share his cleverness with the watching boys. "So you're going to have to help me out a little, tell me which one."

I absolutely love when a teacher on duty actually walks around and shows up at the perfect time. Mrs. Dougherty, in her pink-and-green neon sneakers, was strolling toward us, approaching behind Danny. But she was gazing out the windows and angling toward the other side of the cafeteria. I had to get her attention on us.

I stood up fast. My metal chair scraped loudly across the tile floor. Mrs. Dougherty looked my way and stopped her stroll. I raised my voice, hoping Danny would do the same and she'd hear. "I'm talking about the ignorant word that is a slur against an entire race of people." I glared hard at him and tapped my finger on the table with each word, just as Mom did sometimes. "Don't. You. Say. It. Again."

At least twenty boys—a few of them new ones from nearby tables—waited for his response. The boy with a hoody pulled low on his forehead across the table from Danny noticed Mrs. Dougherty approaching. One nudge, one word, and Danny would be alerted. In my peripheral vision, I could see the hoody boy opening his mouth and bending toward Danny.

I kept my gaze riveted on Danny, daring him not to break our eye contact.

Danny, his pink-cheeked sneer broadening, took the bait. "Hey, Polarity, it ain't a slur against an entire race of people. It's only a slur against dumbass niggers." He elbowed the gamer next to him and giggled at his own joke.

Mrs. Dougherty stiffened, and angry track lines cut across her forehead. "Danny, I can't believe what you just said."

He choked on his giggle.

She whipped out her hall pass pad and started writing.

"Oh, miss, I didn't mean nothing. We were just joking around."

"Office. Now."

"I wouldn't a said it if there'd been any African-Americans close by." His sharp cockiness shriveled into babyish whining. "I wouldn't ever offend anyone."

"You offend me." She extended the pass to him and gave him the look—blank, hard, expressionless.

He opened his mouth as if to give one more plea, gave up, and took the pass. I was still standing, and he glared at me as he grabbed his lunch tray.

It was time for me to sit, but shameful realization gripped me.

Danny had used that word before.

Brad tilted his head upward toward me in a sidelong glance—I guess wondering why I was standing like a statue. I was aware of him and everyone else nearby, but the memory of the first time crashed in on me. *Star Ninth Grade Center, passing period right before history. Danny griping about the civil rights project... using the N-word.*

Mrs. Dougherty headed my way. I dropped into my chair, slammed by regret as a video of what I did the first time I heard Danny say that word played in my head. *I walked past him in the hallway, stared at the floor, and pretended I didn't hear the word.*

Mrs. Dougherty paused by my chair. "Everything okay, Polarity?"

"Yes, ma'am."

"You sure?"

"Yes. Just remembering something."

She strolled back toward the serving area. The boys at my table returned to eating and gaming as if the word had not been said.

I'm no different from them. I ignore racist names unless they touch someone I care about. Why don't I stand up all the time?

Brad said, "Well, you sure made his day." I couldn't tell if he cared one way or the other. He muttered under his breath, "Idiot."

I assumed he meant Danny, but he could have meant me. And he would have been correct. I plowed through the regret about my own double standard. I needed to shake it off and see what I could learn. "So, Brad, you said the dogs aren't allowed to sniff people?"

"Yeah, everyone knows that. They can only sniff lockers, bags, stuff like that."

"So why do you think Ethan had it in his bag?"

"Beats me. I didn't even know he's a doper." He glanced around, as if to check to see who was listening to us. Several of the boys had finished eating and left.

I dropped my volume, hoping he wouldn't be worried about eavesdroppers. "What period did the dog come?"

"Um." He squinted while he opened a pudding cup. "Last period, 'cause I was in PE. Yep, last period of the day."

Ethan had been in world history last period. So was I. And so was Danny.

"Early in the period or late?"

He drained his third carton of milk. "They brought the dog to the gym right at the beginning of class 'cause we were still dressing, and after that, someone watched through the window and saw it go to the band hall. So they probably went to Ethan's class next."

"Do you know ahead of time when the drug dog is coming?"

"No." He rolled his eyes. "You don't know till it shows up. That's why people get caught."

"Do you think some kids know?"

"You ask a lot of questions." He pressed closer and smirked. "Worried about the dogs sniffing your weed?"

I shrugged as I stood to leave. "Just curious." Maybe it would make it easier for me to dig out information if people pegged me as a druggie.

I still had the card that Mrs. Sanchez had given me with the counselor's name. I went to the office and asked to talk with her. A nice thing about this small school was the easiness of actually talking with a counselor. I had to wait only a few minutes.

"Come in, Polarity. Please sit." She had the softest gray eyes I had ever seen. She closed the door to her office and pushed her bobbed gray hair behind her ears as she sat with me on a sunflower-upholstered puffy sofa. She was one of those older counselors, with lava lamps and a little stone water fountain.

"Thank you, Mrs. Gamez, for seeing me. Can you tell me why some students get sent to Beauty for a year and others only go for twenty-to-thirty days?"

"Is something wrong?" She settled back ready to hear a long story. "Are you in trouble?"

"No, I'm asking for a friend—Ethan. He got sent to Beauty for the whole year for having a baggie of marijuana. Why so long?"

"Oh." She shook her head sadly. "I don't know the particulars of Ethan's case, and I couldn't talk about them if I did. But I do know that students get longer terms if they have multiple offenses or if the principal considers them a danger to the other students or themselves."

"This was Ethan's only offense, and he's never hurt anyone—ever. He's kind and mature." Of course, I really didn't know anything about Ethan's actual record. I was following my heart.

"Polarity, sometimes we don't know all the facts." She pushed back her hair again. "Only the student's family and the principal and the police are allowed to know all the facts. There could be a number of reasons for the length of placement."

"Can you give me Ethan's phone number?" I knew she couldn't.

"I'm sorry. I can't do that."

"How can I get in touch with him?" My mind raced frantically for a way to convince her to help. "I'm trying to prove his innocence."

"If you have information about his case, you should inform the principal."

"I don't have it yet. I need to ask Ethan some questions so I can check some rumors. It's still a murky mess, but someone set him up. And if the principal gets involved now, everyone will shut up forever. And the truth will never come out." She didn't stop me, so I kept going—not sure what I would say until I said it. "Ethan didn't push for an appeal because his father was killed in Afghanistan, and his mother is in nursing school in San Antonio. He doesn't want her to have to worry about this, so she doesn't even know. His grandmother is his guardian, and he doesn't want to put her through the appeal process. Mrs. Gamez, I know what the rules are—I know what the system is—and I know it's not fair to students who—" I didn't have the words to explain why some students seem to have everything stacked against them. She waited patiently until I finally finished with the only thing I could think of. "Who don't have assertive parents. I know I can help Ethan. Is there a way you could fax some information to Beauty and have it delivered to him like an assignment?"

Her steady, gray eyes studied me.

"Mrs. Gamez, it is the right thing to do."

She took a deep breath, processing everything I had said. I read a sadness and resignation in her eyes. "Do you have the fax ready?"

"May I use your computer and printer? It will take just a moment to type it."

She gestured toward her computer desk. I pulled up Word and tried to remember the format of the assignment sheets we received at Beauty. At the top of the page, I typed "Reminder of Important Reports Assigned September 23." That was the date that we had lunch together—his first day at Beauty and my last.

I couldn't believe she was going to do this. Now I had to think of something to put on the page—fast, before she changed her mind. I just wanted to get my phone number to him—wanted him to call me so that we could talk about what happened that day, figure out who could have planted that baggie. And I craved the sound of his voice.

I formatted my message to mirror the assignment sheets I received at Beauty, so the teachers there wouldn't get suspicious, but I wanted him to see my name and phone number. I threw in words that would tip him off that it was from me. For once, my weird name came in handy.

Biology—*Polarity of silver lining—review of positive/negative (254) elements*

English—*Poetry, Emily Dickinson, (6444) color themes: orange, apple red*

History—*appeal processes (908), new information*

Geometry—*segment division provided 2546444908*

Assignments due October 30; response required.

He had been in my English class that first day I came to Star Ninth Grade Center. I hoped he'd remember the Emily Dickinson jokes people made about me. Everything else, aside from my name and phone number, came out of our thirty-two-minute lunch.

While I stood out at the printer in the entryway to Mrs. Gamez's office, two girls came in—one with her arm around the other, who was crying. Something about someone looking at her ugly. Mrs. Gamez settled them on the sofa and closed her door.

I could have left the printed sheet in her overflowing in-basket hanging outside her door, or I could have interrupted her talk with the crying girl. Instead, I marched out to her secretary, whose fingers were flying over her keyboard while she simultaneously chewed a bite of her sandwich.

I said, "Mrs. Gamez needs this faxed to Beauty immediately."

"Okay." The secretary took another bite before standing up and grabbing a fill-in-the-blank fax cover sheet. "Whose attention?" she asked, skimming over the page.

"That sophomore, Ethan Rawls."

"Does she want a return receipt?"

"Yes, I'll wait for it." While I waited for the fax to go through, the tardy bell rang. When the secretary handed me the receipt, I said, "Thanks, and I'll need a late pass for class."

She filled it out without a question.

Yes!

When last period rolled around, I sketched the room, listing all the desks and the names of the students sitting in them. During a break in our Ancient Greece video, I asked Rachel, a red-haired girl who sat near me, if the teacher ever rearranged the seating, or if it had been this way all year. Luckily, he was one of those teachers who didn't bother to do regular rotations. I asked her who sat in my desk before I came. *Ethan.*

That night, while we were cleaning up after dinner, I showed Mom and Dad the sketch and told them that Ethan got a whole year and that I had convinced the counselor to send him a fax with my—actually, Mom's—phone number. I didn't tell them about the questions I asked Brad in the cafeteria. Dad would worry about me becoming a target of angry druggies.

We were barely into the discussion when Dad got a text.

He stood. "Oh, sorry. I need to take care of this. See you two later. Don't wait up."

"Bye, Honey." Mom held up her face for a kiss.

Dad bent, kissed her, mussed my hair, and stepped out the door.

Now I was worried. This was the third time this week that Dad had gone out in the evening like this. And the other two times when he came home, the odor of cigarettes and beer drifted in with him. It wasn't like him to go out without us.

Fear gripped me. Maybe the months of stress were driving him back into his drinking problem. But I couldn't ask Mom because she'd know that Grandma told me about Dad's DUI. Mom would be furious at Grandma.

"Where's he going?" I asked.

"He's playing pool with some new friends here in Garcia."

I scrutinized her for those subtle signs of resentment, like stiffness or eye-rolling, that she would usually show if Dad were socializing without her. Nothing. "I didn't know Dad played pool."

"Oh, he used to play a lot. He was just too busy until lately."

A chime from Mom's phone stopped my questions. That was the ringtone she used for unknown numbers. Her eyes got big. "Maybe it's Ethan."

Ethan, Ethan. Let it be you.

She answered and handed me the phone.

"Ethan?" I asked.

Mom nodded, picked up her laptop, and went back to the bedroom.

"Hey." His deep rich voice set off tingling in my body. "Thanks for the assignments. They're all finished except the poetry. I'm hoping for some expert help with that one."

I laughed and worked to keep my voice normal in spite of the thrill that danced through my every cell. "Thank you for calling me. I was so afraid you wouldn't get it or it wouldn't make sense to you."

"It made sense. As soon as I read it, I got a big smile."

"I hope the fax didn't get you into trouble."

"Nah. They don't pay much attention to me anymore. Too many high-maintenance kids. So what's going on?"

I told him everything I'd learned and everything I'd done. "I'm not giving up—sooner or later, I'll overhear someone let it slip about who planted the baggie. I think it must be someone in world history class."

I could see Mom propped up on her bed with the laptop. Did she still think I had a crush on Ethan? I positioned my pen on my yellow pad, trying to make myself appear more businesslike.

"I guess anyone at any time can drop something in your backpack, but they have to be quick and lucky."

I could hear his sisters chattering in the background. "Ethan, why did they give you a whole year?"

"They said they think I was selling it." Anger roughened his voice. "It was a large baggie—they said too large for just using."

"That sucks." A lump formed in my throat. He could stay away for the rest of the year.

I made myself get back to business. "Well, maybe someone in the gym or band hall texted the person with the baggie, so he had a little more time. Where was your backpack? Was it open?"

I caught myself writing *Ethan* over and over.

"Floor—right side—main part was half open—the rest was closed. Baggie was in the open part."

"Who in that class do you think might be a user or dealer? Let's go over each person." I called out their names one by one, and we talked about each. Two students were absent that day. Ethan remembered because it had been his turn to take roll. This history teacher ran his class like a government—everyone had responsibilities. Four students, including Danny, were highly likely, and twelve were maybes. Eight were just no way possibly guilty.

We talked for an hour. Amazingly, Mom didn't try to hurry me, even with Dad out playing pool. She spent the whole time on her laptop.

Before we hung up, I spoke more softly and angled my face away

175

from Mom. "Ethan, I want you to know that no matter what happens, I believe you're innocent, and you will not stay there a year."

He lowered his volume, too. "That means a lot, silver lining, but you be careful." His voice filled places inside me that I didn't know were empty. "Don't ask questions around school—just listen. Okay?"

"Sure."

"You said that too easy. I mean it—don't ask the other kids questions. That kind of stuff spreads quick, and druggies don't like anyone messing with their business."

"I promise." I loved his protectiveness.

As soon as we hung up, I remembered that I had planned to ask once and for all if Shanique was his girlfriend. But, again, the right moment never came up.

"Polarity," Mom called from her bed. "You have another message from Zada's page."

I walked back to her bed and sat beside her and read, "Why do you want to know where she is?"

Mom said, "We'll just say 'Want to get in touch—please let her know.'"

Another message popped up. She clicked it open. "Got sumthin for ya—nice and big—whats ur #"

In a huff, Mom deleted it. "You see why we protect you from this stuff?"

"Yeah, I see." Fear filled me for Zada. "But who's protecting Zada?"

"Heartbreaking. Fill me in on your sleuthing. What did you and Ethan figure out?"

We talked about the list of students for a while before we went to bed. I woke about midnight to the key clicking in the doorway and the shuffling of the door as it slowly opened. I didn't have to look to know Dad came in. The stink of cigarettes and beer filled our small trailer.

CHAPTER 12

STUCK. I WAS STUCK. AFTER the first weeks of so much progress with Ethan, I hit a wall. I couldn't ask questions at school anymore—not after I promised Ethan I wouldn't. I could only eavesdrop and wait. And nothing was coming my way. The only good thing was that Danny, absent or suspended, hadn't come back to school after his mouthing off in the cafeteria.

At least Dad had let go of the idea of moving home before the end of the semester. In fact, he was out playing pool—again. Mom was in bed asleep, and as I lay in the dark, hoping to hear the sound of Dad's key in the door, I counted my worries, starting with Dad. *He's out late almost every night and still asleep most mornings when Mom takes me to school. Is he fed up with us, past his limit with Mom's borderline issues and the naked picture? Is he drinking too much?*

And Mom. *She's too mellow about Dad's late nights. In fact, she's too mellow about everything. Is she on drugs? Having a nervous breakdown? Withdrawing from reality? Over dosed on herbs from her* curandera?

I rolled over to my stomach and hugged my pillow. My mind skipped to Ethan. *Does he have any idea how I feel about him? How does he feel about me? About Shanique? When he calls me his silver lining, am I just someone who is trying to help clear him, or could a boy as gorgeous and good as he is really care about me?* If he'd had the same length of time I had at Beauty, he'd already be out. *Even when he gets out, something like this could happen to him—a black boy—again.* My time at the safe house and Beauty taught me that black students were more vulnerable to tough situations. *How will he make it, with no dad, a busy mom, and little sisters to help take care of?*

And Shanique—I still hadn't been able to talk with her. Lots of mornings, I caught a glimpse of her at the end of first period. Always bright and animated, she boarded a van with about five other United students. I'd figured out she was in band at United first period—including the hour of marching practice before school. Then she was at an early-college-start co-op program in the neighboring town of Vuelta. That school was sort of like Beauty, in that lots of small districts fed into it. After that, she returned to United for athletics at the end of each day. *It's still hard to imagine how one person can be so beautiful and smart and musical and athletic.*

I flipped to my side, facing the shelf that held my poetry book. *Emily Dickinson seems perfect and wise. In all of her verses, why doesn't she mention her servants in her poetry? Why did she say that Irish immigrants should be scientifically destroyed?*

On the shelf next to the book was the phone from Integrations Technology Horizons. *Who has its twin that took my picture? I've worked with every app on the phone but can't figure out how it could have stripped me and distorted my body into a dance and my face into a maniacal smile.*

Worrying in the darkness reminded me of the night I met Zada in the safe house. *She has a child by now. How is she? Is she still alive? If she were white, would there have been publicity and searchers for her when she went missing? Will I ever see her again?*

I had run out of people to worry about, and the aquarium divider at Star Ninth Grade Center floated through my mind. *Even though the aquarium divider is gone, the mollies act as if the barrier is still there. Are we like mollies, stuck in the world we're used to?*

Somehow, things people didn't know about, like invisible barriers, reminded me of bad breath. *Mr. Hill's repels; Ethan's intoxicates. Why don't people know how their own breath smells?*

I flopped over onto my back and stared at the ceiling. My thoughts converged on my most convoluted, complex worry—me. *I'm a kind-of pretty, somewhat talented poetry writer who has grown up a lot in the last few months. Am I going to be borderline like Mom? Am I already? I do get suspicious of people—Arvey, for instance. I keep thinking she knows something about the picture, even though she doesn't have a phone and isn't in the clique. I'm suspicious of her. Why is there a naked picture of me on the Internet, likely to pop up at any time? Maybe even after I'm in college or married or a mom myself. How can I love Emily Dickinson's poetry when she regarded her servants as less than human? Why did I ignore the N-word before I had feelings for Ethan? Do I love Ethan? Do I have bad breath? Am I kidding myself and I'm not kind of pretty, somewhat talented, and learning a lot?*

The wall clock glowing in the darkness showed 2:14 a.m. *Where is Dad?*

I turned on my little reading lamp and took out my journal and began to write.

> *Visible barriers unseen by choice,*
> *Trip and trap innocents who have no voice.*
> *Why choose not to see clear inequity?*

When Mom woke me for school, a new aroma—grilled rice cakes—filled the trailer. She enjoyed experimenting with gluten-free recipes. Oddly, today she wore old jeans with a large T-shirt hanging out. And her hair hung down on her shoulders. Mom was always more put-together than this. Alarms clanged in my head, and I sneaked peeks at her face, searching for the sign that something was wrong. This calmness, these old clothes, the plain hair—were these warnings of a building explosion?

"Dad never came home." I looked out at his empty parking spot while I folded up my bed. I held my breath for her answer, expecting my question to spark the fuse.

Mom nodded. "All-night pool tournament. He'll be home soon." She flipped the cakes on the grill.

"Mom, I know something's wrong. Why won't you tell me?" Again,

I wanted to talk about his drinking, but I couldn't risk her fury at Grandma for telling Scooter and me about it.

"Dad's got a lot going on right now, but it's nothing for you to worry about. We can talk when you get home from school."

Her easy answer made my breathing get shallow, as if I were tiptoeing across a field of hidden mines. When Mom was this cool about something so out-of-the-ordinary, she was getting ready to explode. "I don't want to go. Let me stay here with you today. We can all talk when Dad gets here, work everything out."

"Nope. You're going." She set our plates on the table, sat down, and serenely arranged her food on her plate.

At the risk of sticking my head into an electrical storm, I said, "I've never seen you wear that before."

She shrugged as she cut up her rice cake. "Thought it might be fun to blend in with the locals today."

Somehow we got through the meal without an explosion. Tired and worried, I dragged myself to school, hoping I might get a chance to eavesdrop at lunch and learn something today that could help Ethan. To make the day even worse, Danny was back and acting as ridiculous as ever. On the way into second period, he even barked at his friends—just as he'd done at the ninth-grade campus.

One of his buddies asked, "Hey, how's your breath today, Danny?"

"Dog breath. Ruff, ruff!"

Unbelievable.

At the beginning of Mrs. Dougherty's class, we were writing essays when Mr. Justin, the principal, opened the door and came in—no knocking or anything. "I need everyone to stand with your palms up."

The only times I'd seen him before were in the mornings before school. He stood outside the main entrance smiling, giving high-fives, shoulder-bumping boys, and firing *good mornings* to everyone on their way in. Now he was serious. His stocky bulk that seemed jolly before school each day was ominous as he stood before us demonstrating the palms up with his own hands. "Don't pick up any of your objects—no jackets, purses, or book bags. Everyone walk into the hallway. This row out first."

We all stood, even Mrs. Dougherty, with our empty palms up. Mr. Justin and the assistant principal, who had slipped into the classroom behind him, inspected us. They scanned back and forth—they were trying to see every student at once. Row by row, we went into the hallway. The students reacted as if accustomed to the routine.

As soon as I stepped through the door, I saw the dog a few yards down the hall from us. A beautiful blond German shepherd sat beside an older, grizzled man. The dog watched us, alert with ears up, as we stood in a clump in the hall.

Every school I had attended conducted regular dog inspections, but I had never been in a room that got sniffed. Excitement buzzed through me—I could observe the process and figure out how someone planted the baggie! I started thinking about the way we exited the room, leaving all of our stuff out. Lots of students left backpacks open on the floor or hanging across the backs of their desks. It would be simple for someone to drop a baggie in an open backpack as they walked out of the room. We exited so slowly, row by row, that there would be plenty of time to plant one. Maybe no other students would notice, and if they did, maybe they wouldn't tell.

I stopped myself. I was building a fantasy solution. I was ignoring the way the principal and assistant principal scanned us. The way we held our palms up. Could someone drop a baggie into a backpack without them seeing it? My theory all along had been yes, they could. But a sinking gut feeling told me it would be almost impossible for someone to pull that off.

The dog with his handler followed Mr. Justin and his assistant into the classroom. The principal shut the door. Most of the other students were quiet, maybe like me, wishing they could witness the dog work. But Danny and his buddy were acting like immature fools —smirking, nodding, and snickering at each other.

Wait. *Dog breath. Ruff, ruff.* Even an idiot like Danny wouldn't coincidentally use the same stupid phrase two years in a row. And I had never heard him say it except for those two times. Did the dog come to Star Ninth Grade Center that day last year after Mr. Hill sent me to the principal's office?

It hit me like the most obvious thing in the world. Danny knew the dog was coming, and that was his code to warn his friends. *Dog breath*.

He snorted, bounced on his heels, and elbowed the boys around him. The more I watched him, the more obvious it became.

After a few minutes, the door opened, and the dog, the handler, and administrators came out. Mr. Justin thanked us and said we could go back in.

All day, I monitored Danny. He was even more cocky than usual. Of course, I couldn't get close enough to him to overhear him talk— he made sure of that, after the cafeteria incident. But he spent too much time whispering to his friends. Danny typically blurted out every stupid notion in his head loud enough for everyone to hear.

By last-period world history, defeat squeezed my heart. Danny probably got tipped off that the dog was coming. He probably planted the baggie. He probably used the "dog breath" code to warn his friends. But how could I prove it? Even if I reported this to the principal, Danny would deny it. Unless some of his friends would rat him out, it was hopeless. I vowed that the next day at lunch, I'd pin down Brad again. Maybe he knew something. I could even bring up the subject of the dog breath.

I was still mulling all this over after school when Tilly and I sat together on a bench in the parent pickup area. I'm not sure how, but she sensed my sadness. I smiled and asked her about her day, but I didn't fool her.

She patted my shoulder and said, "Mean gulls." She hadn't done that since last year.

"Hey, Tilly. Hey, Polarity." It was Raymond, the security guard from the ninth-grade campus. Instead of his old blue cap, he wore a new black one, shiny, almost like plastic.

"Hi," we both said.

"Got a promotion. Guard the high school, now." His hand rested on his holstered walkie-talkie just like last year.

Tilly said, "Mean gulls."

How could this day get worse? Tilly's words would start Raymond on a fishing expedition, trying to figure out who did what to whom. I didn't want deal with his questions.

"What girls? What did they do?" Raymond asked.

Luckily, Tilly's mother pulled up, so Tilly wrapped her arms around me and squeezed tight with her head on my shoulder for a moment and skipped to her mother's car. Right behind her car, Dad's truck rumbled in.

"Bye, Officer. We'll talk tomorrow," I said, to discourage him from following me to the truck.

Raymond pulled off his cap, rubbed his hand across his head, and frowned. "What girls?" he asked again, but he didn't follow me.

Dad was driving. That was a first. Mom always picked me up alone. As I walked toward the truck, I could see that Dad was still unshaved, and Mom was smiling and chatting to someone in the back seat. I squinted at the tinted back windows to figure out who it was when the person popped open the back door. *Ethan.*

Ethan was in the back seat of Dad's truck. Ethan. I couldn't feel my body as I climbed in. My gaze skipped from Ethan to Mom and Dad and back to Ethan. *Ethan.* He filled not only the back seat, with his long legs and strong shoulders and thick arms, but the air. He filled my spirit.

Magnetism pulled me toward him. He was even more gorgeous, more touchable, more intoxicating, more Ethan than I remembered.

I wished the rest of the world would vanish and we could be alone. And the longing in his eyes made me feel that he had the same idea. Even with Mom and Dad right there, I leaned over, put my hands on his shoulders, and gave him a hug. He wrapped his arms around me, and we were cheek to cheek. His rough stubble made me want to rub my face against him. I heard a soft exhaled moan—too low to be me. He turned his head a little so the corners of his lips were on my cheek. His lips pressed in a wonderful corner kiss. My head was on my parents' side, so I couldn't angle my face or lips toward him. It stayed our secret corner kiss. I wanted to melt into him, hold onto him forever.

We separated. My heart thudded in my throat.

"How was your day?" Mom asked. "Any interesting classes?" Her sense of humor glittered sometimes.

I sat back and buckled. Even while I answered Mom, I couldn't take my eyes off of him, bouncing from his warm eyes to his full lips that still had my cheek tingling. "Great day, Mom. Excellent lecture on linear equations. How was yours?"

Dad shook his head. "See what I deal with, Ethan?"

"Okay, who's going to tell me what is going on?" I asked.

"I like your mom and dad," Ethan said. "And your dad is a hero."

Mom said, "I'll tell the story."

Her tale zigzagged like an espionage movie with Dad cast as the heroic undercover agent and Mom as his clever, sneaky sidekick. If I could have wished for a better solution, I wouldn't have had the imagination to come up with what happened.

Mom, like an excited child, unraveled the story. "We researched the drug dog company and found out that the owner, Max, plays pool at a local bar. Hence, Seth's new hobby." Max, I realized, was the grizzly older guy I'd seen at school that day with the dog. "So Max never decides which school he's going to until after he has the dog loaded—no pattern, no plan. It's all random and in his head. His contract requires him to hit each school ten times a year, but he picks the times. When Max gets to the school, the principal decides which classes to check—again, no pattern, no plan."

I tried to keep my eyes on Mom, but Ethan's knee and thigh, just below my line of vision, tugged at my attention.

"So Seth figured the only way a student could have advance notice would be if someone spied Max's truck coming and if that person phoned or texted kids at school."

Ethan's nod caught my glance. Mom went on explaining that, as I was gathering information at school, Dad and Mom reviewed the route Max took when he went to United High, scoping out houses or businesses that had a good view of the street, hoping to spot someone well positioned to see passing vehicles.

While they continued to work on that aspect, Dad expanded his night work. Max had mentioned which bars he avoided, the known drug hangouts. Dad started bar hopping night after night.

There were several businesses with views of the street that Mom and Dad had on their list of possibilities. And when Dad overheard the name of one, Gus's Gas and Tires, while playing pool at a druggie hangout, he checked my list of suspected students just in case there was a connection. Danny's brother, Chuck, worked as a tire changer at Gus's.

Now Mom almost bounced up and down with excitement. "Last night, after Seth heard a second tip about Gus's, he went to the county sheriff's office to report his suspicions."

Dad was driving us into a part of Garcia I had never seen before. I had no idea where we were headed, but I figured Mom would get to that soon enough.

"Of course, the sheriff knows us from the picture investigation. And guess what!" She didn't wait for us to guess. "Seth wasn't the only person doing undercover work at the pool halls. The sheriff was already building a trafficking case and had a search warrant to check out Chuck's house. So Seth asked if they could wait and let the dog do one more sweep first—to see if Danny was involved in selling at school. Max's visit to United High this morning was set up by the sheriff, who had a spy waiting at Gus's, getting her tires rotated."

She paused to get her breath, and Ethan said to me, "Amazing, isn't it?"

Before I could answer, Mom said, "We weren't supposed to watch, but we were in the coffee shop down the street at a table by the window—that's why I dressed like the locals today. It was so cool! Max actually pulled up in front of the station to pretend he was checking his tires, to make sure Chuck noticed him. And bingo, the scum stood right there in broad daylight and texted."

I asked, "Where are we going? And how did Ethan get here?"

Mom said, "We're going to the sheriff's office. After we told him about all the information you two had gathered, he wants to talk with you. He called Ethan's grandmother, who gave permission for us to pick up Ethan at Beauty. And here we are."

Dad spoke up. "So they arrested Chuck this morning and found pounds of marijuana at his house that they think will be a match to the baggie from Ethan's backpack. And they're supposed to pick up Danny after school for questioning. We hope he'll admit the rest once he finds out his brother has been caught. The problem is even though they know Chuck texted Danny, there's no proof that the text meant anything—it was just some weird letters—or that Danny even used it. So unless he admits it, we still may not have the answers we need to clear you, Ethan."

We waited for a few hours in a dull, gray conference room for the sheriff, who was still with Danny. Mom had anticipated a delay, so she spread out an array of nutritious snacks on the large metal table in the center of the room and explained to Ethan in excruciating detail all about my food intolerances. I sat next to him, and he gave Mom the same polite attention that he gave everyone. Everything she said seemed to genuinely interest him.

Once when she interrupted her lecture to prop a pillow behind Dad, who was snoring on a gray vinyl stuffed chair next to the wall, Ethan whispered to me, "Thank you, Polarity, for everything you're doing." He ate all the food Mom offered.

A large older man dressed in jeans and a plaid button-down shirt lumbered into the room. "Hi, Stanley," Mom said. "Ethan and Polarity, this is Sheriff Chapa." I was surprised that Mom was on a first-name basis with him. It reminded me that all the time I was at Grandma's, Mom and Dad were working with the legal system.

The sheriff sat down at the table with us, and Mom tried to get him to have some protein. Dad woke up and stretched, and Mom plied him with carbs.

After she quieted down and everyone settled around the table, the sheriff sighed. "I wish I had better news." He sagged in his chair as he addressed Ethan. "We believe that Danny has been taking product to school and selling. We believe Chuck warned him when the dog was coming. We believe it's likely that Danny planted the baggie on you.

But he won't admit to any of it. We've got a case against Chuck, but that's it."

No. This cannot happen. Ethan cannot go on being punished for what Danny did. "Where is Danny now?"

"We've got him in an interrogation room. Thought we'd give him some time to think before we let his mother take him home."

I could get him to tell the truth. "Can I talk to him? I know how to work him."

The sheriff leaned back and folded his arms across his stomach and observed me. Without taking his eyes off of me, he said, "Seth, Jennifer—what do you think about that?"

Before Mom or Dad could answer, Ethan said, "I don't think you should be in the same room with him. He's capable of bad stuff."

Mom and Dad listened with their eyes riveted on Ethan. Knowing their off-the-chart overprotectiveness, I suspected they'd agree with him.

Dad said, "Ethan's right."

Mom patted Dad's hand. "Stanley, could we view? Would it be a room that we could be right outside the door?"

He nodded slightly, still studying me.

Mom didn't give Dad or Ethan a chance to object. "Good. She should do it. Not only to get the truth for Ethan, but to give Danny a first step toward restorative justice." It was times like this that I could forgive my mother's many failings. Only she would come up with something like "restorative justice."

A muscle in Ethan's jaw flexed. "But if it doesn't work, he'll have a grudge against Polarity. He'll pull something else on her."

They had probably all read my incident report, so they knew Danny was the one who pulled up the naked picture and showed the class.

Mom shrugged. "If it doesn't work, he won't have a chance to get at Polarity again. We'll move back to Houston immediately."

Dread washed over me. It had to work.

The sheriff pushed himself up from the table and grabbed a handful of Mom's organic assorted nuts. "Let me check with his mother."

Ethan said, "Wait. Sir, could I talk to Danny instead?"

I remembered Ethan's clenched fists and his banging-on-the-floor chair after Danny said *Whoa, poetic Polarity.* Ethan was smart, so smart, but his protectiveness put me on edge a little. It was too much like Mom and Dad, always holding me back. And I was afraid Ethan would get too angry.

Before the sheriff could respond, I blurted, "No."

Ethan's brow furrowed.

"I've watched Danny. He'll get defensive with you." *For good reason* I didn't add, remembering Danny's scared face that day as Ethan approached him. "Danny likes to tell me stuff. He doesn't feel threatened by me. He'll spill. I know he will."

The sheriff, standing with his hand on the doorknob, said, "Thanks, Ethan, but you're minors. I have to get parent permission. I've got Polarity's here and Danny's mother down the hall, so we'll go ahead with what we've got."

My adrenaline surged. I wanted to face Danny right now. And I hoped that we didn't have to wait another two hours. I felt sick, remembering Danny, snorting about needing an updated picture—pantomiming boobs on the front of his chest. He had shut me down. *This time, no matter what he says, I can't let him rattle me. I have to get the truth out so that Ethan is cleared.*

Ethan rotated his chair so he faced me. "What are you going to say to him?"

His question threw me off balance. I wasn't sure what I'd say until I saw Danny—until I took in his face and got a feel for his mood. And if I started a discussion about what I would or wouldn't say, Mom and Dad might change their minds about letting me talk to him. I wanted to put my hands on Ethan's worried face and tell him not to worry about me. I wished we were alone.

Sheriff Chapa opened the door. "We're good. Let's go." We all stood. "Ethan, you'll have to wait here for us."

Ethan, his face full of worry and disappointment, put his hand on my arm. "Polarity, you don't have to do this." His touch surged through me and mixed with my already pumped adrenaline. I felt charged, ready for anything.

I put my hand on his, even though we were being watched by all three adults. "It will be okay."

The sheriff led us to a viewing room where a small, faded woman sat in the corner alone. Frazzled, straw-colored hair framed her pale, splotchy face. The sheriff introduced her as Danny's mother. Through the viewing window, I could see Danny sitting at a small table in a plain, bare-walled room.

I didn't wait. I walked into the interrogation room where Danny had his head resting on his folded arms on the table. When he heard me step in, he raised his red tearstained face. His mouth dropped open in shock.

I closed the door and sat in the chair across the table from him. I folded my hands together on the table in front of me and simply looked at him.

He could never let silence hang. "What are you doing here?"

"I came for the truth."

He squinted at me and deepened his frown. "I don't have to talk to you."

I nodded once.

"I didn't have nothing to do with your picture." He was picking at his fingernails. They were chewed with little red, bloody creases at the corners. "It was just like I said. I was messing with the history on that computer, and your picture just popped up." He had clearly been questioned about this before, and he must have been thinking that I was here because of the picture. "It wasn't my fault. It was Cynthia and those girls that spread it."

"I forgive you for that, Danny."

His face froze, as if he were watching a rattlesnake and waiting for it to strike him. For a moment, our gazes connected.

I made myself smile. "In fact, I'm glad you had the picture on your screen that day. I'm glad you let Mr. Hill see it. Otherwise, I might never have found out about it."

He nodded and his face relaxed. "That's right. If it hadn't been for me, Cynthia and them would have kept sending it around."

"Who posted the picture?"

"Don't know. She wouldn't tell me. She's the cause of all this trouble. If it weren't for her, I wouldn't be here. She made me—" He caught himself and changed directions. "She ruins everything."

"What did she make you do? How did she cause all this trouble?"

He folded his arms. "Not telling you anything."

My mind raced. How could I get him talking again?

When Nelda Sims questioned me at the Baker sheriff's office, she used different strategies to try to trick me. She circled me from different angles and dived in with surprising approaches. "That 'dog breath—ruff, ruff!' signal is clever. All your friends can dump their weed whenever you let them know the dog's coming."

His eyes widened.

Bingo! "They really liked the way you let them know, and they're sad that it won't work anymore, after this."

He squirmed in his chair and blew out a loud, frustrated groan. "I shouldn't have listened to Cynthia."

"Yeah, Cynthia messes up a lot of people. Sending my picture all over the place. Ruining your 'dog breath—ruff, ruff' that's worked forever. Now I hear your brother was arrested. She totally ruined everything." I wasn't sure whether Cynthia was connected to Chuck's arrest or not. I was trying to say enough to keep him talking without letting him know how little I really knew.

He groaned again, and tears rimmed his eyes. "Chuck—" His voice broke. "In jail because of her."

"Yeah, she messed up everyone." My mind snagged on Cynthia. Maybe she really did mess up everyone. Maybe she made the picture and somehow got Ethan framed.

He nodded. "Even Ethan."

My breath caught, but I kept my face blank and my eyes steady.

Danny couldn't leave a silence unfilled for long. "You think I don't like blacks because of what I said in the cafeteria, but I was just kidding around."

I nodded as if I agreed.

He imitated my nod, and he hunched forward. I kept nodding with him and leaned in to help close the distance between us.

"Cynthia said he was too damn nosy about her texts," he whispered, nodding. "She told me to get Ethan to stop if I wanted her to be my girlfriend. It's easy to stash a baggie—I should have put it in the trash can, like Chuck always told me. Or in a toilet paper roller." He gritted his teeth and clenched both fists on the table, still peering into my eyes as if trying to make me understand. "It was *her* fault that I put it in Ethan's bag." His head's nodding graduated into bouncing. "*She* told me to go sit in his desk while he was out of the room, you know... taking the attendance slip to the office, like I needed to see the board better."

Tears welled in my eyes. Relief flooded over me. He had admitted to framing Ethan.

His own eyes overflowed. "Chuck in jail—" He dropped his head onto his hands, and his final words were muffled.

I trembled with relief, but my mind raced. *What else? What else do I need to get him to say?* "Poor Chuck—all he did this morning was let you know the dog was coming."

Danny kept his head down, but his words were clear. "I never missed one of his texts. I was always on alert. No matter what time of day, I got the signal out to everyone. We had a good plan until Cynthia messed everything up."

"Did Cynthia post my picture on the Internet?" *Come on, Danny. Spill it. This is the last piece. This is all I need to be cleared along with Ethan.*

"Don't know," he said without looking up.

I swallowed the hard lump of disappointment. If he had no more information, I wanted to get as far away from him as I could. My metal chair, scooting away from the table, made a startling screech in the small room. Danny jerked his red face up, squinting at me as I backed to the door. Relief poured through me when I escaped Danny's presence and shut the door on him.

The sheriff was beaming in the outer room. He reached for my hand.

I shook hands with him and whispered, "Anything else? I could go back in." As much as I hated the idea of more time with Danny, I'd go back if it would help Ethan.

Mom and Dad were looking at me strangely, as if I were a Martian who had just landed in the room.

Danny's mother still sat in the corner, holding a tissue under her nose. She stared at Danny through the window.

Fortunately, Sheriff Chapa said, "Nope. You pretty much covered everything."

Mom and Dad recovered from their awe at my interview skills. Mom hugged me, and Dad squeezed my shoulder.

"Some girl, huh?" Dad said to the sheriff.

I escaped from Mom's hug and started down the hall. "Let's tell Ethan."

I reached the conference room a few steps ahead of the others. Ethan was sitting, still alone, at the table. His worried eyes met mine. I wanted to fly into his arms. Ethan stood and took a step toward me, but the sheriff walked past me and reached for Ethan's hand.

"It's over. You're cleared. I'll phone your principal. They'll expect you back at United in the morning."

My eyes welled up, but through the blur, I could see the relief on Ethan's face. And for once, Mom's need to report helped me get through an emotional moment that could have been awkward. She launched into exaggerated play-by-play of my short conversation with Danny. And her story gave everyone, myself included, a little time to adjust to the joyous relief that Ethan was cleared.

Dad put his hand on Ethan's shoulder. "We'll help you with your hearing, Ethan. I have an attorney who's familiar with school regs."

The sheriff shook his head. "He won't need a hearing. Ethan's removal was based on legal charges. I'm dropping the charges, so the school can cancel the action without a hearing."

Ethan said, "Thank all of you, Mr. and Mrs. Weeks and Polarity. You went out of your way. I appreciate it. Okay if I call my grandmother?"

His voice was calm and strong. I couldn't speak.

Mom handed him her phone. I couldn't believe this had happened so fast. This gave me hope that I'd find the answer to my own question: Who made that picture? I needed to start analyzing and eavesdropping about Cynthia as I had done for Ethan's case.

Ethan stepped to the other side of the room to phone his grandmother.

While the rest of us stood by the doorway, waiting, Dad asked, "What's the status of tracing the picture?"

Sheriff Chapa's smile drooped. "Nothing since I sent them that second link that Polarity found. I'll give them a call in the morning." He turned toward me. "I'm glad to finally meet you, Polarity. I've known your parents since last May, and I've never seen two people work harder than they did to get you back. I'm sorry for all you had to go through. At the time, we just didn't have a way to know that your parents were innocent. And now I'm wondering…"

I figured he was going to ask how I could have posed for that picture. The prospect no longer hurt so much because Ethan believed me.

"…If stubbornness runs in your family, after all you did to clear up this marijuana incident."

We laughed.

"And your scoop about the 'dog breath—ruff, ruff' came at just the right time. That's the piece that made him break. And Chuck's text was *dbrr*. So good work, Polarity."

We drove Ethan home, which was far out into the country. In the dark backseat, I wished I had the courage to slide my hand across to Ethan. Was he thinking the same thing? My ever-present urge to touch him was intensified by my desire to be closer to him during this happy hour.

Mom said, "Now we just need to figure out who posted the picture, and the world will be right again." She didn't say *who made the picture*, which was the question in my mind.

"Ethan, would you mind?" She passed a folder of papers over the seat to him. As he took the folder, she said, "These are Polarity's reports on what happened that day and on the TeensterBlast activity afterwards. Would you read through them—see if you think we've missed anything?"

That was a good idea. Ethan was smart and had lived in Garcia a couple of years. He would probably have insights that I didn't. But

I felt a little embarrassed and exposed that my reports were in his hands.

"Love to," he said. And in the shadowy darkness of the backseat, I could tell he was looking at me. He repeated very softly, "Love to."

I gripped my hands together to steady myself. It was hard for me to talk about this. "Any random person could post a picture—I figured that out at Grandma's. But who created it? Distorted my face? Stripped my clothes? Wrote the poem? Drew the graffiti? Spelled my name wrong?"

Before we solved Ethan's case, I didn't have the courage to dissect my own embarrassing mess out loud with Ethan, Mom, and Dad. But now my voice filled the truck. No one moved.

"Is Danny smarter than we think—patient enough to make the picture and clever enough to lie about it tonight, even while his world was falling apart? Did Cynthia and her crew do it and manage to keep that part of their scheme a secret even though they took the fall for texting the link?" Explaining the next part slowed me down because instinct more than logic guided me. "And I get the strangest feeling that Arvey knows something. She tried to let me know about the picture that day. She won't talk to me. She runs hot and cold. But she's not in the clique. Doesn't have a phone. Probably doesn't have a computer."

Ethan said, "She'd have access to computers at school."

Mom faced us. "Oh, yeah. That little girl we tried to give a ride to in the rain. She seemed happy at first and for no reason backed away from us."

Ethan said, "Sir, the drive up to the house is by the next mailbox on your right. It's easy to miss in the dark." There were no streetlights on this narrow country road.

Dad slowed down and turned into the long driveway that led up to a single-story house with a few buildings around it. A dim light glowed on the chair-filled front porch that stretched across the front of the white wood house.

"What a lovely farm," Mom said.

"My grandmother is hoping you'll come in," he said as Dad pulled up to the house.

Before we were all out of the truck, the front door swung open, and Ethan's three sisters came running out, clad in pajamas. They threw themselves on him like appendages as he walked toward his grandmother, who lingered on the porch. He picked up the youngest one, Keisha, as he reached her.

His grandmother put both hands on his face and kissed him. She waved us forward. "Please come in. Please. I can't thank you enough for what you did for Ethan. Thank you. Thank you."

We stepped into the homey living room, filled with stuffed chairs and a sofa, lit by shaded lamps on tables around the room. The two older girls were bombarding Ethan with questions.

Keisha slid down from his arms and grabbed my hand. "Do you want to see my room?"

I started to go with her, but Mom said, "Another time."

It was late. Dad and the grandmother were deep in a conversation I couldn't hear.

I'm not sure whose eyes were first to settle on the large picture of Ethan's father above the fireplace, but we suddenly were all locked on the handsome man in uniform who resembled Ethan so much that a heaviness flooded my chest. We stood in silence in front of the picture for long moments. My eyes brimmed, and Mom dug in her purse and pulled out a tissue. I felt as if we should whisper. Hearing from Ethan that his father was killed had been sad, but seeing the man's face that looked so much like Ethan's made the death more real.

Dad touched a glass case of medals propped below the picture. "I thank you for the sacrifice your father made." He looked at Ethan and his sisters. "He died making us safer. It's an honor to know his family."

CHAPTER 13

THE NEXT MORNING, MY SPARKLING, bubbling elation about seeing Ethan at school got diluted with unsure, pit-of-my-stomach troubling questions. Should I go up to him if I see him in the hall, or should I just nod and smile? Are we casual acquaintances now, or are we special? Where should I go at lunch? What, oh, what should I wear?

Mom always dropped me off at the last possible minute, so I could go immediately to first period. When I approached the office area, I could tell by the surprised expressions in the hallway that Ethan had to be checking in. He sat in the same chair I'd used when getting my schedule. His back was to the windows, but there was no mistaking the shape of his head and his broad shoulders.

Apparently his check-in went fast because he walked into my first-period geometry class right after the tardy bell. There were no empty seats. I'd taken the desk where he sat before. So Mr. Jeffrey, the teacher, called to have another desk brought in. I let my eyes rest on Ethan as he waited for the desk. He had on a white polo shirt, a leftover from Beauty, but instead of the khaki pants, he wore jeans that hugged his butt and thighs just right.

As if he felt me looking, his gaze met mine. The room was silent.

I glanced down at my yellow highlighter that I was rolling between my fingers, but my eyes couldn't stay away from him. When I peeked up again, he smiled at me. I had no idea what the other students were doing or whether they were paying attention to us. But I gave up trying not to stare at Ethan. He pulled absentmindedly at a strap hanging from his backpack. His thigh pressed against a bookshelf by the door. I don't know how much time passed before the door swung open and a custodian popped his head into the room.

Ethan stepped out into the hallway and picked up the desk. "Where would you like it?" he asked Mr. Jeffrey.

The teacher pointed toward the back of the shortest row—my row. Two desks separated us. Even though Ethan sat behind me and I couldn't watch him, the room was different with him in it. At the end of the period, I took my time gathering my stuff, so he could talk to me if he wanted to. But before I stood, Shanique and another pretty black girl burst into the room.

In a low voice, Shanique said, "Ethan, Ethan, Ethan."

The other girl squealed and made little skipping jumps as she rushed toward him.

When I stood, they were on either side of him. Ethan had his arms wrapped around both their shoulders, and he flashed them that same warm expression that he gave me.

What an idiot I had been. Ethan was a friendly guy. A hugger. A smiler. Nothing he shared with me was unusual for him. It was all just Ethan being Ethan. An ache in my chest warred with anger at myself. It crushed me to see that I wasn't special to him, but I was also disgusted with myself for wanting him so much, for not facing the Shanique question.

Students were jammed at the doorway as my class exited and the next one came in. While I waited to get out, I tortured myself by spying on the joyful reunion.

The squealing girl bobbed up and down. "So happy you're back! Missed you so much!"

Shanique, with elegant smoothness, wrapped both arms around Ethan. Her embrace was careful and tender, as if she were holding pure preciousness. They stood for long moments in a full-body embrace. Shanique was only a few inches shorter than Ethan. He tilted his head downward so they were cheek to cheek, and he angled his head toward her—giving her, I suspected, the same secret corner kiss he'd given me yesterday in the backseat of our truck.

Tears blurred my vision, but I could see well enough to break through the crowd at the doorway. On the way to my locker, I lectured myself. *Shape up. Get a grip. Focus on your classes. Finish this semester. Go back to Houston. Get over it. Be happy to have him as a friend.* I kept my teary eyes down, hoping no one would notice as I passed through the crowds of students changing classes. I turned into my locker wing.

A strange silence blanketed this hallway. It was full of students, as always, but they weren't talking. I glanced around, wondering why, and all eyes were on either the floor or me. It was a replay of last year. My stomach heaved. *Have they figured out I have a deflated crush on Ethan? Does everyone know what a fool I am?*

I walked faster. Looked away from the gawking students and onto my locker. My breath stopped from what I saw, stuck at a careless angle on the front of the green metal locker.

White paper. Pink and yellow zigzag lines. Crazy smile. Skinny naked dance. Obscene hand-waving. Poetic Polaritey.

The reason for the silent hallway.

A printout of the naked picture—the first one, taped on the front of my locker.

Feeling as if I were dying inside from disappointment and humiliation, I snatched it off, crammed it into my book bag, and for some insane reason, opened my locker and did my book exchange as if I were going to second period. I closed the locker softly and rushed through muted students all the way to the office wing.

This period, the office had five student aides stationed up and down the counter. The adults were back at desks. I approached a short guy with thick glasses. "May I use the phone?" My voice scraped. "I need to go home. It's an emergency." At some schools the "emergency" ploy would get girls out quick—especially when the line is used on a male. I hoped he'd assume I had some mysterious feminine product need and he'd let me use the phone. I still didn't have my own cell.

Instead, he called out to all the other aides, "Where's that form for going home?"

The four other student aides, with sidelong glances, starting shuffling through shelves on their side of the counter.

I felt on the verge of exploding as Mom would do. I whipped around their counter and crossed over to the Counselor's Corner receptionist. Just as Shanique had done on my first morning, I told the receptionist I had to see the counselor. It was an emergency.

Mrs. Gamez stepped out immediately. "Come in, Polarity."

"I have to go home," I whimpered, my voice weak and childlike. "Please let me call my mom."

She gently took my arm and guided me to the sunflower sofa. "Dear, tell me what's wrong. Are you ill?" Her soft gray eyes assured me of her willingness to receive anything I would say.

I sat gripping my book bag on my lap to stop the trembling in my hands. "I just have to go home," I whispered, voice shaking.

She reached into a little fridge beside her sofa and pulled out a small bottle of water. She twisted the cap off and touched my hand with it. I accepted the cold, damp bottle, took a sip, and handed it back to her with a quivering hand. The coldness in my mouth was hard to swallow.

"Polarity, we're going to take three deep breaths together." She softly counted through our breathing, in and out. In and out. By the third breath, my shoulders started shaking, and a groan forced its way out in choppy beats. "That's okay, dear. You can cry."

She scooted closer with one arm around me. My head found her safe shoulder.

She continued to hold me, as if she would sit there with me all day long if I needed to. But I pulled myself together, took the tissue she offered, and dried my face. I opened my book bag and pulled out the picture. "I found this stuck on my locker."

"I'm so sorry this happened to you, Polarity." Unfazed, Mrs. Gamez took the wrinkled printout from me and gently folded it over, as if to protect the poor naked girl. "Do you know who put it on your locker?"

I shook my head. "It was there just now when I went to change books after class. I don't know who did it."

She handed me her phone. "Call your parents."

After I called Mom, Mrs. Gamez phoned the principal and told him about the picture and that we'd come to his office after Mom arrived.

She let me sit quietly while we waited. She didn't pressure me to talk. She just kept watching me and urging me to drink the water. I was thankful for her silence. Talking about the picture would have been doubly difficult because my heart was breaking over Ethan.

Mom arrived in minutes, and Mrs. Gamez escorted us into the principal's office. My only brushes with him had been during the drug dog search and an occasional "Good morning" as I arrived at school.

Mr. Justin invited us in and asked us to sit. Even though he was a bulky guy, a former football player, he'd be no match for Mom's tirade about all the things the school had done wrong.

But Mom acted oddly subdued. "We aren't sitting, Mr. Justin. Polarity is not ready to talk about this. She's shocked and upset." This did not sound like Mom.

"I understand, Mrs. Weeks," he said gently. "But I'd like to see if Polarity has any idea who might have put this on her locker." Somehow the folded printout was in his hand. "I want to hold that person accountable."

Mom clasped my arm and started backing us out of his office. "I'm taking her home, and after she's had a chance to recover, we'll talk."

"Wait," he said, just before Mom opened the office door. She stopped with her hand on the doorknob. "I just want you to know, I checked the security footage, and unfortunately, Polarity's locker is about five lockers out of range. But tonight I'll adjust the camera so that it's in center view."

"Good thinking," Mom said flatly, and she pulled me out the door. As we walked to her car, she muttered to herself, "As usual, the school is helplessly reactive."

Our short drive home was as silent as the hallway had been. Even with the misery of the picture on my locker and the Ethan-Shanique moment, my stomach churned with worry about what was going on with Mom. The lull scared me far more than her screaming.

My heart pounded as memories of past silences flashed: the time

I woke up to her stare, her explosion after the hearing with Dr. Stone, her cold calmness when she accused me of dancing naked for boys.

She rushed into the trailer ahead of me, pulled out my folder of reports, snapped open her laptop, and sat down at the table. "Sit." She pointed to the seat across the table from her. "I've figured out who did this."

I lowered myself onto the bench. "Who? How do you know?"

Fast as bullets, she shot out questions. "Who is the one person who might be smart enough to use a proxy server or floating IP address or wireless air card? Who is the one person that no one would suspect?" She grabbed and shook my pages of TeensterBlast logs. "Who is the one person too smart to get into this blather?" She slapped the papers down and scanned her laptop screen. "Who is the one person with a reason to get you out of school?"

I stood so I could see her screen: picture after picture of Shanique on the Internet—receiving a trophy as captain of the volley ball team, singing in a Christmas program, receiving a scholarship award to the early-college start program, leading a campaign to help abandoned dogs and cats.

"Who"—Mom beamed a jubilant smile—"is too good to be true?"

Denial stunned me. "No. That can't be." But for the briefest moment, a question nipped. *Could Mom be right?* Maybe Shanique was, in fact, like Mom—full of contradictions. Famous too-good-to-be-true borderline personalities I'd found on Google searches skated through my mind.

I joggled my head to clear out Mom's twisted thoughts. "Shanique is amazing, but she has no reason to want to hurt me."

Mom stood and grabbed both my shoulders. "Polarity. Ethan has a crush on you. It's been plain from the first time we met him. I see the way he looks at you. And the way he did all that phone research. He's smitten with you. Shanique is jealous, pure and simple."

"I think it's Cynthia or maybe Arvey."

"Arvey has issues for sure, but she's not smart enough to do it. And Cynthia, from her dumb TeensterBlast posts, is a mindless bimbo who just forwarded a random text." She let go of me and sat back down to her computer. "All we have to do is figure out a way to trap Shanique."

Ethan would hate me if I accused Shanique. He cared about her. He even had her help him borrow people's cell phones.

My stomach twisted at the idea of Ethan discovering Mom's theory. "Mom, we—"

Her phone rang.

"Stanley," she said instead of hello.

No. I didn't want her to tell the sheriff about her crazy theory.

She quietly listened to him. "Oh." Disappointment shadowed her face. "And the first picture?"

I froze. *He must be telling her what the tech lab found out about the IP address for the online pictures.*

She clicked off her phone and tapped her fingers on the table. "That doesn't make sense."

"Mom, what? What did he say?"

"They're still working on the first picture—something about the IP address being masked. But the second picture—the one you found with the tile showing—was posted from a computer at the Star campus eight days after you left." She frowned, put her elbows on the table, and rested her chin on her hand. "Why would Shanique use two different computers?"

"It wasn't Shanique. It couldn't have been. Ethan wouldn't be with someone evil enough to do that picture. He just wouldn't." But as I said the words, a big truth smacked me.

My good, patient dad stayed with Mom even though she did monstrous things.

Ethan phoned that evening. Mom and Dad were finishing dinner and rehashing the move-back-to-Houston debate, so I took Mom's cell outside. They didn't object. I leaned against the trailer and gazed out over the darkening vacant field.

"Shanique told me about the picture on your locker" was the first thing he said.

The words stabbed. Whether Shanique was involved or not, I hated that he and she were talking about me. "How did she know?"

"Someone told her right before she got on the Vuelta bus this morning. I hate it." His voice dropped into something low, threatening. "I'm going to find out who did it."

"That's okay. You don't have to—"

"Polarity. I do have to. I have to put an end to it for you. I gave Shanique a copy of your papers."

My stomach sank, and my jealousy of her churned with my suspicion of her.

He raced ahead. "She's lived here her whole life, and she's a brain. I want her to go through them and see if we're missing something."

Dusk blurred the pile of junk dumped in the corner of the field, but I could still see the peeling RV Resort sign propped at an angle against the rusted lawn tractor. My life was as wrecked as that junk pile. "I wish you hadn't given them to her."

"Why?" Keisha must have approached him—she was asking him to open something.

I waited too long to answer his question.

He asked, "What's wrong? Has something else happened?"

"No." I pushed myself off the trailer and turned away from the field. "I have to go."

"I can tell something's wrong. Let me help you."

I rested my forehead against the trailer and closed my eyes. "It's nothing. I don't know what to say."

"Let me help you the way you helped me."

I squeezed my eyes tight and made my voice hard. "No. Don't help me anymore. I appreciate all that you did, but it was enough. We're done. Bye." I cut off the phone and wept with my head against the trailer.

After first-period geometry the next day, Shanique came into our classroom again. But instead of heading back toward Ethan, she paused by my desk. I didn't stop for her. I moved fast, hoping to hoof it out before a crowd jammed the doorway. When I got to the door,

I could see Ethan and her in my peripheral vision. They were both doing their best to catch up with me.

I had packed all my books for the morning into my book bag to avoid stops at my locker, even though Mr. Justin had promised the camera would now have a direct view of it. I passed by the locker—fortunately bare this morning—but I didn't want to dally in the hallway and give Ethan or Shanique the opportunity to talk to me. I dived into the girls' restroom to hide out until it was time to step into my next class. My feelings about Ethan and Shanique were confused and embarrassing.

For the rest of the day, avoidance kept me away from Ethan. But he must have figured out I was dodging him. During our seventh-period world history class together, the teacher put us into groups to outline a chapter. Ethan and I were in the same group of three. Our desks were in a circle, and as always when I was near him, I wanted to drink him in. I averted my eyes and stayed focused on the work. But when Rachel, the third person in our group, left us for a few minutes, Ethan said, "You don't have to keep avoiding me."

His sad face was heartbreaking. "I'm not going to bother you. Just wish I understood what's wrong."

I stammered. "It's nothing. Just—nothing." I couldn't tell him Mom's insane theory about Shanique. I couldn't confess fantasizing there was something more than friendship between him and me.

He nodded and lowered his head. Rachel returned, and we got through the period.

I was drained by the time Tilly and I sat on the bench in the parent pickup area after school. As usual, Arvey stood ten or fifteen feet behind us. Tilly was explaining how she pasted wooden quills on a porcupine picture when a tap on my shoulder startled me. It was Shanique, dressed in her team shorts and shirt.

A flash of understanding hit me, about why Ethan cared about her. Her glowing face warmed me even while I tried my best not to like her.

Tilly jumped up and squealed. "Sheekie! Sheekie!"

Shanique stepped around to the front of our bench, and with the same elegant tenderness that she'd used on Ethan, she wrapped her beautiful arms around Tilly and lay her face on the top of Tilly's head. I could hear Shanique faintly crooning, "I love you, sweet, sweet, Tilly."

After Tilly let her go, they settled on the bench with Tilly squeezed in the middle. Tilly's full squinty-eyed smile bounced back and forth from Shanique to me. "Pohlee. Sheekie." She rocked from side to side, giddy with joy to be with both of us.

Tilly's mother drove up, and we had a round of hugs again before she skipped to the car.

Shanique and I sat back down. What was she was doing here? She should have been in athletics.

"Polarity, I just have a couple of minutes, but I wanted to tell you that I read your incident report and the TeensterBlast log. Nice work." She flashed her glowing smile again.

"Thanks," I murmured. Her compliment may have been genuine, but my stomach twisted with Mom's too-good-to-be-true theory, and my heart squeezed with the vision of Ethan hugging her.

"There's one thing I noticed that might be helpful." She lowered her voice and glanced back where Arvey was standing. "You have Tracey's name wrong. Students call her 'RV' as in 'RV Resort.' They've called her that since third grade. She used to cry about it. There was a big sign by her trailer."

Numbness crept through my body. That was why Mrs. Sanchez said there was no Arvey. That was why Arvey—Tracey—started to get into our car that day in the rain, but when Mom and I said *Arvey*, she backed away.

I'd seen the RV Resort sign myself. Why didn't I put it together? I glanced back at Tracey, standing alone. Regret washed over me.

"And Tracey has only one comment on TeensterBlast. It was a question on the day you left Star. *Sup with cops at school?*"

A rugged, handsome guy, wearing a senior football practice uniform, jogged toward us, his focus locked on Shanique. His skin was almost as rich and dark as Ethan's, and his head was shaved.

Shanique followed my gaze, and her face brightened. She leaned closer to me and whispered fast. "I don't want to be unkind, but Tracey's always struggled. She has issues. I think her TeensterBlast message could mean that she's somehow mixed up in the plot against you."

The senior put his hand on Shanique's shoulder.

As she rose, she took his hand in hers and brought it to her lips, giving it a quick kiss. "Did you have a good day?"

Something sizzled between them as their eyes locked.

Still holding his hand, she said, "Polarity, this is my boyfriend, Jed. Jed, Polarity."

"Hi, Jed. So nice to meet you." *She has a boyfriend—a gorgeous senior boyfriend. Of course she does.* I could have levitated with joy as I stood to meet him... except now Ethan hated me for the brush-off. Relief and regret crashed in on me.

"Hey, Polarity—cool name." To Shanique, he said, "Coach is looking for you."

She waved at me as they sprinted toward the gym.

Mom pulled in, but I held up one finger, signaling her to give me a minute. Tracey was still standing in her spot. I approached her. "Tracey."

She jerked to look at me with surprise. Her gaze shifted from side to side as if she were off balance.

"Tracey," I said again. "I'm so sorry I called you RV. I thought your name was Arvey. I didn't know that your real name is Tracey."

She dropped her eyes to the ground.

"Tracey, I have to go now—my mom is here. Would you like to ride with us? We can talk about this some more if you want to."

She didn't look up. I lifted my hand to touch her but sensed that contact might overwhelm her. A single tear slowly flowed down the side of her face that wasn't covered by her hair. When I got into the car, she was still holding herself stiffly, as if balancing on unsteady ground.

"What was Shanique doing with you?" Mom asked as soon as I shut the door. "What did she want?"

I told her everything Shanique had revealed, including the part about her having a boyfriend.

"You said she was Ethan's girlfriend."

"I was wrong." About so much. *Will I be able to make this up to*

Ethan and Tracey? And I had other unfinished business. "Mom, would you stop at the ninth-grade campus on the way home? I need to talk to Mrs. Sanchez."

"No. I will not. I don't want you to talk to that woman."

"I need to tell her about Danny using the code word last year. He or his friends might have planted marijuana on some student at Star."

"I don't care. Last year is over, and I don't like her. We owe her nothing. Nothing after what she put us through."

"Mom, she helped—she interviewed all those students. She sent Cynthia and her friends to Beauty. And don't you see? If I don't tell her what I know, I'm the same as those eighty students who never reported the text to anyone."

Stiff and quiet, Mom kept her eyes glued on the road until we reached Star. Mrs. Sanchez stood in her usual after-school spot, near the front entryway, monitoring the students getting picked up. Mom pulled over, and I got out.

"Hello, Polarity. How are you? How's high school?" Mrs. Sanchez asked as I approached. She had lots of questions about my classes and my writing.

I thanked her for connecting me with Mrs. Gamez and told how the counselor helped yesterday when someone put a picture on my locker. After we got through that, I explained about Danny putting marijuana in Ethan's bag and how Danny had used the code word last year, too. "I wanted you to know in case anybody got framed in ninth grade like Ethan did."

She thanked me and said nice things about my thoughtfulness, and I started toward the truck. But I stopped. The uplifting news that Ethan and Shanique were not a couple had totally brightened my universe, and big ideas danced through me. "You know how you kept saying someday I'd benefit from all this—this picture stuff? That it would make me smarter somehow?"

"Yes. I believe that we can find lessons everywhere and benefit from them."

"You were right. I never knew what it's like for..." I started to say "students who are black and Hispanic," but it wasn't their color that was the bad thing. It was that a lot of them didn't have privileges that some white students had. "Students that don't have the same advantages as I do."

She nodded and held still. She was one of those people who listened so well that it made you want to put out even more. Even though students and cars and buses were moving around us, she focused on me.

I continued, "And most people don't even see it. Don't even see the differences in privileges."

After I stopped, she waited a moment then softly said, "You are remarkable. Your vision and understanding are beyond your years. I'm privileged to know you, Polarity."

Well, that was a little over the top. "I'd better go. Mom is waiting."

Mom, still frowning, drove home in silence. A few months ago, my talking with Mrs. Sanchez would have resulted in a major sulk scene on her part. But the positive steam of her and Dad's marijuana success helped her get over her irritation quickly.

That evening, I took Mom's phone outside again and called Ethan. Instead of saying hello, I blurted, "I'm an idiot—a total idiot."

"I don't agree with that," he said. "But I don't understand what's wrong—what happened. I want to help you the way you helped me." Anger tinged his voice. "I want to get to whoever did the picture."

I lay my forehead against the trailer and closed my eyes. "Ethan. I'm going to say this fast because it's stupid and embarrassing." His sisters' voices chattered nearby, and knowing that he couldn't speak freely made it easier for me to plunge in. I could just say what I wanted to say and be done. "So please listen because I don't think I'll ever be able to say it again."

"Polarity, it's okay. Whatever it is—it's okay."

I took a deep breath. "So, I had a crush on you, but I thought Shanique was your girlfriend, and Mom came up with a crazy idea that Shanique did the picture—which Mom no longer thinks after today, but she did think it yesterday, so I distanced myself from you and Shanique because I was jealous, and at moments even suspicious— and I apologize from the bottom of my heart, and you don't have to answer or say anything because I'm going to hang up now that I've revealed the depth of my stupidity, and from here on out we can be friends with no more me avoiding you, and Shanique is the kindest, most amazing girl I've ever met, and I'm ashamed for every moment I didn't trust her, and you've been thoughtful and helpful from the beginning, a hero, a true hero, and I appreciate everything you've done for me, and now I really am going to hang up, but I hope that when we see each other at school you won't feel uncomfortable around me, and we can be friends. Good-bye." I squeezed my eyes shut tighter and bit my lip.

I expected he'd pause a bit before saying good-bye or anything. But instantly, in his low rich voice, he said, "Polarity..."

And somehow just his voice saying my name, despite my tense embarrassment over my awkward confession—somehow his voice saying my name reached so deep inside me that he found places to be touched that I didn't even know I had.

"... I'll see you tomorrow."

The next morning at school wasn't as awkward as I had feared. A geometry test first period and the video of Julius Caesar in second kept us busy, so Ethan and I didn't have to talk to each other. But on the way out of second period, he said, "I'm glad you called me last night." Before I could answer, a crowd separated us, and our schedules kept us on different paths for the rest of the morning.

But lunch came—an entire hour to fill. I stalled at my locker and cleaned out some trash, using up as many minutes as possible before I had to find some place to disappear and eat until fifth period. I didn't want to go into the cafeteria and invade Ethan's space yet or deal with the awkward where-to-sit decision, especially with him there. At least it was good weather. I could stroll around outside.

His warm hand touched the back of my neck and rested on the center of my shoulders. "So, in addition to my desks, you also have my old locker." His smile went all over me, and his eyes connected with mine in a way that made me feel he shared my warm gush of feelings.

All my self-lectures had been useless. I could never think of him as just a friend.

I concentrated to make myself speak normally. "Want it back?"

"Nope. But can I leave my stuff in it during lunch?"

"Be my guest."

His books thudded when they hit the bottom. "Where do you eat?"

"Oh, anywhere—brown bag." I held up my sack.

"Your mom made everything gluten- and soy-free, right?" He grinned.

"Yeah."

"Okay to eat in the cafeteria? My grandmother doesn't pack lunches, so it's the line or starvation for me."

"Sure." I couldn't believe he expected me to go with him to the cafeteria—and his books were in my locker, so he'd be coming back to it with me after lunch. I tingled all over.

"Ready?" he asked before he shut the locker door with a clang that rang out extra loud because the hallway was empty except for us.

"How were your classes?" I asked as we walked.

"Okay, especially first and second periods." He took my breath away.

Be calm. That could mean so many things. And you saw the way he was with Shanique. He's just a friendly, happy, outgoing guy.

And just as if we'd been doing this for years, just as if it were the most natural thing in the world, just as if I were special to him, he took my hand in his, with warm, solid pressure. For once he didn't look at me as he usually did. Instead, he faced forward. And when I peeked at him out of the side of my eye, he had shaded to burgundy dark chocolate. Maybe he was trying something out—something special he wasn't used to doing. I wanted to bring his hand to my lips and kiss it.

Suddenly we were there—in the cafeteria—walking through the center, holding hands.

Talk stopped. Heads turned.

I didn't care about the gawking—I was used to it by now. But I gripped his hand tighter—maybe for support, or maybe for the pure joy of squeezing him.

When we came to the tray line, I asked, "Is there an area where you like to sit?" Oh gosh, there I was, assuming that I should find a spot for us while he was in line. *What if he doesn't want to sit with me?*

"Nope. Any place is fine. I don't care, as long as I'm next to the silver lining."

Our eyes locked again. My doubts were gone. I connected to Ethan. Totally, completely connected.

I squeezed his hand. "That will be arranged."

He squeezed back, and we unclasped hands. Every part of me resisted moving away from him.

I headed toward the tables, and he joined the tray line. I looked around for a few empty spots not jammed in with a noisy group. For the first time, I noticed that most of the black students—maybe twenty or so, in this school—were in a corner area. Funny, that was one area that I had missed, in all my eavesdropping rotations. Would he want to sit there?

I found an in-between spot, on the invisible line between the white and the black students.

My eyes feasted on Ethan as he came out of the serving area and glanced around for me. Our eyes met. His warm, smiling face, as he headed in my direction, totally reaffirmed that he wanted to be with me. He, Ethan, wanted to be with me! This kind, handsome, perfect guy, who had just held my hand, walked toward me. It was a dream come true.

As he passed by the table filled with Brad and some of the other jocks, someone called out to him. "Hey, Ethan. You're back. We need you on the team, man. You gotta play football."

Ethan gave them a slight wave. "Thanks, not my thing."

Brad said, "Hey. Come on—you bruthas are made to play football."

Ethan never slowed his step or lost his smile or took his eyes off me. But irritation flashed across his face.

The hour flew by. We talked about our classes, our families, and our after-school routine. He rode a late bus to his grandmother's farm.

We figured out we could spend time together after school before his bus and my mom arrived.

He put his arm around the back of my chair and whispered, so close to my ear that I could feel his lips move, "It's a date—you and me—after school, today?"

I angled my face toward him so that my cheek touched his. "Yes." The rough stubble and fresh, masculine scent of his skin drew me to him. I closed my eyes.

Mrs. Dougherty tapped both our shoulders. I had been oblivious to her approach. "Polarity and Ethan, enjoying your lunch?"

We pulled apart. Ethan said, "Yes, ma'am."

"Do I need to remind you two—no PDA at school?"

A few months ago, this encounter would have embarrassed me beyond belief, but I was so happy about being close to Ethan, I didn't care what anyone said. "Consider us reminded."

She strolled past us.

The crimped blond girls huddled with a group at the end of our table. Their pointed stares and energetic whispering made it clear they were gossiping about us.

Ethan said, "People are watching us."

For once, I absolutely didn't care. I was bursting with happiness and wanted the whole world to know I was with Ethan. *I, Polarity Weeks, am with Ethan Rawls.* "Yeah. Are you okay with that?"

He lowered his voice and moved closer to my face. "Sure. They'll get tired of us after a while. Something else will catch their attention."

Joy rippled throughout my body.

He turned back to his food and said with a hard, determined tone, "Besides, I don't care what it takes." His jaw clenched. "I'm going to stop the picture stuff."

My joy crashed to a stop. *He's the hero, saving the underdog. Even if it takes being stared at. What if he doesn't have feelings for me? What if the hand-holding, locker-sharing, and sitting together is all about protecting the poor little victim or paying me back for helping him?*

He stood to return his tray. "Be right back."

As he walked away, I bolstered myself back up by filtering through all the special things he'd said to me. Even Mom had proclaimed

Ethan was smitten with me. But phrases from the crimped girls' gossip pierced my self-lecture.

The girl wearing the Sue necklace said, "Someone stuck her naked picture on her locker. Ethan's her locker guard."

A different girl shrieked hysterically. "Maybe Ethan…." I couldn't hear the rest as she went into a whisper.

I stood and left their giggling behind. Ethan came out of the tray area. Friends approached him. The bell rang. We pushed through the crowded hallway. I went into fifth period with my crumbling fantasy.

Between fifth and sixth, he was at my locker before me—standing guard with his arms folded across his chest. His protectiveness was noble, but his stance made me even more afraid that he was drawn to me because he was a hero, not because he had feelings for me. One way or the other, I had to know the truth.

I spent the afternoon rehearsing the question to ask him after school. *Do you have feelings for me, or are you with me because you want to save me or pay me back for helping you?*

I mentally rehearsed all the ways I could ask him. I worried about whether we'd get enough alone time after school to even talk about it. Tilly usually sat near me until her mother came. I worried if I was getting too intense—even paranoid—by questioning our relationship on the very first day of it. *Am I turning into my mother?*

All these worries were a waste of energy because he dashed out of seventh period without saying a word to me. By the time I got to my locker, he was nowhere in sight, and he didn't show up in the parent pickup area after school.

I phoned him that night. "What happened, Ethan? Did I misunderstand?" I had my eyes closed and my back flat against the hard metal of the trailer. "I thought we were going to talk after school?"

"You didn't misunderstand," he said.

Relief flowed through me. "Oh, I—"

"I made a mistake. You were right last night when you called. We should just be friends—nothing else."

The relief skidded to a sickening stop. "Did I do something

wrong?" I opened my eyes to see the dim outline of the junk piled in the corner of the field.

"No. It's like I said—my mistake. I have to go."

I stood in the darkness and listened to the dial tone after he hung up. I hadn't read Emily Dickinson lately—not since Mom pointed out the poet's bigotry—but now a line about the cost of ecstasy echoed through me like a taunt. I didn't have a relationship with Ethan yesterday, and I had been sad about that. But after having a few golden minutes with him, today's loss was anguish.

CHAPTER 14

I PROPPED MYSELF UP THE NEXT morning with lame excuses about Ethan. *There must be some mistake. The feelings we shared yesterday—even though for only a few hours—were real. Maybe a little time, patience—things will work out. Maybe we just need to move slower.*

But at school, all my excuses crashed. He came into first- and second-period classes late. Both teachers gave him a warning. He offered no excuse, no apology. Instead of his usual laid-back smile, he scowled. He didn't participate or talk to anyone. And to make things even worse for himself, he walked out of second period before the bell rang.

Mrs. Dougherty's jaw dropped. "Ethan, you are not..." She let her words trail off and finished, "dismissed," after he left. She looked questioningly at me, as if I could explain.

The bell rang, and I slinked out. There was nothing I could tell her.

At lunch, I peeked into the cafeteria, and Ethan was nowhere in sight. He sauntered near my locker a few times during passing periods, but he always averted his eyes. By the end of the day, his message bulldozed me down: He didn't just want to change our connection to simple friendship. He hated me.

Maybe he had seen a full copy of the naked picture. *Maybe he now shares everyone else's belief that I posed and lied about it.*

It broke my heart to see him so angry and on edge, but I couldn't be the one to help him. After school, I went into the gym, which is absolutely forbidden territory when the varsity athletes are in practice. The volleyball girls rotated setup drills, but before the coach noticed me, I caught Shanique's attention and mouthed, "We need to talk."

She nodded from her line and pointed to the door. A few minutes later, she came outside where I waited.

"What's wrong?" The worry lines crossing her normally sunny face showed that she sensed my alarm.

I raced through the concerns, knowing she'd probably have to return fast. "It's Ethan. Something's not right. He came late to classes—even walked out of a class without permission. He didn't even show up in the cafeteria to eat, and he always eats. He's mad and upset about something. And I can't help him—he won't speak to me. Could you talk to him?"

"Did you break up?"

How did she know we were together? It was only about five hours?

Before I could answer, she said, "Oh, I guess it wasn't a public thing, but I could tell you two had something. So he won't tell you what's wrong?"

"No, he won't talk to me."

"Okay, I'll talk to him. Got to get back in."

"Thanks," I said to her back.

Mom was already in the parent pickup lane. She practically hopped in her seat when I opened the car door. "Guess what!"

I hated her game. "I give up."

"You got an e-mail today from someone who knows Zada. It said, 'I'll tell Zada you're looking for her.' Isn't that exciting?" She pulled out of the lane and onto the street.

"Mom, how can you even believe what some random stranger says in a TeensterBlast message? We'll never hear from Zada again. She'll be one of your thousands of missing that never show up."

"What's wrong?" She gave me a sideways frown. "Are you sick?"

"No, I'm not sick. I'm just realistic."

"Did something happen with Ethan?" She was a bloodhound sniffing at the one thing that could totally destroy me.

"No. Let's just go home. I have homework."

With her excitement squashed, she stayed unusually quiet for the next few hours. For a change, she tiptoed around my mood, instead of me trying to keep her on an even keel. After Dad came home, the weight of my depression made dinner long and awkward. They went outside and whispered together after we ate, while I cleared the table and cleaned up the dishes.

They came back inside, and Dad said, "Let's go for a ride."

He said it to me—not Mom and me. I looked up in surprise.

Mom said, "Yes, you two should take a ride."

Okay. So they'd planned this. I shrugged and walked out to his truck.

We weren't even out of the trailer park before he asked, "What's going on?"

As if I would tell either of my parents about Ethan. "Nothing."

"Mom thinks something happened at school today."

"She needs to get a life. Just because I'm not over the moon about some random TeensterBlast message doesn't mean something happened."

The pointless conversation went on for several miles outside the Garcia city limits until he gave up on persuading me to bare my soul. "Your mom and I are giving you your own laptop. You've been through a lot these last few months—a lot that we still don't understand. But you're old enough to have more freedom than we've given you."

"Thanks," I said. But my bitter heart whined, "Yeah, about five years later than everyone else my age."

He turned down a road we had taken before that led to a small lake. "And with Skype and e-mail, you can keep up with your Garcia friends after we move back to Houston at the end of the semester."

"Thanks." *I don't have any Garcia friends to Skype with.*

The sun was setting over the lake. He cut his engine. "Let's sit on those rocks awhile."

We settled a few feet apart from each other on the edge of the water.

"I'm sorry that I'm not more help with Mom." He gazed out over the water. "She spends more time with you than anyone else, so I know that you catch the brunt of her rough edges." He turned to me. "She loves you. That doesn't excuse how she hurts you, but I hope it makes it easier."

I scooted closer to him and lay my head on his solid shoulder. He put one arm around me and squeezed. With the unsolved naked picture mystery, he probably thought I was as messed up as Mom. But he cared about me, anyway.

Dad was one of those people who were comfortable just being quiet. With Mom, we normally had constant, accelerated, energetic chatter. It was nice to be silent while the late sun sparkled on the rippling water. We sat still, with only the gentle sound of water splashing against the rocks, until the sun dropped below the horizon.

The drive home took us past the high school, which was deserted—no games or activities on that night. About a mile farther, our headlights picked up the distinct form of Tracey, walking home alone in the dark.

"Do you know that girl?" Dad asked.

"Tracey—she lives in that double-wide."

He started slowing down. "Should we go back for her? It's late for her to be walking down this highway alone."

"She won't ride with us. I've asked her before." I stared back into the darkness until I could no longer see her. Minutes later, when we passed her double-wide, there were two cars parked in front. Two men and a woman, with bright cigarette tips glowing in the dark, sat outside in lawn chairs.

Weeks dragged by. Ethan's behavior deteriorated. He never did anything bad enough to get kicked out of class, but his lateness and daily attempts to leave class early kept him on the edge of major trouble with the teachers. Shanique was no help. A few days after I asked her to talk with him, she told me he wouldn't spill. She was as puzzled as I was.

The only time he showed that he even knew I still existed was the day Mrs. Gamez called me in for a meeting with her right before Thanksgiving break. She sent the message during second period, while I happened to be facing Ethan's direction.

Mrs. Dougherty said, "Polarity, you're needed in the counselor's office."

He jerked to attention. But when he noticed me watching him, he buried his face in his textbook.

When I arrived in the office, Mrs. Gamez invited me to sit with her on the sunflower sofa. "Some of your teachers are concerned that you've become too quiet and withdrawn since that picture was on your locker. Are you having trouble?"

I perched on the edge of the puffy seat, resisting her subtle invitation to relax. "No. I'm fine."

"Who are your friends?"

I hated questions like this. Other than Tilly, I had no friends—except possibly Shanique, who was gone most of the day. "Tilly and Shanique, I guess."

"You're alone a lot. Why is that?"

I shrugged.

"Are kids bullying you?" Her soft gray eyes peered into mine.

"Not like last year. No name-calling to my face. They still gossip about me, and someone put the picture on my locker, but mostly they leave me alone."

"Leaving you alone—ignoring you—can be a form of bullying, too."

"If it is, I'm fine with it. I don't mind being left alone. I'm moving at the end of the semester anyway." I wanted this conversation to end. I had to refrain from shoving myself up and off the sofa cushion.

Mrs. Gamez sighed and pushed her bobbed gray hair behind her ears. "You feel that you're okay being alone since you're moving away. But, Polarity, don't leave things on a negative note. Even though you're moving to a new school, trouble here"—she put both hands on her heart—"will follow you."

She mumbled something about brochures on bullying and started shuffling through papers on top of her fridge.

Good grief. "Thanks. I really need to go now. I have a test."

She sighed. "The six girls who were sent to Beauty for distributing the text about you are being released. They'll be here when you return from Thanksgiving break. Will you be okay with seeing them?"

"Sure." Seeing them again would not be fun, but I was so over being bothered by anything Cynthia could say or do. Reflecting about it, I looked forward to quizzing Cynthia face-to-face about the picture.

After Mrs. Gamez gave up on her guidance efforts, I headed out of the Counseling Corner, carrying a stack of bullying brochures, and through the office reception area, where Ethan was asking one of the office aides for some kind of form.

I swished past him. The frustration of Mrs. Gamez's probing plus the weeks of agonizing over what could be wrong with Ethan piled up. Anger at him flashed through me. My two-inch-heeled ankle boots click-clacked with my fast, hard steps.

Ethan abandoned the office aide and followed close behind me. "What happened? What's wrong?"

"How dare you?" I stopped and whirled around—too fast for him to adjust. We slammed into each other—full body contact.

The bulging muscles of his thighs pressed against my legs. His chest, like a warm, magnetic haven, pulled me into him. His dark brown eyes with the secret streaks of gray, locked with mine. His breath warmed my face. His hands held my arms, steadying us after our collision.

"Take your hands off me."

He dropped his hands. But every cell in my body screamed, "Put them back."

Neither of us moved. He spoke close to my face, and my undisciplined eyes dropped to his lips. "What happened in the office?"

His proximity made the hollow place he'd left in me throb with pain. Backing away and spinning around, I filled that emptiness with roiling fury. "None of your business." I looked over my shoulder at him. "I'm moving back to Houston at the end of the semester. So why don't you just drop whatever game you're playing and pretend I'm already gone?"

I walked rapidly down the hall back to English class.

Ethan never came back into the classroom for the rest of the period.

Mom and Dad let me fly to Dallas for Thanksgiving week while they drove to Houston to get our house ready to move back into. I didn't realize how wound up I was until I'd been at Grandma's for a few days and started to relax and feel normal. Her house was an oasis, and I kept thinking about Mom's rant that Grandma was irrationally in love with me. Mom meant it as a negative thing, but I loved that Grandma didn't want to change one thing about me and that she was thrilled to have time with me.

We had Thanksgiving dinner at Scooter's house, with all four of his children and their families. It was a riot of gorging, laughing, and playing with his youngest grandchildren—three-year-old twin girls. But among all the craziness, I found a private moment with Scooter— we were unloading the dishwasher for the third time—to thank him for his help with my case. His approach and the report writing had helped, even though I still didn't know who made the picture.

The highlight of Thanksgiving Day came in the evening with a phone call from Mom. "Check your e-mail. Zada sent you a message. It has to be her because she used your name."

On Grandma's computer, I pulled up the TeensterBlast page, and there was a private message: "Polarity, is that you?" The message was from a page with a different name—Molly M.—but the message had to come from Zada.

Grandma was as excited as I was. We both did what I used to call the jiggling dance—just a silly, hoppy craziness—accompanied by squeals. I sent Zada a message and included details that only she and I knew, so she wouldn't be afraid that I was a stranger.

"Yes, Zada, it's Polarity. We talked that night in the little bedroom next to Hannah's. And the next day before I left, you whispered, 'Things will get worse before they get better.' You were right about everything. How are you? Where are you? I'm back with my parents, but the picture mystery is still out there. Sometimes I'm afraid I may never know how it happened. But your advice to just keep telling the truth has helped me. I'm not giving up on my case or on reconnecting with you."

I flew into San Antonio Sunday night, and Mom and Dad picked me up on their way from Houston to Garcia. I laughed when I got into the truck. My new laptop and Gypsy—both wearing glitter-covered pink bows—rested on the backseat. Gypsy snored, and I played with my very own computer all the way back to the trailer park.

Before Thanksgiving, my efforts to figure out who made the picture had slumped. My sadness about Ethan's turnaround had derailed me. But the week at Grandma's let me recharge and refocus. There were only three weeks left in the semester to figure out who made that picture, so I set out a plan, just as I had done when I tried to figure out who framed Ethan. If I didn't find out before we moved, I was afraid I might never know. Long-distance sleuthing from Houston would be next to impossible, and the police progress, as Scooter had predicted, dragged at a crawl.

First, I reviewed all the TeensterBlast chatter, searching again for clues. Shanique had been right about Tracey. As far as I could tell, Tracey had made only that one entry on the day Danny showed the picture in class. Before and after that she was silent. I figured there must be a reason why that was her one and only TeensterBlast comment, *Sup with cops at school.* I would keep asking her—try different approaches to get her to talk to me.

I also resolved to work on Cynthia. Maybe now that she'd been away a while, she'd be willing to spill information about who sent her the original text. I wasn't the same shy girl I'd been back at Star. Maybe I could figure out a way to connect with Cynthia. After all, I wore makeup and had highlights now, which were her greatest interests in life.

And I made up my mind to have a frank discussion with Ethan. Something changed for him that day. He'd gone from putting his books in my locker, holding my hand, making a date to talk after school, then bam—a complete reversal. If my worst fear had come true and he'd seen the whole naked picture, I needed to find out where and when. Maybe that would help me solve the mystery. And if he hadn't seen the naked picture, I needed to know what went wrong—why he changed from a breathtaking boyfriend to a game-playing jerk in the course of one hour.

Pumped and ready to solve the picture mystery, I had Mom take me to school thirty minutes early so that I could talk to students before class. I strolled into the large common area in the center of the campus, and immediately the achingly familiar lines of Ethan's back caught my eye. He faced the wall, standing near a classroom door with one arm braced against the bricks. His head was tilted down, as if he were reading something.

I rushed toward him, and my plans to be frank crumbled. His shoulders, the back of his head—so familiar, strong, and beautiful—made me want to press my body against his back, to wrap my arms around his stomach and work my way around to the front of him. I wanted to touch his beautiful face and say, "Let's start over. Whatever went wrong, let's just fix it. There's too much feeling between us. We have to fix this."

I wanted him to smile at me and say, "Yes, let's start over." I wanted him to say my name.

With only a few steps left before I reached him, my eyes dropped to his lower legs.

He was not alone. A girl's legs faced his. She was leaning up against the wall. She had stepped out of one of her pink pumps, and her bare foot rubbed his ankle up under his jeans.

I veered to the right, so I wouldn't run into Ethan's back.

They must have heard me because the girl called out, "Polarity."

Her familiar voice shattered my heart. And as much as I wanted to keep walking away, I couldn't stop myself from turning to confront the horror I never would have imagined in my worst nightmare—Ethan and Cynthia, together, facing me. Cynthia's pale hand clasped Ethan's dark, strong arm. She tilted her head so her blond crimped hair touched Ethan's chest, and she flashed me her big, glossy smirk, "Hey, sup?"

My eyes bounced from her to Ethan. His face was blank. If I had been alone, I would have wailed in frustration at my stupidity for my pathetic daydream two minutes earlier. Instead, I nodded and spun around, walking toward the cafeteria.

I found an empty corner and opened a book—pretending to read. I focused on staying calm and figuring out how to make it through the rest of this long day.

Within minutes, Ethan sat down beside me. "Let's talk. I need to explain some things to you."

I gave him my coolest glance. "Whatever for? You owe me nothing." I hit my head with the heel of my hand. "Oh, why didn't I think of this sooner? You and Cynthia were together at Beauty. You rode the bus together every day. That's when this started." Now I understood his on-again-off-again game with me. He was a player. All that time I'd suspected he was juggling old feelings for Shanique with his new interest in me, I had the right game—just the wrong girl.

"No." His jaw clenched. "It's not what it looks like with Cynthia."

"Well, thanks, Ethan. That's good to know." I dropped my book into my book bag and stood. "Have a great day." I jerked around so fast I almost collided with Cynthia.

She quickly plopped into the seat I had vacated. "There you are, hunkie. Want to eat?"

Hunkie. Somehow I managed not to groan as I left them. I survived the day by putting one foot in front of the other and counting off the hours until I'd be out of Garcia forever.

After Tilly's mother picked her up that afternoon, I approached Tracey, who was standing in her usual spot about ten feet behind the benches. "I think you know who made that naked picture."

She stared straight ahead.

"I'm moving away in three weeks, and I'd really like to know before I leave." Her lack of response prodded me to switch tactics. "We drove by you walking along the highway alone after dark. Aren't you afraid? Don't your parents want you to be safe? Won't anyone at your house come and pick you up?"

Her expression never changed. Her puzzling behavior reminded me of Ethan. *Is she playing some kind of devious game, too?*

"You have only one posting on TeensterBlast, and it was the day Danny showed the picture—*Sup with cops at school.* Why did you post that? You knew what was up—you were in the classroom when it happened." Mom drove in. "My mom is here. Would you like to ride with us?"

Still staring ahead, Tracey said, "No." Her low voice had a brittle quality that jolted me and made me hope I wouldn't hear it again, even though I needed information from her.

"What can I do to get you to tell me what you know?"

She slowly angled her face toward me, and her bland expression shifted into her chilling, thin-lipped smile. Wordlessly, she started walking in the opposite direction, which led to the deserted practice field.

I gave up and headed to Mom's car.

Mom, beaming brightly, slapped one of her hands on the steering wheel as soon as I opened the door. "Guess who I ran into today at the grocery store?"

"I give up."

"Ethan's grandmother." She popped her hand again as if it were an exclamation point.

"Cool." I used my flattest voice, hoping she'd abandon the topic.

"And, guess what she said?"

I was so frustrated with the universe, I could weep. "Just tell me, Mom."

"They're moving at the end of the semester—to San Antonio, where his mother will be working. Isn't that something—you're both moving? I'm surprised you haven't mentioned this to me. Are you and Ethan not speaking to each other?"

"We speak, but only about"— *Cynthia*—"casual stuff."

She nodded and glanced at me with raised eyebrows. "And moving is not the only coincidence."

Silence hung in the car. Mom liked to make me pull information out of her. We were coming up on our trailer park in the distance.

I sighed. "What's the other coincidence?"

"Ethan got a laptop, too. I'm surprised you didn't know this. Don't you two want to e-mail and Skype after you move?"

"Guess not," I said, bitterly thinking that Skyping with Ethan might work better than an in-person relationship. It would be easier for him to keep Cynthia and me both dangling.

That night, Ethan phoned me. I was burning with curiosity about what he might say, but I shook my head at Mom when she offered me the phone. My pride was bigger than my curiosity. To be dumped for Cynthia was beyond bearable.

Mom stared at me as she talked to Ethan. "Oh, I'm sorry, Ethan. She's not available."

After she turned off her phone, she came and sat next to me. "Polarity, I don't like lying to your friends. Tell me what is going on."

"Nothing. I just want to end all connections in Garcia. No point in gabbing with people I'll never see again after we move."

By the time my final week at Garcia arrived, Ethan and Cynthia were the hot item—together everywhere—Tracey was as tight-lipped as ever, and with only days left in Garcia, I was frantic to know who made and posted the picture.

One day, Ethan wasn't in first or second period. I was furious at myself for caring, but all morning, he and Cynthia were missing. At lunch, I peeked into the cafeteria a couple of times, and they weren't there, either.

After lunch, when I walked past the office, Cynthia was sitting in the waiting area, with one of the school security guards standing nearby. She raised her red, watery eyes to meet mine.

Alarms went off in my head. *Something must have happened to Ethan.* I barged into the waiting area. "Cynthia, is Ethan okay?"

The security guard stepped forward. "You'll have to go outside—move on to your class."

I looked from Cynthia's raccoon mascara stains to the guard's stern, blank expression and back again. "Ethan," I said louder. "Where is he?"

She glared at me. "Don't act like you aren't in on this. You probably put him up to it."

The door to the principal's office swung open, and Ethan came out. He was not injured, but his concerned gaze locked on me. In two long, quick steps, he was by my side. "It's okay. Everything is okay." He put his hand on my arm.

Mr. Justin followed close behind Ethan, and the security guard edged closer to me, still saying something about going to class.

Mr. Justin said to the guard, "That's all right. I actually was going to send for her. She can stay." He said to Cynthia, "Okay, you can come in now. Then, Polarity, after we're done, I'll talk with you."

Cynthia yanked herself to her feet. But instead of heading into the office, she made a beeline to Ethan. "I hate you, Ethan Rawls. You're nothing but a pathetic snitch. I hate you." She hadn't even glanced at me during her angry attack, but Ethan put one arm in front of me and eased me behind him, using himself as a barrier between us.

A moment later, Ethan and I were alone—or as alone as possible, in a glassed-in reception area with student aides, office staff, and passing students gawking our way. I stepped out from behind Ethan. "What's going on?"

"Over the Thanksgiving break, friends told me that Cynthia made a stack of printouts of your picture. She's been playing little games with them, giving them out as jokes."

Nausea washed over me. *Would this ever end?*

"I was hanging out with her, hoping she'd spill, and she did. She brought a stack to school today, and I narced."

I sat down. "So you aren't really her boyfriend? It was just to trick her?" Hearing this and being so close to his body at the same time had my heart stuttering.

He sat next to me and looked into my eyes. "No. Never. And I wanted to tell you. I didn't want you to believe I was with her."

"That's why you followed me into the cafeteria the day she came back from Beauty and phoned me later?"

He nodded.

Okay. His news thrilled me, but it didn't explain why, on the day he held my hand, he so abruptly broke up with me. "Long before Thanksgiving, before Cynthia came back to United—that day you put your books in my locker and we had lunch together, what happened?"

He frowned and something like pain flashed in his eyes.

"It was like you flipped a switch on us. Turned us off."

His jaw clenched. "Yeah. There's that. I still need to explain that." He rested his elbows on his knees and tilted his head downward. "I'll clear that up, but right now I want Cynthia to tell who made the picture and sent her the link. I've pushed her this far. Now I want the principal to get the rest out of her."

"Ethan, tell me why you stopped hanging out with me." I didn't want another minute to pass with my question unanswered.

"Okay." He straightened up and looked at me again. "You deserve to know the truth." He reached into his back pocket and pulled out his wallet. He stared at it for a moment then back at me with concern in his eyes. "You being with me was calling attention to you. The wrong kind of attention. I broke it off hoping that—"

The door to the principal's office opened. Ethan quickly put his wallet back into his pocket. Mr. Justin came out, glanced at us, and signaled the security guard to come closer. "Ethan and Polarity, I'd like to talk with you now. Come with me." He turned to the guard, who was now standing next to us. "Cynthia will wait in my office— just stay close in case she needs anything."

Mr. Justin, with an air that this event was a normal part of his routine, led us into a small conference room. Ethan and I sat on one side of the table with the principal across from us, facing us.

"Did she tell you who sent her the link to the picture?" Ethan asked.

Mr. Justin shook his head. "No. And I think she may truly not know. I think at this point, she's so mad she'd snitch on who sent it to her if she knew."

Ethan clenched his fists on his thighs. "Unless she did it herself."

"Yeah." He nodded respectfully at Ethan, almost as if Ethan were a staff member instead of a student. "You're right." But Mr. Justin's expression shifted slightly, and a hint of irritation crept into his voice when he addressed me. "Polarity, I'm sorry for all that you've been through with this picture, and I'm grateful to Ethan for making sure that the stack she brought to school today didn't get out of her book bag."

I took his tone to mean that he, too, assumed I had posed for the picture.

"Kids just don't think when they make a picture." Having confirmed that he believed I'd done it as a prank, he shifted into lecture mode. "These days, once a picture is made and shared digitally, it never ends."

Ethan put one fist on the table and leaned forward. His words came out in a deep growl. "Polarity didn't pose for that picture."

Mr. Justin's expression froze, and he pulled back slightly. "Okay. How did the picture get made?"

Ethan glared at him. "We haven't figured that out yet, or you'd know. But while we're here, I have one more person to narc on." He reached for his wallet again and quickly pulled out a folded sheet of paper.

I held my breath. This had to be a copy of the naked picture.

With the sheet in one hand, he put his other hand on my shoulder. "I'm sorry you have to see this. Are you ready?"

His eyes locked with mine, and we breathed in and out in sync.

I nodded. "Ready."

Ethan unfolded the sheet and laid it face up on the table. He or someone had blacked out my private parts. The picture was a copy of the original one with the textbox:

Hi, I really need my own special hotie.
Come on and get me. Poetic Polaritey.

Below the textbox, someone had written in red magic marker. "Got her hotie now—a big black brutha."

Ethan flipped the page over and pointed to a date and time written on the back—right before seventh period on the day he dumped me. He must have found it on my locker. That was when he rushed out of class at the end of the period and didn't show up for our after-school date. "This was taped on Polarity's locker at this time. If you check your camera surveillance records for the ten minutes prior to this time, you'll see who put it on."

Mr. Justin took the picture. "Do you know who it is?"

Ethan nodded. "Brad Philips."

Why would Brad have put out the picture that day? The only conversation I'd had with him was on the day Danny got busted for saying the N-word in the cafeteria. And then the day Ethan and I held hands in the cafeteria, Brad had called out, "Hey. Come on—you bruthas are made to play football."

Mr. Justin headed out the door. "I'll check it and be right back."

Ethan scooted his chair closer to mine. "When I found that picture on your locker, I realized that being with me was making things worse for you. Some guys are really torqued that I won't do athletics. Seeing us together gave them one more way to dig at me."

"And you started leaving classes early so you could watch my locker."

He nodded.

"But why didn't you tell me?"

"I know how protective you are. You would have gone after whoever labeled me a 'big black brutha.' I heard what you did with Danny while I was gone. And I want the root of the picture—not just who the idiot was who taped it onto your locker. It was easy to find out that Brad taped it on, but it took some digging to find out he got the picture from Cynthia."

"How did you find out it was Brad?"

"I suspected because he's always called me 'brutha.' I found out for sure by just asking around. Several people saw him stick it on. But it wasn't until Thanksgiving break at a cookout at Shanique's house that I caught on to Cynthia. Some students sort of crashed—including Cynthia. She dropped hints that she was planning a comeback with your picture."

Mr. Justin swung open the door. "Bingo. Good work, Ethan." He stood in the open doorway and motioned for us to come out. "I'm going to send you two to class. We'll keep working with Cynthia and Brad. We've got someone coming from the sheriff's office to review what we're doing. Hopefully, we'll get to the source." He led us back into the main reception area and told a secretary to give us passes to class.

I stopped before going to the secretary's desk. Scooter's guidance about keeping people accountable rang in my head. I wanted to be sure that some other issue didn't push my business off the principal's plate. "Mr. Justin, will you let me know what you find out? Keep me updated?"

"Yes," he said too quickly.

"When? When will you give me an update?" Scooter's voice said *Get it in writing*, but I settled for a verbal statement in front of witnesses.

"Um. I'll give you something by the end of the day, for sure—if not sooner. Okay?"

I nodded. "Thanks."

He was good for his word. Toward the end of seventh period, Ethan and I were called to the office. Mr. Justin invited us into his private area and asked us to sit. "I'm afraid I don't have anything on the origin of the picture. But the good news is that Cynthia named other students that she gave a copy to. A couple of those kids said they threw their copy away, but the rest brought them in. They'll all be getting consequences here on campus, and Brad and Cynthia will report to Beauty tomorrow."

I asked, "Did anyone from the sheriff's office talk to Cynthia?"

"Yes."

I stood. "Thanks." There was nothing else here that would help me figure out who made the picture. I was disappointed but not surprised. It was still going to be up to me to get to the bottom of it.

Ethan stood and stepped toward the principal. "What else are you going to do?" His jaw clenched. "Someone started that picture, posted it online."

Mr. Justin sighed. "I guess a case is never actually closed until all questions are answered, but I don't have any next steps at this point.

Maybe something else will come up. We could offer a reward, but that would call a lot of attention to it." He glanced at me. "I don't know if you want that."

He was right—I wouldn't want a reward posted. I walked out, and Ethan followed me.

CHAPTER 15

AFTER SCHOOL, ETHAN WALKED WITH me to the parent pickup area. Tilly wasn't there yet, so we sat on the bench alone.

I clutched my book bag on my lap. "Can I ask you something?"

"Sure." He curved his arm around my back and shifted closer to me. "Are you okay?"

"It's just I want to talk about the picture and what it, what it means to us—you and me."

His jaw tensed. "I won't stop until I figure out who did it."

"I won't forget it, either, but I don't need to be rescued."

"I know you don't need to be rescued. But I need to do the same thing for you that you did for me."

There must have been sounds and movement around us, but all I could see was this beautiful boy who I wanted in my life. And all I could hear was a voice in my head. *He doesn't have feelings for me, he just needs to save someone—to pay me back.* I made myself ask the hardest question I've ever asked anyone in my life. "Ethan, is that the reason you're hanging out with me today?"

He looked at me, shocked.

"Are you with me just because you need to save me and pay me back, not because you really care about me?"

Anger sparked in his eyes. He jerked his face towards the parent pickup driveway for a moment, and his chest heaved.

Slowly, he turned and locked eyes with me. He was ready to speak. I made myself ready to hear.

Tilly plopped onto the bench, wedging herself between us. Frowning, she looked up into my eyes. "Where's Mama?"

We scooted apart to make more room. Tilly's anxious face was a reprieve from the heart-breaking words I was expecting Ethan to say: *Yes, it is about payback—that's all.*

I tore my attention away from him and scanned the area. Raymond, who must have been with Tilly, was approaching us. All the other parent-pickup students except Tracey were gone. "Oh, Tilly, Mama hasn't come yet? She's just a little late. She'll be here soon."

Raymond stopped next to the bench. "Don't you worry, Tilly. I'll stay here until she comes. You won't be alone."

Ethan kept his gaze focused on me. Tilly looked with concern at Raymond and back at me. She took my arm in her short, soft hands and held on tight.

I made brief eye contact with Ethan over her head. As much as I needed his answer, I was afraid of what the answer might be, and I couldn't tell if the scowl taking over his face was from anger or concern.

We spent the next few minutes distracting Tilly by talking about the papers she had done in class. Even though she nodded and commented about her worksheets, she kept one hand gripping my arm. Mom drove up, but Tilly wouldn't let go of me, so Ethan went to Mom's car and explained.

Mom parked and joined us in the wait. She, Ethan, and Raymond stood in front of Tilly and me, as the two of us sat on the bench, talking about her drawing of a blue butterfly from art class. Tracey stood quietly about ten feet behind us, bleakly pointed toward the parent pickup lane.

Suddenly, an electronic voice said, "Tilly, get your phone and push Mama button."

We all looked at Tilly. Her eyes opened wide, and her mouth formed an O.

"Tilly, get your phone and push Mama button."

She raised her loose, long shirt and attempted to unzip her fanny pack. I helped her open it, and inside was a bulky, pink phone with one bright, blinking, happy-face button on it. The phone was the same shape and size as the black one from Technology Integrations Horizons.

"Tilly, get your phone and push Mama button."

Tilly always wore the fanny pack, but I'd never seen what was in it. I figured it was her crayons or something personal. With her short, chubby pointing finger she pushed the large, blinking button.

"Tilly, are you okay?" asked a human voice, on speaker. "It's Mama."

Tilly nodded and smiled up at me.

"Tilly?" The voice sounded worried and a little frail. "Tilly, are you there?"

I said, "She's here, ma'am. She's nodding. Tilly, say hello."

"Lo, Mama."

Her mom asked, "Is she okay? Still at school?"

"Yes, ma'am, she's fine."

"I'm so sorry. I dozed off and just woke up. I'll be there as quick as I can—I'm just a few blocks away. Can someone wait with her until I get there?"

"Sure. Take your time." I took Tilly's phone from her hand.

Raymond said, "Tilly, I didn't know you carry a cell phone. Did you have it last year? At Star campus?"

Tilly nodded and pointed to the phone. "Mama."

Chills washed over me. I rotated the phone in my hands and found a seam in the pink covering, and next to it was a barely visible slide switch. I caught it with my thumbnail. The pink case popped open with a soft click, and I removed the cover and handed it to Ethan. The phone inside was identical to the one Dad had brought home from Technology Integrations Horizons.

I went to the picture and video files. Tilly would never have been capable of removing the pink cover or using the photo apps. Some eerie force drew my eyes back to Tracey.

For once she wasn't staring ahead. Her steady eyes met mine. And her mouth was curled into the beginning of her thin-lipped smile.

"Look," said Ethan, bending down to get a better view of the phone in my hands. "Video. E-mail. Edit. Zoom. Forward. Reverse. File. Print. Quite a little camera."

There was a video in the File section. I pushed Play. Immediately, girls' voices giggled and whispered as the camera focused on a single curtained shower stall in the Star locker room. The distance and angle of the camera told me that the person filming was standing back, about ten feet, probably in another shower stall across from the one being filmed. Girls in varying stages of dress crossed back and forth, not seeming to be aware that they were being filmed.

"Oh my gosh," Mom said. She pointed to Ethan and Raymond. "Both of you—over there. You two can't see this."

They wordlessly backed away.

Mom's interruption had startled me into stopping the video. I fumbled through the start process, and the video restarted from the beginning. The camera zoomed in and back out once, not targeting any particular girl—still holding steady on the shower curtain. This went on for minutes, and I began to think maybe this was all there was—just the curtain with an occasional locker door clang or giggle or muffled voice in the background.

Mom reached for the camera. "This is ridiculous. Who would make such a stupid, time-wasting—"

"Wait," I said, blocking her reaching hand with my own. "Something might happen. I need to see it all."

Her hand froze. In my peripheral vision, I could see her struggling to keep her public niceness as she dealt with my defiance. But I kept focused on the shower curtain. *There has to be something here. There has to be. This must be the phone that took the original picture. This filming took place in the shower room. There has to be something here.*

Then a clear voice spoke up in the video—Cynthia's distinct in-charge command: "Okay. Now."

The camera slowly turned to capture her standing next to the shower curtain, surrounded by a crowd of girls.

"Mama," Tilly said, swinging her legs back and forth on the bench.

Her mom, a thin, white-haired lady, approached us. She stood next to Mom, where Ethan had been. Mom whispered something to her.

In the video, Cynthia and another girl positioned themselves on either side of the shower stall. Each girl held one hand poised by the curtain, ready to yank it open. With her free hand, Cynthia directed the others, who crowded around the front of the curtain.

The taunts of my first day at Garcia rang out, mixed in with more giggling.

"Yoohoo. Poetic Polarity. Where are you?"

"You looking for the Poet of the Park?"

The voices piled atop each other—some repeating taunts, others throwing out new ones.

"Yeah. The trailer park."

"You must mean Bean Pole Polarity."

"Polarity, come on out. You need us to help you in there?"

A voice—it took an instant for me to recognize as my own—said, "No. I'll be out in a minute. Almost finished." My familiar but oddly foreign-sounding speech yanked me back into that terrible day.

Cynthia loudly whispered, "Now!"

She pulled one curtain open to expose the left half of my naked body. The bottom part of my body was covered by the heads and shoulders of the crowd of girls. My hand flew up, grabbed at, and missed the curtain.

The stark terror on my videoed face made me gasp. The whites popped out all around my irises, and my mouth opened in a scream that rose above the wild giggling of the other girls. The second curtain jerked open, and my towel fell from my other hand as I grabbed at the second curtain. Girls rushed past the stall, blurring the video, hooting and laughing.

One clear point gave a full shot of me. My hands, which in the Internet picture appeared to be waving, were widespread and reaching in desperation for the curtains on both sides. For a split second, my open, terrorized mouth slipped into an embarrassed grin.

One curtain fell shut, then the other.

Cynthia high-fived her curtain partner, and with wicked smirks, they went out of the camera range. The only sound left was my crying.

Slowly the camera rotated past a blur of walls, lockers, and showers, as if the person holding it rolled the camera over. The automatic focus shifted as the lens pointed to a close-up of green and orange checkerboard tile.

Keep rotating the camera. Show your face.

A dark curtain blurred out half the picture, and before the lens could refocus on the curtain, the film stopped.

I clicked into the "stills" file and found both pictures that had been posted: the original and the "Sorry Polaritey" one.

I turned off the camera and set it gently in my lap. Adrenaline had kept me focused during the viewing, but now I trembled all over. Relief at having proof of my innocence collided with my shock at the viciousness in the scene. Feelings swirled.

Ethan rushed forward and put a hand on my shoulder. "Are you okay?" His touch grounded me.

Tilly patted my other shoulder with her soft little hand. "Mean gulls."

Raymond, who like Ethan must have guessed what was on the video even though they had only heard it, said, "I knew it. I knew that there was something about the mean girls. I knew it. I told Mrs. Sanchez we needed to follow up on what Tilly said. I told her."

I put my hand up on Ethan's, which was still caressing my shoulder. "This proves I didn't do anything. This proves my innocence."

He squeezed my shoulder, and the caring in his eyes touched my heart. Tilly laid her head on my other shoulder and held onto my arm.

"Yes, it does, but who filmed it?" Mom snatched the camera from me. "I want to know who did this. After all I've been through with this mess, there's still nothing to prove who took the picture."

It didn't surprise me that Mom had completely glossed over the impact of this video on my life. She single-mindedly focused on finding the guilty and getting rewarded for her part in the drama.

I looked back at Tracey, who met my eyes without moving or showing any facial expression. That dark curtain that covered part of the lens at the end had to be her long hair. But I couldn't make myself call her out. She looked so alone, standing there watching us. And I couldn't stop thinking about all the times I called her Arvey and how Shanique said children started taunting her in third grade because of the sign by her trailer.

Ethan was still holding the pink cover with his free hand. "Here's a tag inside that says, 'Tech Friends, San Antonio, TX.'"

"Yes," said Tilly's mom. "It's a non-profit—business people that make assistive technology for the handicapped. I wanted Tilly to have an emergency phone, to always be able to reach me. But we didn't even know about the camera. We never used the phone until today."

Mom started digging into her purse, as if searching for her car keys. "I need to take it over to the ninth-grade school. This video was made last year and caused a lot of problems. Mrs. Sanchez will need to see it."

"Oh, certainly. I'm so sorry this happened. Who is that little girl in the shower? Poor child."

Little? When I had seen my naked picture, I saw my five-foot-eight frame. I'd been so tall—towering even over my own mother forever—that *little* was not a word that remotely fit what I saw in the photo. But hearing Tilly's mother made me understand that with nothing else in the picture to serve as a ratio to my true size, it did look like a little girl.

We were quiet for a moment, leaving the question unanswered. Raymond studied the ground, and Ethan said, "A new girl who went to school there last year."

"Poor child," she said again. She reached for Tilly's hand. "Let's go home, dear."

Tilly and I stood, and she wrapped her arms around my waist and laid her head against my shoulder. Her soft little hands patted my back. The embrace was beyond her usual good-bye, and it filled me with awe at her intuitive ability to tune into my emotions. She couldn't read or do math or work through technical processes like most people her age, but she was always on the pulse-beat of the deep-down real things.

Mom, with her keys in hand, thrust the camera at me. "We're going to the ninth-grade campus."

Ethan said, "I'm coming with you."

Mom handed Ethan her phone. "Okay, but let your grandmother know."

Raymond started sprinting toward the staff parking lot. "I'll meet you over there."

By the time we were rolling, Ethan had finished talking to his grandmother. "Mrs. Weeks, okay to Google Tech Friends on your phone?"

"Sure. I was thinking the same thing."

While he searched, Mom fumed. "I can't wait to show that evil woman this video. After all she put us through. After all her idiotic assumptions. After all her goody-goody speeches. I can't wait to show her the truth."

Good thing other concerns held Ethan's and Mom's attention. I rolled my eyes. *And what about your idiotic assumptions about me, Mom? What about all the times I told the truth and you didn't believe me?* But I didn't want Ethan slammed with a full dose of how warped Mom could be.

I fast-forwarded to the end of the video again. That dark curtain had to be Tracey's hair.

Ethan read aloud, "'Non-profit devoted to making technology work for the handicapped. Show us the need, and we will find the way.'"

Mom asked, "Do they list the people who work for it?"

"I don't see anything like that, but here's a list: 'Donors Who Contribute Engineering and Resources.'"

"Check for Technology Integrations Horizons."

I leaned closer to Ethan to look at Mom's phone with him. "It's the first one listed."

Ethan said, "This is the company I found with reverse lookup."

I nodded. "Right. The owner must have donated the phone to Tech Friends before he died. Dad said no one noticed some missing phones or took them off the company's billing package."

The ninth-grade campus grounds were clear, with just a few cars in the faculty parking lot. When we entered the reception area, Mrs. Sanchez was still in her office, sitting at her desk.

"We need to talk with you. Now," Mom said marching toward her open office door, ignoring Miss Smart who stood to intervene. Ethan and I followed, and within seconds, Raymond shot in behind us.

"Shut that door," Mom said to Raymond. "You two stay over there." She didn't have to tell Raymond and Ethan they weren't allowed to see, but she was in take-charge mode, full speed. "Polarity, you don't have to put yourself through this again."

I stayed beside her. I needed to see the whole thing again. The first time I watched it, I was reeling from the idea that Tilly had a phone, someone sneaked it out of Tilly's fanny pack, and videoed me. Seeing my horrified face was like viewing something from a dream. I knew it was me. I knew it was my face. But it didn't look like me. Back on my first day at Garcia, in the moments that the video was taken, I was so distracted by the girls' name-calling and my embarrassment, I had lost touch with what I looked like. Now I wanted to see it again to drill into my understanding how my naked picture came out of that video. And I wanted to see the long-awaited evidence one more time that would guarantee that everyone would believe me.

Mom started running it with Mrs. Sanchez and me on either side of her. "Just wait until you see this—see what happened in your school, see how you wouldn't believe us all those months. Just wait until you see."

Almost immediately, Mrs. Sanchez brought both her hands to cover her mouth. She turned her head from side to side. Raymond pulled off his cap and rubbed his head. Ethan's fists clenched. His chest heaved. I lost track of everyone in Mrs. Sanchez's office as the video got closer to the part that was used to create the photo.

Mesmerized with the video, I realized that the truth had been there all along. I'd known the girls had jerked the curtain. I'd known that anyone at any time could take a picture. But I could never see myself doing that wacky pose. So, instead of trying to figure out logically how it happened, I resisted believing it actually happened. A surge of anger at my own blindness howled inside my head. *Like your own bad breath. It's easier to assume it isn't there than to dig deep, find the truth, and fix it.*

"Here," I said. I took the camera from Mom and pushed pause—that slender slice of video when my horrified mouth for one second turned upward into an embarrassed smile. A smile that was toothy and exaggerated by my fear. My hands still splayed, grabbing for both sides of the curtain, I looked like a clownish dancer. All I had been thinking about was how to cover myself and not let them see me cry. I never thought grabbing some curtains quickly could look like a waving pose.

Mrs. Sanchez pulled a copy of the printout from her file cabinet. The center of my body had been cut out, but when she held it next to the camera, my face, hands, and the textbox were a perfect match.

I pushed play. "There's one more thing to see." We viewed the aftermath, including my crying. When we reached the final moments where the camera focused on the up-close orange and green checkerboard inside a shower stall, Mom and Mrs. Sanchez drew nearer to the camera. I think they were hoping to see a face, as I had. The dark curtain blurred across half the screen.

I pushed Pause. "I think Tracey filmed. Her hair always falls over her face like a curtain. She was probably turning the camera around as she got ready to pause it, and accidentally filmed her hair. And she was in our gym class—she could have easily snooped into Tilly's fanny pack while—"

Mom's face lit up, like a child's on Christmas morning. "That's it. Of course, it had to be her." She conveniently forgot her earlier claim that Tracey wasn't smart enough to pull it off. "She did it because you called her the wrong name."

Mrs. Sanchez frowned. "What wrong name?"

"I called her Arvey—thinking that was her real name. I didn't know her name was Tracey. Shanique told me that students started calling Tracey 'RV' in elementary school because of an 'RV Resort' sign by her trailer. She hates that name, and I think for some reason making the picture was a way to get back at me for not calling her Tracey."

Ethan, still standing with Raymond in their out-of-viewing-range corner, said, "Some of the teachers even call her 'RV.' In Polarity's incident report, she quotes Mr. Hill using 'Arvey.'"

When she faced me, Mrs. Sanchez's eyes were red-rimmed, sad. "I saw 'Arvey' in your report, but I thought you just had a student's name wrong because you were so new to the campus." She didn't say it out loud, but she surely remembered the day at Beauty when I asked her about Arvey. Before we could dig into the mix-up, Mom had stormed in and ordered Mrs. Sanchez out. "I wonder, though, why she spelled your name wrong. The next day, when I had all the students write about what happened, none of them, including Tracey, used the *ey*."

Mom huffed and put her hands on her hips. "Mrs. Sanchez, it is so obvious. You clearly have no understanding of human behavior. Tracey is fed up with people getting her name wrong. *Of course* she would deliberately post Polarity's wrong. It's a tiny way of getting back for all the years of people bullying her by calling her 'RV.' Even your teachers are engaged in the mindless bullying of the child. She has no other defenses. Nothing."

I gazed down at the final frame—at Tracey's dark curtain blurred over the orange and green tile. I had been bullied in school, especially while we lived in Garcia. But she'd had a lifetime of being labeled by everyone, of living in the out-of-place double-wide in a park for sleek travel trailers, of witnessing the park deteriorate into—

"Polarity."

I had forgotten all the others in the room. At first I wasn't sure who had spoken my name.

"Polarity." Tears covered Mrs. Sanchez's face. "I am so, so very sorry. You were telling the truth. You did the right thing, every step of the way. I am so sorry that I didn't know. So sorry for all that you and your parents went through. I will follow up immediately with all the girls in the video. And we'll use the process of elimination to figure out which girls in the class could have had the opportunity to use this camera that day."

Hard sobbing—gasping, moaning, loud, out of control—broke through my daze. *Who is that? Is that me?*

But in the next heartbeat, I knew it was Mom.

Mrs. Sanchez put her hand on Mom's shoulder. "I'm so sorry, Mrs. Weeks."

Mom and Mrs. Sanchez wrapped their arms around each other, and Mrs. Sanchez, patting and soothing Mom, looked over Mom's shoulder toward Raymond. Softly she said, "Officer Raymond, you were right all along."

Raymond sniffed loudly and waved his hand as he left, shaking his head.

Ethan's eyes—full of relief and something else, deep and stirring, that I couldn't identify—linked with mine.

I stepped into his warm, protective arms and wished I could stay that safe for the rest of my life. He guided me out into the waiting room, and we left Mom and Mrs. Sanchez working through their tears.

Miss Smart popped up and beamed at Ethan. She pantomimed quick clapping motions. Mrs. Sanchez, who'd apparently freed herself from Mom, stepped up from behind us. "Oh, Miss Smart. You can go home now."

I could hear Mom still in Mrs. Sanchez's office talking to Dad on the phone.

Mrs. Sanchez put her hand on my arm and lowered her voice. "I'm going to place a call to the sheriff while your mother is still in my office. You are welcome to join us, or you may wait out here with Ethan."

Duh. "Thank you. I'll wait out here."

Miss Smart slipped past us, smoothing back her ponytail and winking at Ethan on her way out. Mrs. Sanchez went back into her office and closed her door.

Ethan put his hands on either side of my face and looked into my eyes. "Are you okay?"

"Yes, I am."

"What are you thinking?" he asked as he lowered his hands from my face.

"The truth was there all along, and I didn't see it." We walked to

244

the bench in the corner. "What else is going on around me right now that I don't see?"

"You've got a lot going on in there." As we sat, he tapped my head with his finger and gently slid his hand down until his palm was against my cheek.

My cheek, of its own free will, burrowed into his cupped hand for a moment.

The muffled voice of the sheriff on speakerphone, talking with Mom and Mrs. Sanchez, drifted through the closed door.

We sat, and even though my heart was racing from our proximity and every fiber of me just wanted to lean closer, I made myself confront hard questions. "Ethan, when you were still at Beauty, and I was circulating in the cafeteria, I never even landed in the corner where the black students sit. I didn't make a decision not to sit there, I just never noticed or considered sitting there. Until you came back. Why is that? Why didn't I see what I was doing?" I glanced down at Tilly's phone still in my hands. "And I never realized before I went to the safe house that there are more black students in protective services than white. And I never noticed before Beauty that more black students get kicked out of school."

He studied me, and I could see layers of understanding and patience in his eyes—as if he had a deeper knowing of the world than I did, but he wasn't holding my ignorance against me. "I guess people don't see their own way of seeing. They don't mean harm by it. They just don't see."

I said what was in my heart. "I'm glad that all of this happened— not just because of what I've learned but because it gave me you."

"Polarity, I—"

"Wait, let me finish." I had to go back to the question I'd asked him before Tilly wedged between us earlier, but I couldn't look at him while I did. I faced the aquarium where the mollies were still swimming on their side only. "The whole picture thing... There's nothing left to do. Nothing you can do to help. So if that's why you've hung out with me, you're free now."

He exhaled sharply. With my eyes still on the mollies, I waited for his answer.

One little molly darted past where the barrier had been and into the old betta's side. I gasped.

"What?" Ethan asked.

"Look," I whispered.

The molly immediately swam back into the home territory and glided back and forth along the line where the barrier had been.

For an instant, all movement in the aquarium stopped.

The single molly crossed the line again.

Soon another and another molly crossed over, and within seconds, the whole aquarium was full of mollies.

Ethan put one arm around my shoulder and the other hand on my chin. He pulled my face toward his own. He lowered his lips close to mine and looked at me with questioning eyes.

I answered by closing my eyes and the gap between our lips. Warmth. Connection. Ethan.

When nothing could possibly have been more wonderful, his lips started parting, and my own lips, with some instinctive knowing, followed his lead. I heard a moan—too high-pitched to be Ethan. Even though only a small part of us was touching, my whole body melted, and a core part of me pulled closer to the solid, magnetic warmth of him. Time stood still or sped or ceased altogether.

Too soon, the sheriff's call ended, and the women's conversation moved closer to the doorway. Our lips separated despite the powerful force that pulled them together.

Still close to my face, Ethan said, "It was never about paying back. Never."

It was three days before my withdrawal date. The nightmare of my picture had been resolved, dropping a boulder from my shoulders. I knew today, I'd see Ethan, talk with him, and touch him—and knowing that, especially now that the picture mystery was solved, was the most uplifting experience of my life.

I wasn't even worried about Tracey. I didn't think she'd be able to upload anything else. Her somber gaze at me yesterday somehow made me think that she knew I was on to her. And I had confidence that Mrs. Sanchez would follow up with her.

Five minutes into first-period geometry, a student aide came into the room with a note. Mr. Jeffrey read the message. "Polarity, you're needed in the office."

I stood, and as I passed his desk, he said softly, "Mrs. Gamez's office."

From the back of the room, Ethan gave me a questioning, concerned frown. I shrugged on my way out, hoping he wouldn't worry. But, walking down the hallway, I remembered the horror of the time Mr. Hill sent me to the office at Star. I hoped this was just another bullying discussion session.

The door to Mrs. Gamez's office was closed, but her receptionist, who was talking on the phone, angled her head and pointed to the door, signaling me to go on in.

Mrs. Sanchez, Tracey, and Mrs. Gamez sat on the sunflower sofa. Tracey, with her head tilted downward, seemed smaller than ever, pulled back into the sofa between the two women. Her hands were fists on her lap. Her feet and legs were pulled into the sofa, as if she were trying to slide them underneath her.

Mrs. Sanchez said, "Polarity, we're going to talk about the picture, and we were wondering if you'd mind joining us?"

"Sure—I mean, no, I don't mind." There was no place for me to sit. Mrs. Gamez stood and rolled her desk chair from behind her computer and parked it in front of the sofa, so that it squarely faced Tracey.

Mrs. Sanchez, in her kindest, gentlest tone, asked, "Tracey, can you tell us about the picture?"

Tracey didn't move at first. Her curtain of hair covered her face. Still with her head down, she shrugged.

Probably a full minute went by with no one speaking. At one point, Mrs. Sanchez and I made eye contact, and she shook her head slightly, as if she didn't want me to speak.

How much easier to be the victim here and not the one who did the crime! It would have killed me at that moment to be in Tracey's place. Despite all the pain she'd caused, a part of me wanted to say, "Let's forget it. It's over. She won't do it again." But Tracey needed to own the consequences.

Mrs. Sanchez repeated her question in the same soft tone three times.

The last time she asked it, Tracey rolled one of her fists on her lap so that it was now facing palm up. She opened her hand. There was a small silver pen drive in her palm.

"I confess." After so long a silence, her brittle voice was loud in the small room.

Her head was still down, and her face was covered.

Mrs. Sanchez asked, "Did you load the picture on this?"

Tracey nodded.

Mrs. Sanchez took the pen drive. "Did you film the video and extract the picture and do the graffiti and textbox?"

She nodded again.

"Did you upload it onto the Internet?"

Another nod.

"Did anyone help you?"

Tracey gave Mrs. Sanchez a sidelong look, as if surprised by the question. "No. I did it alone."

"Is there anything you'd like to say to Polarity? If not, we'll send her back to class now."

Tracey raised her head up and pushed her hair behind her ears. "I'm sorry, Polarity." Her voice was flat, and before I mumbled a thanks, her head went down again. "I mean it this time. I didn't mean it in the textbox. That was just my sorry note like the one you stuck on my desk."

Mrs. Gamez said, "Polarity, it's best for you to go back to class now. Thank you for coming in."

Tracey remained frozen.

Mrs. Sanchez nodded in agreement. "We thought we might need

your help in understanding what happened, but Tracey has been cooperative and truthful, so we can work with her from here."

"May I ask Tracey a question first?"

Mrs. Sanchez asked Tracey. "Is it all right with you if Polarity asks you a question?"

Tracey nodded, raised her head, and met my eyes.

"Why did you do it, Tracey?"

"To help you." Her voice was hard and vulnerable at the same time.

"I don't understand." This was the last thing I expected her to say. *Was she trying to teach me a lesson?* "How would it help me?"

"Cynthia and them bullied you all day, and I heard them making a plan for P.E., and I borrowed Tilly's camera and filmed them doing it. I waited to give you the pen drive after school, so you could take it to the principal. That's what we're supposed to do when someone gets bullied. We're supposed to tell."

The memory of that afternoon rushed back. *She was sitting on the curb about a block from school. She smiled when she spotted me and fell into step with me.* "But Danny came by on his bike, and you ran home."

She nodded. "And I was going to give it to you and your mother the next day when it rained…" She lowered her head again.

"But Mom and I called you 'Arvey,' and you thought we were bullying you just like everyone else does. Is that why you made the still shot?"

She nodded. The two women continued to inspect her closely, almost as if they were on alert for any sign that she might be getting too upset by the questions.

"And you spelled Polarity wrong because you wanted my name to be wrong, too?"

She nodded.

"Why did you use two different computers to upload the picture?"

Talking to her chest, she said, "The first one I used, someone left at my house. But it stopped working. So the second one I had to upload at school."

"Why did you send the text to Cynthia?"

She shrugged.

Mrs. Sanchez met my gaze. "Thank you, Polarity. That clears up everything. Would you like to leave now?"

I started to stand, but I needed to say more to Tracey. "Tracey, I apologize again for calling you 'Arvey' all that time."

Her whole body, already still, stiffened.

"I wouldn't have done it if I had known your real name."

One hand slipped up under her hair, as if swiping a tear.

"I hope you never do anything like the picture again because it caused a lot of trouble, but there's something important I want you to know."

She slowly raised her head and faced me with damp, red eyes.

Memory took me back to that night Grandma explained why she was so happy in spite of the horrors she had survived. I wanted to do what Grandma had done—leave the bad times behind so I could enjoy the good times. I wanted to close the door on this whole drama.

"Tracey, I forgive you."

I stood and rolled Mrs. Gamez's chair back to her desk. I stopped with my hand on the doorknob. Tracey's head hung even lower, and her hands were wrapped around her own stomach.

"Tracey—one more thing."

She raised her eyes to meet mine.

"If you have to go to Beauty"—I glanced at the two women, leaned forward as if to tell Tracey a secret, and whispered—"it's not so bad."

For just a moment, her mouth slipped into her small thin-lipped smile.

I was almost out the door when Tracey said, "She's the leader."

I stopped and tilted my head, puzzled.

Tracey's jaw jutted out. "Cynthia is the leader. I knew she'd do a good job of spreading the link." Her answer, although honest-sounding, sent a chill through me. "That's why I picked her."

Her grateful smile shifted into something creepy that made me shudder inside.

I stepped through the doorway, and relief flowed through me—there was more oxygen outside that room.

Saturday morning, Dad made the trailer travel ready, hitched it onto his truck, and hooked Mom's car behind the trailer. When we eased up to the entryway of the park, Mom said, "Look, maybe that's Tracey's mother."

Through my backseat, tinted window, I witnessed a scene I'd never expected. The same child protective services lady who'd driven me led Tracey down the steps of the double-wide. Tracey wore her backpack and carried a grocery bag full of what looked like clothes. "No. That's not her mother. That's Lacy Wright, with protective services. She's the one who drove me to the safe house."

I rolled down my window, so Tracey could see me if she raised her head. But she stayed behind her curtain as she followed Miss Wright to the car.

Mom shot a sharp nod to Dad. "Oh my gosh—after all those calls I made they are finally doing something." It didn't surprise me that Mom had reported her suspicions, and I hoped Tracey would find a better life wherever she was going. But things would get worse for her before they got better.

Dad started us out of Garcia, toward the Houston connection. Gypsy snored softly with her head next to my leg, and I had my laptop and my journal. After we were on the highway, Dad said, "I always love this feeling—heading home with both my girls and the dog."

"Dad, may I—"

Before I could finish my sentence, he passed his phone over the seat to me.

"Thanks, Dad." When I could get Internet, Ethan and I e-mailed and messaged along the way. I loved having this ongoing connection with him.

And Grandma's e-mails, full of her and Scooter's excitement about my mystery being solved, kept me pumped with that positive joy she sparked.

Zada's page on TeensterBlast had some more likes but no new comments. My message to Zada was still unanswered, but at least she had found the page and remembered me. She could contact me if she needed to.

I Googled "Emily Dickinson's servants" and read that later in her life she did care about them. In fact, before she died, she asked that six Irish immigrants carry her coffin to her grave.

During the five-hour drive, I did some journaling, reflecting on everything that had happened and Ethan, Ethan, Ethan.

On the last day at school, he'd led me around the corner of the gym where we had brief but precious privacy. It was the best moment of my life. With his back against the wall, he wrapped his strong arms around me and pulled me to him. He looked into my eyes and then at my mouth. "I wish we had more time together, but we can make this work long-distance."

Our lips came together, and I put my arms around his neck and melted against his body. I could have stayed there forever.

"Rawls, what are you doing back here?" one of the male coaches boomed from the corner of the building.

We pulled apart, and I looked into Ethan's beautiful warm eyes and squeezed both his arms. "Yes, we can make it work."

Ethan, his gaze still locked with mine, called out to the coach, "Just telling my girlfriend good-bye before the holidays, Coach."

We walked in the opposite direction, and I brought Ethan's hand to my lips and kissed it—first on the palm and then on the other side. A sound came from deep in his chest—sort of a soft growl. I wanted to kiss all the way up his arm to his neck and face, but I peeked back, and the coach was still glaring at us with his hands on his hips.

So that was our last kiss... so far.

I ached with the distance between Ethan and me. But the familiar light-filled, sprawling skyline of Houston gave me a rush about everything that could happen in the future. Somehow we'd get together again. The lines I'd written a few weeks ago started to jell for me. In the darkness, I squinted at my journal:

Visible barriers unseen by choice,
Trip and trap innocents who have no voice.

Why choose not to see clear inequity?

My question had not gone deep enough. There were lots of people who deliberately ignored inequity, the same way they pulled a curtain over those barriers that stopped Zada and Tracey and Ethan from having an even playing field. And some people, like Tracey, hid behind a curtain even though refusing to see things didn't really make them go away. But in addition to people who deliberately used a barrier, there were others, like me, who just weren't aware that they weren't seeing.

An instant message popped up from Ethan. *Thinking about you.*

Before I could answer, the connectivity bars disappeared. But his words made every cell in my body sing. And the answer to the question about why people don't recognize inequity sailed into my mind. Ethan gave it to me before our first kiss in the Star office, when I asked him why I hadn't noticed the area where the black students sit in the cafeteria. He said, "I guess people don't see their own way of seeing." Using his wisdom, I rewrote the poem.

> *I tore the curtain down and roared, "I see inequity."*
> *But countless veils, shifting and sheer, deftly blinded me.*
> *So I, pumped with pride, still failed to see the way I see.*
> *Veils, unseen and unnamed,*
> *Remain unremoved.*

I re-ordered the last two lines into the style that Emily Dickinson used sometimes, with the verb at the end.

> *Veils, unseen and unnamed,*
> *Will unremoved remain.*

Which closing works best? I decided I liked the rhythm of the Dickinson style. I closed the journal and e-mailed Ethan, "You are my poetry."

Streetlights in our old neighborhood glowed on the white-rock fences and giant pecan trees that welcomed us home. But I fantasized about a new home in San Antonio, near Ethan. "Mom, have you ever thought you might like to try living in San Antonio a while?"

Uh-oh, did I cross a line? Mom had been so happy and easy lately that I'd forgotten—reminding her of her need to frequently move might set her off.

Dad must have had the same worry because he looked at her with his brow furrowed and waited to see what she would say.

Mom, with both of her hands clasping the back of the seat, gave the same girlish, shrugging-shoulder grin that Grandma always did. I'd never seen it on Mom before.

She gave a happy giggle. "Well, I hadn't thought about that before. Might be fun."

What a relief. Sooner or later, the borderline curtain would again cover the mother I love and blind her to my and Dad's feelings. But right now, in this moment, we were happy.

DISCUSSION QUESTIONS

- Consider/discuss the title. Why would a girl be named *Polarity*? What is the significance (literal or figurative) of *Motion*?

- When does Polarity first realize there is something special about Ethan?

- What does the aquarium with its invisible wall symbolize to Polarity?

- Barriers can be visible or invisible, and many are denied. Are there barriers between Ethan and Polarity even though they care deeply for each other? If you care about someone of a different race, can you still be influenced by racism?

- People like Polarity's mother are complex. In the story, what are her mother's strengths and weaknesses? What do you think of her question at the end of the family therapy session? ("Doctor, is mankind a borderline collective?")

- Polarity and her mother have an emotional fight scene that is defused when Polarity says, "My name is Polarity." In what ways is their argument normal? In what ways is it excessive/extreme?

- How does Polarity's father deal with her mother?

- Tilly had the truth all along, but no one recognized it. Are there other truths in the novel that were there all along but are unrecognized?

- Why didn't Polarity immediately realize when and where the nude picture was taken?

- Why wouldn't the authorities believe her when she said she was innocent? And why did the authorities suspect her parents might be involved in child pornography?

- Do you think the actions Polarity and her parents took to investigate the case were appropriate or necessary? To get better results, should they have worked more closely with the system or less closely?

- What do you think happened to Zada? Why did Polarity's mother insist on adding the quotation below to the Internet posting?

According to the National Center for Missing and Exploited Children (NCMEC), nearly 800,000 children under the age of 18 are reported missing each year in the United States. Of that number, 33 percent are African-American.

With the rare exception, the unprecedented number of African-American girls who disappear from their classrooms, communities, and churches...end up exploited uncounted.

Invisible.

Forgotten.

- In the end, why does Polarity say that she is glad the nude picture was published?

- What do you think of how each principal handled Polarity's case? Was there more they should have done? If so, what?

- Do you think school environments like Beauty are useful or necessary? What are some of their benefits and flaws?

- Why was Polarity jealous of Shanique? Were her feelings reasonable?

- Discuss the grandmother's role. Does she support Polarity, and does she enable Polarity's mother to engage in borderline behaviors?

- How do you think Polarity changed over the course of the story? Do you consider these changes positive or negative?

- Do you feel sorry for Tracey, or does she make you angry?

- Polarity sums up her experience in a poem. What do curtains and veils symbolize to her? Where did she get the idea for her phrase "still failed to see the way I see"? Do you agree with the last two lines of the poem?

I tore the curtain down and roared, "I see inequity."
But countless veils, shifting and sheer, deftly blinded me.
So I, pumped with pride, still failed to see the way I see.
Veils, unseen and unnamed,
Will unremoved remain.

- What do you predict is next for Ethan and Polarity?

ACKNOWLEDGEMENTS

Writing the acknowledgement page is like scattering chocolate sprinkles on top of the published novel. I get to joyfully call out all the wonderful people who have touched my work. Many of you have no idea that your chance comment or act of kindness or late-night discussion wove its way into the complex process of producing a work of fiction. But here you are!

Family—Your love and encouragement are the core of everything. You bless me. Molly, Lacy, Jed, Justin, Jeff, Rachel, Mabry, Zach, Quin, Emery, Arden, Vicki, Dan, Emily, Brian, and Christian.

Cherry Steinwender—Your persistent mantra to "make the invisible visible" pulses on every page of this novel.

Dawna J. Vicars Posey—Your vast Vicars' genealogy opened my eyes to the role that history plays in our present. Your Robert "Robin" Vicars site energized my latent drive to write fiction. Thank you for the years you invested in research.

Gloria Conerly—Your insight about one special passage of the manuscript was invaluable. Thank you.

Enlightened people—You who never waver from your passion to bring equity into the lives of children and youth, I can't begin to count the moments when your actions or words have elevated my understanding of the work we do in support of students. A few of you have moved on to the better place, but your names are included anyway— Jane Swann Nethercut, Jim and Lee Davis, Gordon and Kay Shultz, Liz Harris, Beverly Reeves, Maurine Perino, Dr. Bergeron Harris, Mary Thorngren, Michael Lofton, Janice Johnson, Linda Perez, Dianna Groves, Margaret Hester, Amelia Palacios-Gomez, Barri Rosenbluth, Terrence Stith, Mel and Sari Waxler, Roy Larson, Jim Lehrman, Dr. Susan Millea, Dr. Cinda Christian, Dr. Holly Williams, Eric Metcalfe, Jose Del Valle, Michelle Wallis, Grace Gonzales, Jean L. Synodinos, Auturo Hernandez, Gail Penney-Chapmond, Willie Williams, John Rosiak, Dr. Jane Ross, Myra Waters, Dr. Paul Cruz, Jennifer Hill, Phil and Linda McAnelly, Diana Resnik, Sandra Jolley, Donna Hagey, Lewis and Marsha Stroud, Shirleen Justice, Dr. Semonti Basu, Cathy Boring, Renee Walker Dougherty, Melodye Watson, Wendie Veloz, Bob and Joyce Bendele, Zachary Wilson, Allen and Julie Weeks, Barbara Ball, Angela Ward, Dr. Jason Laturner, Kevin and Cindy Brackmeyer, Claudia Kramer Santamaria, Kemal Taskin, Suzanne Hershey, Vincent Torres, Michelle Bechard, Cheryl Bradley, Belinda Rubio, Tim Dunn, Dodie Sims Maddox, Jim Lax, Carla Grace Roberson, Cathyleen Requejo, Virginia Potter, Sue Carpenter, Jacquie Porter, Tracy Diggs Lunoff, BiNi Foster, Suki Steinhauser, Sybilla Irwin, Doug McDurham, Craig Shapiro, Patsy Brady, Paul Turner, Mike and Gloria Sullivan, Eric Mendez, Wendy Carr, Dennie Schmidt, George and Martha Wall, Richard Malone, Betty Morgan, Don Thomison, Anita Mitchell, Rosalinda Carranza, Karleen Gauthier Noake. There are hundreds more—teachers, social workers, counselors, non-profit and school administrators—who contribute daily toward the goal of making the playing field even for all kids.

Dr. Andri Lyons—You taught me everything I know about school disciplinary rules. (Forgive me for any procedural errors in this novel. They are my mistakes—not yours!)

Juliana Tran Castillo—You are one of my favorite people in the world—a young person with an old soul.

Ron Seybold and critique group members: Jasmine Patterson, Nancy Warren, Shannon Stewart, Druzelle and Rob Cederquist, Adam Carduff, Debbie Eynon Finley, Julie Rennecker. Your thoughtful reflections and feedback on this manuscript and subsequent ones continue to shape my writing.

Students—You, more than my college degrees, added to my learning. A rich new group of faces and ideas came with each of my teaching roles: a junior college teacher in San Antonio, a prison teacher at the Torres Unit, and a public school teacher at Kirby, Lackland, and, finally, Devine. And serving as principal in Natalia was a rich and rewarding experience—not only because of the students but because of the incredibly dedicated staff and involved parents. Although this book is entirely fiction, I wouldn't have been able to write it had I not been privileged to work closely with young people.

Elizabeth Buhmann and Claire Ashby, outstanding authors—You continue to teach me how to write. Elizabeth, you were the first to say that this manuscript was a mystery, and as soon as you said it, I realized you were correct. And, Claire, you, with your relationship expertise, taught me how to rev up the romantic appeal in the story. This book would not have been nearly as interesting without your guidance.

Charlotte Sheedy—Thank you for believing in and accepting the manuscript I submitted to you. Your belief in the message and your assertion that it should be published, together with all the editors' feedback you provided, paved the path for *Polarity in Motion*.

Amy C. Durall—Thank you and all the victims' services staff and volunteers of Travis County Sheriff's Office for your tireless and inspirational work.

Oprah—I'm grateful that my time on this planet coincides with yours. Super Soul Sunday is woven into everything I write. This novel, I hope, arcs some of that light into a story that appeals to young people.

My friend, Melissa Rupert, queen of one-liners—Your encouragement, honesty, humor, and friendship are priceless gifts I never expected to find in this writing journey. Thank you also for your most amazing one-liner of all, the title of this book—Polarity in Motion.

ABOUT THE AUTHOR

Brenda Vicars has worked in Texas public education for many years. Her jobs have included teaching, serving as a principal, and directing student support programs. For three years, she also taught college English to prison inmates.

She entered education because she felt called to teach, but her students taught her the biggest lesson: the playing field is not even for all kids. Through her work, she became increasingly compelled to bring their unheard voices to the page. The heartbeat of her fiction emanates from the courage and resiliency of her students.

Brenda's hobbies include reading, woodworking, gardening, and Zumba.

Made in the USA
Middletown, DE
10 March 2022

62400164R00158